Kat

BY

Michael B Fletcher

AND

Paula Boer

Kat

ISBN-13: 978-1-922856-52-4

V1.0

Printed in Palatino Linotype and Gismonda FG.

IFWG Publishing International
Gold Coast

www.ifwpublishing.com

Michael B Fletcher is a writer of adult and YA speculative fiction including fantasy, science fiction and horror. His first book *Kings of Under-Castle*, a collection of humorous adventures featuring two rogues living under a medieval castle, was published by *IFWG Publishing Australia* in 2013.

Book 1 of his *Masters of Scent* fantasy trilogy was released in 2022, with *Tumblers of Rolan* and *Shadow Scent* will be released in 2024.

Fletcher has had over 100 short stories published, many with a 'dark' or fantasy bent, in magazines and anthologies in Australia, USA and the UK. An anthology 'A Taste of Honey', containing 43 of these stories was published by Double Dragon in 2021.

He lives in Tasmania, Australia with his wife, Kim.

Paula Boer cares about all animals and runs her 500-acre home in Australia as a wildlife sanctuary. She has many novels, short stories and non-fiction articles published about horses. She has always loved fantasy, especially unicorns and dragons, and the weird and wonderful creatures to be found in science fiction.

Paula's other passions are travel and the natural environment which also feed her non-fiction writing. After the devastating bush-fires of 2020, Paula published her observations of the recovery on her property, including 1,300 photographs covering 400+ species. In 2023, Paula's essay on the impact of climate change that she witnessed in Antarctica was published in Ocean Geographic magazine.

For more info about Paula's writing see www.paulaboer.com.

IFWG Titles by
Michael B Fletcher and
Paula Boer

Michael B Fletcher
    Kings of Under-Castle (themed short fiction collection)
    Masters of Scent (Book 1, Masters of Scent trilogy)
    Tumblers of Rolan (Book 2, Masters of Scent trilogy)
    Shadow Scent (Book 3, Masters of Scent trilogy - out 2024)

Paula Boer
    The Bloodwolf War (Book 1, Equinora Chronicles)
    The Stealthcat War (Book 2, Equinora Chronicles)
    The Harbinger of Death (Book 3 - final, Equinora Chronicles)
    Brumbies (Book 1, Brumbies series)
    Brumbies in the Snow (Book 2, Brumbies series)
    Brumbies in the Mist (Book 3, Brumbies series)
    Brumbies in the Outback (Book 4, Brumbies series)
    Brumbies in the Mountains (Book 5 - final, Brumbies series)

Michael B Fletcher and Paula Boer
    Kat

Chapter 1

The brush of the early morning breeze brought the scent of a herd of striped zeena, soft herbs, and salt licks. The scarlet moon sank as the sun rose, the remnant catner bushes dotting the plains in red and gold.

Kat and Tar, her partner, crept forward on all fours, bellies low to the ground, stalking their prey, the animals' elongated shadows reaching out across the ghostly grasses. Other members of the pride watched her for instructions. Although one of the youngest females, her rare, pending ability to breed placed Kat at the top of the female hierarchy during a hunt.

Her whiskers twitched, signalling the pride to sweep left and circle the zeena. Being in feline shape also heightened her senses. She swivelled her rounded ears at a rustle behind her, but all fell silent. She slunk lower, creeping forward, her tail stiff, feeling every shift of sand beneath her paws, every snap of dried tussock, every press of coarse quartz.

Tar, the dominant male of the pride, the strongest and fastest, burst into a sprint, long legs on silent paws streaking across the plains. Kat mirrored his chase, cutting off the retreat of the zeena. Most of the prey bolted for the horizon, but one lone youngster dithered, not knowing which way to turn.

It was the last mistake it would ever make.

Tar pounced and raked the black-and-red hindquarters of the zeena with his claws, bringing the animal down. Kat leapt for its throat, the hot squirt of blood an elixir in her mouth. With a swift twist of her neck, the zeena died. She didn't believe in letting any animal suffer, even when she took its life for food.

Tar purred with satisfaction as he rolled with the carcase and tore into the delicate flesh. Together, they feasted on the fallen beast. Dust rose as other members of the pride singled out the weak, old, or injured.

Natives of Crofta, the feline frenines ruled the plains like the canine dineeth dominated the mountains. The sweet smell of blood overcame the stench of fear from the zeena and the fragrance of excitement from the frenines. As the last prey animal fell, the sounds of crunching bone and tearing flesh filled the air.

*S*hastic Gorind, Lead Enforcer for the Sensuna Policing Corporation, adjusted the screen to give greater clarity to his surroundings. Important men from the Interplanetary Hunters Organisation, IHO, perched behind him in his upmarket r-drive all-terrain vehicle.

Finally. As a result of all his hard work, he could provide these select, well-financed hunters with the experience of a lifetime. And it had to be significant to draw people from around the galaxy to the remote planet of Crofta.

To him, the only redeeming features of this red planet were the native sapient species, living freely in their natural habitat. But their calm and easy lives didn't mean that others couldn't take advantage of any opportunities arising. As Lead Enforcer for the human colony, no one would dare question his authority to hunt intelligent genoids.

Wealthy, jaded people demanded excitement. Pitting their wits as well as their talents against their prey, the danger of *kill or be killed* brought them to this desolate outpost where he had been born. Now it was his turn to lead the real men.

"Gorind!" snapped a controlled voice, "we need to feel the atmosphere, feel the hunt. Open the roof!"

"At once, Lord Baden-Hauf," he replied, instinctively adjusting his equipment belt over his paunch as he touched the control panel. He had taken special care when dressing this morning, ironing his fatigues and polishing his buckles, his weapons always primed and ready, yet the recent years of opulence had taken their toll.

The man next to Baden-Hauf waved his hunting laser. "I want to bag one of those big cats, have a pelt to walk on in my den. It'll match nicely with my Earth cheetah trophies." He turned, the laser pointing back into the r-drive.

Gorind's hairs rose on the back of his neck. He had no intention of being an accidental victim instead of a galaxy-respected trophy provider. "I guaranteed a frenine hunt, Mr Hershung. But those rifles are sensitive, easy to discharge. Best keep it stowed until you need it."

He glanced towards Baden-Hauf, possibly the richest man in the galaxy, for a sign of approval. The tall, slim man ignored him.

"Shut it, Gorind," Hershung continued. "I didn't pay a fortune in credits to get treated like a boy with a new toy gun. I aim to be ready."

Gorind choked back a retort. Using his imbedded optics, he caught his offsider's attention on the rear viewing seat behind the hunters. "Jekar, my second, will help you locate your quarry, Mr Hershung. You won't miss out."

He drove on, ploughing through the fields of tall grass and low scrub, barely registering the bumps of the plains, while a sweeping infra-red detector gave them indications of life in the vicinity. Several blips near a grove of trees appeared on the screen, too small to be zeena. Maybe tek-tek. These men wouldn't be interested in the fragile antelope.

"Gorind! Stop!" Hershung waved at the indications on the detector's screen. "I don't want more zeena. I want to catch a cat front on. Straight between the eyes. That must be them there!"

Jekar didn't move. "Negative. Wrong heat signature."

As he spoke, the blips skittered away at random, not a co-ordinated retreat like a pride of frenines.

Kat raised her head, alerted by tek-tek racing haphazardly from the shelter of boulders. Although Kat delighted in the succulent juice of the tek-tek, she would never hunt them without permission from the dineeth. Wondering what had startled the miniature antelopes that normally ranged the mountains, she stood upright and stared into the distance. The low rumble of a vehicle headed toward the pride, still out of sight but most likely transporting human adventurers.

Humans rarely left Sensuna, the capital city, and lacked the genetic ability to change from upright beings to hunting form like genoids such as frenines and dineeth.

"We should take the rest of the meat home," Kat said. As a pacifist species, other than hunting for food, she had no desire to enter into a confrontation.

Tar continued to wash his paws and wiped his face clean of the last remnants of blood from his tawny fur. "Let the others do that. I have something else in mind."

Raising an eyebrow and throwing him a smirk, Kat called the pride over. "Someone's coming. We don't want to lose our meat to humans. Tar and I will distract them while you head off."

She pulled the shoulders off the carcase at her feet to make it easy for them to carry, leaving the offal and head for the grecka, the carrion lizards, to clean up.

When she and Tar had distributed their kill, she sidled up to him. "That was a quick chase. Lucky that young buck hesitated."

"I'd have caught it anyway." He stretched out his muscled body and invited her to follow as he trotted off. "I had it picked out from when we first spotted the herd."

Kat gracefully loped alongside. "Maybe you mesmerised it, like you do me."

They played as they raced, rounding up the scattered zeena and driving them towards the vehicle sounds, not close enough to cause them distress, but close enough for the people to change direction from the kill site.

When the rumble of the transport sank away in the distance, Tar dropped to a walk. "Let's find a patch of shade. I'm not in a rush to go back."

They found a suitable spot under a clump of catner bushes and lay close.

Kat washed Tar's face with her tongue, aroused by his musk. "Do you think we'll help our species?"

Tar purred. "Of course. You've been going off-planet for those fertility treatments, and I've got solid genes. I'm sure our love will ensure success. The magic ingredient."

His muscles rippled as he stretched his body along the ground, swept the grasses with his tail, extended and retracted his claws a few times. "We should eradicate all other predators on Crofta. That way we'd never have to compete."

Kat licked his cheek. "The dineeth are no trouble!"

Sometimes the dineeth asked to hunt zeena. If the herds were plentiful, the Frenine Council would grant a quota, but frenines and dineeth never hunted together. They had long reached an accord, living in harmony in their separate territories.

"That's not who I meant. They're native, like us. I meant the other species." A growl rose from Tar's chest. "How will our cubs have a chance if there isn't enough food? It's getting harder to find zeena these days. And it's impossible to import living meat like we do salt."

Kat stroked his back, snuggling closer. "We can't help it if other sapient species immigrate here for safety. Many nearby planets have suffered mass extinctions. There's room for everyone if we manage the herds well. It's the predators who take good breeding stock that need to be educated."

She waggled her tongue at him. "Anyway, let's not discuss that now."

Tar snarled. "I'd educate them with my claws, and rip their hearts out, especially if they took food from you or our cubs."

"Tar!" Despite her shock at his words, the image of Tar looking after her and the urge to have his offspring heated her blood.

She stood and paraded around him, her tail held high and her rump angled slightly towards him. "Enough talk. We've had a feast today. Let's focus on expanding the frenine population."

Gorind slowed the r-drive, watching the zeena sprint away in the dust. "Jekar, check the screen. The way those animals are moving, there're frenines nearby."

Hershung stood up, waving his rifle. "Faster, man, faster!"

Without increasing speed, Gorind listened to Jekar's quiet directions in his earpiece. When the track ahead cleared, he glanced at the screen. "There's something there, most likely frenine, but I repeat, they're bloody dangerous. Don't forget they have claws as long as your hand."

Hershung thumped back down on the seat. "I don't need a nursemaid, Gorind. I've hunted on more worlds than you've ever seen. The bigger the challenge, the better. Catch up with those cats and let's get on with why we're here."

"Hershung," said Baden-Hauf, "trust him. Gorind will find you a frenine."

Hershung snarled. "I should hope so. I've paid good credits for this."

Gorind grimaced, his shaven face tightening like the skin on his close-cropped head. "Remember, they're not like the cheetah on Earth. These are genoids, with many of our genes. Smart, too. When we stop, I'll set up the ion rifle and watch from the vehicle. Jekar will lead one of you to begin the hunt."

"Stop the waffle. We all know humans are superior, despite what galactic law says." Baden-Hauf looked down his aquiline nose at Gorind. "Hershung can go first. I can come back another day if necessary."

"This should be near enough." Gorind halted the r-drive and opened the door.

Asudden waft of humans distracted Kat. "There are people near. They must have come from that vehicle."

Tar raised his head from where he had been nuzzling her neck. "You're right. That's all we need. We'd better find somewhere else."

They trotted off through the tall grass, side by side. The scent of the men pursued them. Tar broke into a lope. "Let's get to the outcrop. We should be able to find privacy there."

Kat followed his lead, lengthening her stride, confident in her ability to evade any pursuit. The men couldn't be after them, but might try to track them, thinking they would lead them to zeena.

They reached the outcrop, where no zeena could climb, and leapt onto a high shelf. Tar switched his tail in anger. "They're still following. They must have technology to detect us. Why can't they see we're not hunting?"

Without stopping on the rocks, they wound their way between the outcrop and exited the other side. Two men stood waiting, lasers poised.

Kat ducked back between the boulders, expecting Tar to follow. Instead, he launched at the men.

Screams bounced around the rocks as Tar returned. "Quick! Away from home! From the pride!"

"What did you do? You didn't hurt one, did you?"

"Only enough to scare them off. Let's go!"

Racing across the plains, Kat and Tar outran their pursuers. When they could no longer hear or smell them, they dropped to a walk, the heat of the day pounding on their backs.

Tar licked Kat's face. "I know a pool with shade near here. You're not ready to go home yet, are you?"

Kat smiled and shook her head.

Gorind's earpiece crackled. "Bring the r-drive! Hershung's hurt." He acknowledged Jekar's contact and thrust the vehicle into overdrive, rumbling towards the spot where the infra-red screen indicated their location.

"What happened?" Baden-Hauf snapped.

"Not sure," Gorind looked up from the screen. "Your man's injured."

Smacking Gorind on the shoulder, he grabbed the detector. "Drive faster! I'll direct you."

In short time they reached Jekar and Hershung. The hunter squatted on the ground, both hands over his face. "The damn animal attacked me! Then fled! Dumb beast!"

Gorind bit back harsh words. "They're intelligent hunters, and dangerous, like I told you. I thought you wanted a challenge."

He would have added more, except for the look on Baden-Hauf's face. He didn't want to lose this lucrative customer before he'd even started operations. After grabbing the first-aid kit, Gorind pushed Jekar out of the way and squatted next to the injured man. "Let me see."

Gorind pried Hershung's hands away from his face. A deep vertical gash ran from his scalp to his jaw, but the real injury lay in his ruptured eyeball, dangling on his cheek by its optic nerve. Using a cauterising scalpel, Gorind slashed the jellied mass free and flung it away. "I'll tape this wound, but we need to get you back to Sensuna for proper treatment and a new eye."

Baden-Hauf swaggered over. "Not yet! He knew the risks. I want that frenine. It's my shot now. Put Hershung in the back and get on its trail."

Not wanting to argue, Gorind did as asked and instructed Jekar to locate the frenine.

Kat's pulse raced, harder than if she'd sprinted all the way home. Excitement flushed through her legs, every hair tingled, and Tar's musk overwhelmed her other senses.

He nuzzled her shoulder and gently positioned her in front of him.

She'd anticipated this day for so long, she wanted to savour every moment, but her body thought otherwise. In a rush, she pressed back into him.

Tar lunged, his claws raking her sides.

She ignored the scratches, heat filling her from nose to tail. Her heart swelled with love for her mate, the outside world forgotten in her passion.

A high-pitched whine shrieked into her consciousness.

Tar slumped off her sideways.

Dazed, Kat turned and stared down at him. A hole larger than her paw gaped in his ribs, blood pouring from the wound.

The shriek of another blast startled her.

Instinct kicked in. She leaped into flight, seeking refuge.

Panting hard, more from fear than exertion, she reached the boulders where they had earlier drunk from the pool and crouched behind them. Ruthlessly suppressing her anguish and shock, she raised herself upright and peered with one eye through a gap no wider than her nose.

Three men strode towards Tar. His body remained limp, a dark stain spreading around his body, blood spilling from his mouth.

Chapter 2

Dead.

Pain twisted Kat's gut as if she had been the one shot. Not Tar! Not her best friend, her intended mate, her life partner. She berated herself for not paying more attention to the unusual scent, one she'd never now forget.

From a distance, half afraid to stay in case they came after her, and half afraid to go in case Tar was by some miracle still alive, Kat watched the men as they crouched over her mate's body, two in security uniforms hung with devices and weapons, another in hunter khaki. She couldn't hear what they said, but the large hunter with the ion rifle flicked the barrel at Tar.

The two other men hefted Tar's sagging body between them, his front legs over the shoulder of one, his hind legs over the shoulder of the other, and threw him up onto the vehicle before climbing in and snapping down the plexiglass dome. Behind the transparent bubble another man lay prone on the seat, clutching his face.

Kat suppressed a cry of despair and numbly watched the hunters speed away, Tar's golden body limp across the luggage rack.

She couldn't leave him. Regardless of the danger, Kat kept pace with long, galloping strides as the vehicle sped across the grasslands, keeping far enough out of ion rifle range but close enough to keep them within hearing, if not within sight. Anger and hatred drove her beyond the limits of her usual stamina.

She tracked them all the way to the spaceport in Sensuna where cultural exchanges typically occurred. Traders came for the valuable Crofta gemstones and brought salt from far-off planets to supplement the limited local supplies. Frenines and dineeth had long ago adopted the universal language, enabling communication with visiting species, though few made Crofta their home.

Determined to find out who these men were, Kat entered the customs house at the spaceport in her genoid form, walking upright, her paws transformed to hands and feet, not caring that in her hurry she hadn't donned the clothes normal for a frenine in the city.

She didn't care.

The three men disappeared into the spaceport, one shouting orders for a medic to collect the man remaining in the r-drive.

Ensuring her face and body were clean of the zeena feast, she put on an inquiring smile and sashayed over to an officer at the doorway, swallowing her horror and grief for later. "Who were those men who just arrived?"

The officer looked her up and down with a leer that changed to compassion when he realised what she'd asked. "I wouldn't hang around here if I were you. One's the Lead Enforcer, and another is a big game hunter from Earth. It's an obsession on that planet."

The hair on Kat's nape rose. "But hunting other than for food is banned on Crofta."

The officer coughed and looked away. "The tall man is a diplomat. Special privileges. Nothing I can do about it, especially as Gorind is with him. If I were you, I'd get out of here fast."

Kat dragged herself into the kitchen where a few of the females worked at a marble benchtop covered in sealed bags of zeena meat prepared for storage.

Gorind! So he was Lead Enforcer now. After all these years she hadn't recognised him but might have known he'd be involved. She shivered, her hair standing up along her spine. She pushed away memories from her childhood, troubled more by the greater angst of Tar's death, and slumped into a chair opposite the eldest female, who'd stopped work.

"Whatever is the matter, Kat?"

Tears streamed down Kat's face, streaking her fur. Between gasps, she recounted Tar's murder and following the hunters to the spaceport.

"Kat! How could they kill Tar? He was so vibrant!"

Sashyr, one of the younger females and her best friend, leapt to her feet and hugged her. "Poor Tar! What did he ever do to deserve that?"

Mesat, the older frenine, gaped. "I can't believe it. He was always so strong. This is terrible news, terrible."

Kat sobbed onto Sashyr's shoulder for a long while before straightening up and wiping away her tears, a determined look on her face. "I've got to find out where they've gone. I'll make them pay for what they did."

Sashyr stepped back, still holding Kat's shoulders, and looked hard into her eyes. "You mustn't! I know he was your life mate, and was part of the future for frenines, but it's too risky."

"We'll contact the authorities," Mesat said, nodding in agreement. She was an elder in their tribe, and her opinions were more considered, less emotional. "They'll deal with it. Something like this is too important for you to get embroiled with. What justice can you mete out? We didn't evolve this far to become like humans, fighting and killing outside the law."

"I don't care! This is Tar we're speaking about. Tar! We were just about to…to…you know, *increase the pride*. We…we…" She broke down in sobs.

Mesat strummed her fingers on the table. "Yes, the implications will reach beyond your broken heart. Poor Tar. I can't believe it. But revenge is not yours to take. Leave it with me. I'll call an emergency meeting of the Frenine Council straight away. We weren't going to meet until the new moon, but this is too important to wait."

Kat leapt up and paced the room on two feet. "They won't be able to do anything! The hunters were diplomats. They'll have immunity! I *have* to do something."

Mesat busied herself making a pot of tea in silence, waiting for Kat to calm down. After piling Kat's favourite biscuits on a plate, she patted the back of the chair. "Sit down. If you're really determined to act, there's something else we might be able to do."

Intrigued, but still burning inside with anger, Kat propped on the edge of the stool, drying her tears. "What?"

The elder joined her at the benchtop and took a long, slow breath. "Long before Crofta was discovered, society ran on more informal ways. Issues that occurred within or between species were often directed to a reclusive group of the dineeth, known as mystics. They were said to be in tune with the heartbeat of the planet, knew all and saw all, and would get to the root of any issue. It was they who first dealt with the incursions of spacers, the invasion of aliens who brought enlightenment to Crofta. And it was they who kept their old ways once the planet had been colonised."

The dineeth packs were as varied in form as the environments on the mountains they lived in. Kat knew that the mystics retained knowledge beyond what was commonly understood. "How can they help?"

"I know a mystic who lives in the mountains to the east. One of us could seek him out," Mesat said, pausing, "but we don't know what he may require of us in return."

Kat leapt back up. "I don't care what the cost is. Tell me how to find him."

"Kat, please, I didn't mean for you to go. You could put this to the Council."

"I don't want to wait on them. What if they won't contact this mystic? They'll say this is frenine business. I'll go to him."

"Kat, think this through before you act rashly. I didn't say the cost would be in credits. That, the pride could afford. Mystics are renowned for making strange requests of those who consult them."

The elder stood and waved her arms to include everyone in the pride. "We have no idea what he might ask, how dangerous it might be. We can't afford to lose you, too. Especially you. Not only do we love you, you're our best chance for expanding our numbers. You're precious to all frenines, their future hope. We can't risk you. Let the Council deal with this."

Kat straightened, her hackles rising. "Don't use that emotional blackmail with me. I loved Tar. I'll visit this mystic. And I *will* have revenge, one way or another."

Kat climbed the steep cliffs, her long claws gaining holds on the hard rock. She kept at bay her doubts about whether she was doing the right thing by replaying Tar's death in her mind and going over what she might say to the mystic, unsure whether he'd even be interested in hearing of her troubles.

The further she climbed, the more her hatred of the hunters grew, spreading like a fire throughout her body.

A shadow moved to her left, perhaps a tek-tek. The small antelopes favoured by the dineeth lived in the mountains as well as the plains. She stopped herself from calling out to Tar, expecting him to be climbing alongside her, guiding her to paw-holds or warning of loose stones as he had when they romped here as cubs. She shook her head to clear the memories. The shadow was only the wind blowing the tussocks of grass that clung precariously to their mountain perch.

The sun had climbed high, and by the time the cliff levelled out onto a rugged path she was panting from the heat. Kat heaved herself over the ledge and rested while catching her breath. Far below, the homes of the frenines lay hidden in a fold of rock, surrounded by the grassy plains where the zeena, tek-tek and other prey ran. In the distance, she could see Sensuna, the older marble buildings of Crofta's cultural centre on the northern edge, with the spaceport and human settlement on the opposite side. The occasional spacecraft glinted in the sun as it shot skywards or descended on a cushion of flame.

She growled with the memory of the hunters leaving Crofta. *What had they done with Tar's body?* Determination drove her up the trail. Winding around the mountainside, it gradually broadened, rough footing changing to well-worn stones. She turned a corner and faced a dark opening at the end of the trail.

She was here, but still didn't know what to say to the mystic. *Would he welcome her or chase her away?* Taking a deep breath to strengthen her resolve, she called out, "Hello! Is anyone there?"

"Enter. And welcome." The soft words were spoken as if she were expected.

Kat peered into a small cavern, ambient light showing an indistinct, hooded figure seated among decaying vegetation. Yet the scents were of leaf-fall and rich soil. She bent to go through the low opening, and straightening once she was inside, she held out her hands in greeting.

The mystic waved her to one of the rocks opposite him, which had been carved into resting places and were covered with dried grasses, thick and comfortable.

He gave a gentle clearing of his throat. "I'm Mystic Nivlac. I know what troubles you."

Kat's ears swivelled forward in hope. She opened her mouth to ask how he knew.

The dineeth lifted a brindled arm, almost hairless from age, to forestall her. It was rare for an elder male to be separated from his pack and yet maintain a position of respect. Keen to see his concealed face and hear how he knew why she was there, she settled, as if a game were being played. But she was a hunter, and patience was part of her psyche.

While the mystic leaned forward to pour an extra cup with a tea redolent of peppermint, her eyes adjusted to the dim light. His dark snout merged to lighter brown on his bristly, patterned face higher under the hood. She knew his eyes would be golden brown in the light, but she hadn't expected to see a brown teardrop-shaped mark below them; a sign of someone venerated in dineeth hierarchy.

He cleared his throat with a small cough. "Kat, your coming has been foreseen. It marks a turning point for genoids, both here and on other worlds."

"How—?" Her voice trailed off as the mystic again raised an arm.

"The years of peaceful co-existence have come to an end. The intrusion of humans on Crofta has also brought the less desirable attributes of that species. Crofta was settled while continuing to allow sapient species such as ours to live our natural ways, but human values, or lack thereof, have spread outside of Sensuna. It's now up to us, among others, to reset the balance." He took a sip from a small cup at his side.

"So you know what's happened to me, to us, to my pride," interrupted Kat, her tail swishing through the leaf litter around her. "Tar—" She gulped.

"Kat, Kat…" The mystic leant forward again, his golden-brown eyes growing in her vision, catching and holding hers.

She tried to look away but couldn't. A feeling of warmth encompassed her, spreading through her body, pushing away her hurt. Something was happening but she was loath to make it stop.

A soft hand touched her knee.

She came back to herself and shivered, eyes narrowed. "What did you do?"

The mystic smiled and sat back against the wall. "Relax, Kat. While your emotions are raw at the moment, you have much before you which will require courage and patience. I have merely given you strength to help you with what you may have to face. This is a time for action and you have the motivation to do so, with help."

No longer anxious, Kat shook her head. "As you know so much, you'll know I must have revenge for Tar's death. I'm happy to participate in whatever you have in mind if it helps me achieve that, but I'll need more than platitudes to convince me."

Mystic Nivlac rested back into his leafy nook, hood falling forward, again becoming a mysterious figure. "I am satisfied you will prove beneficial to our needs. As to what you will have to do, time will tell, but you will have to travel off-world."

"You mean follow the murderer throughout the galaxy? I don't even know where they've gone. Do you? If so, tell me. What else do you know?" Kat struggled to maintain her calm and keep her seat, wanting to leap up and head after Tar's killers immediately.

"All in good time. And you will be aided. First, a short flight to a transit waystation that will bring you face to face with your enemy. After that, you will require patience and intelligence, which I know you have. Even so, your path may have unexpected consequences." The mystic poured himself another cup of peppermint tea.

Kat declined, having barely sipped at hers. *What was he saying? That he, a figure of significant influence within the very fabric of Crofta, was condoning an attack on a human, and a diplomat at that?*

So many questions buzzed in her head, but before she could ask any, the mystic gave a barking cough, signalling the end of discussion.

Instead of providing more information, he reached into the side of his robe and removed a black tek-tek leather choker studded with precious stones and a carved canine tooth, yellow with age. "Take these," he said, handing them to her. "The stones are hollow, each a different shape so you can recognise them by feel, each with a different purpose. They're a reliable, but secret, way to carry illicit substances."

She held out her hand for the gifts. "What do I do with them?"

Mystic Nivlac stroked his bearded chin. "At this time, all you need to know is that the largest stone, the emerald, contains a powerful, tasteless poison that will rapidly disintegrate in a body."

"You mean for me to kill the hunter? As much as I desire that, I'll be ostracised from the pride! I want to catch him and get him to confess to the authorities, or at least face trial." Kat barely gave the choker a glance before she slipped it in her pack. She couldn't see herself using it.

The mystic shook his head. "He would never be found guilty. You are up against humans, and the Sensuna Policing Corporation is corrupt. You will need to mete out your own punishment."

Kat's hackles rose. "I can't do that! I can hunt for food, but frenines don't eat humans."

The dineeth sat back. "Do you want revenge or not? You are a catalyst for greater change. You need to do this for the sake of all genoids, no matter the cost."

Was that what Mesat had meant about a cost she might not be willing to pay? She couldn't think about that at the moment. She'd vowed to do whatever was necessary. Kat turned the tooth over in her hand, looking at the indecipherable markings on the ancient enamel. "And what about this?"

"The tooth identifies the holder as a trusted emissary from me. When you arrive on K-Astar3, you will meet a barman, a dineeth. Ralvan is his name. Ral will help you with the next step, including the provision of accommodation and work within The Hub while you wait for the hunter. Be patient, and you'll have your revenge."

Chapter 3

Kat made her way down the short corridor to The Grotto, the circular entertainment area clinging like a stinger's nest to the spaceport hub. She was already becoming familiar with K-Astar3, the high grav asteroid that acted as a waystation linking the major trade routes between all the inhabited systems within 200 light years.

Having arrived a week earlier after assimilating the mystic's instructions and securing a flight from Crofta at short notice, she still found it hard to believe the enormity of the task she had undertaken, as well as the reality of Tar's death. From a life of hopes and dreams she had plunged headlong into an interstellar hunt amid overwhelming grief. Whether it was the mystic's influence that had strengthened her, or her own desire for revenge, she knew she was ready to kill Tar's murderer, no matter the consequences.

She had met her contact, Ral, a dineeth from a different pack to the mystic's, more upright and paler in colour, who worked as a barman in The Grotto. He had known of her mission and, although accepting the tooth token with some trepidation, quickly arranged serviceable accommodation among the workers and entertainers near The Hub while she waited for Tar's murderer to arrive on the asteroid.

Now here she was at the start of a new day, dressed like a call girl, waiting on interplanetary travellers. A band, whining like a blood-blot fly seeking a meal, played on a small stage against the curved walls of The Grotto.

Kat flicked an ear in irritation but her eyes remained steady, her attention on any humans in the room. Ral watched her as she sashayed between the booths around the stage, clearing tables and avoiding the groping hands of patrons. Careful to always stay where she could see the entrance from The Hub and the exit to the outside adjacent to the unisex relief station, she watched every newcomer who entered. Since working here, Kat had come to know which girls operated in the place, but had kept herself to herself. It didn't pay to ask questions in a place like The Grotto.

Ral held up a glass, to which she nodded. Despite her feline patience, the waiting for her quarry to arrive was dragging on. *Soon,* she thought, as she accepted the non-alcoholic drink and slid into a booth as if waiting for a customer. As much as she wanted revenge, killing without the need for food was anathema to frenines. The thought wouldn't leave her mind, roiling around with her desire for vengeance, her need to make sense of Tar's murder. She shifted on the cushioned bench, seeking comfort, but that did little to ease her inner turmoil. *What would she become when she murdered the hunter? Was she no better than him? Would the pride ostracise her? If so, where would she go?* Lost in her quandary, her head drooped over her glass of juice.

A noisy group of men entering the room snapped her to attention, their barracking drowning the substitute for music, their large leader young and fit, jaunty and puff-chested. They gravitated to the bar and shouted for the most expensive drinks on offer. Bar girls, some non-human, followed the aura of wealth.

Kat studied the tallest of the men. All of them were big for humans, who were normally only slightly taller than her, but he stood out from them all. He leant in the middle of the bar, his arm slung around the body of a regular, openly caressing her enhanced chest.

Kat's nostrils flared, tongue dipping in and out of her mouth. *That smell!* She recognised the mixture of sweat and body odour. She'd only had a brief waft when Tar was taken away, but she had been sure she would recognise his murderer's scent anywhere. Her pupils shrank to thin, vertical slits in her golden eyes, body tensing. She inhaled deeply to be sure.

It was *him! It had to be,* she thought, *the alpha male.*

Kat restrained herself from leaping up and confronting him. Instead, she sauntered up to the bar, pretending disinterest in the group of men, and ordered another drink. She had to follow the mystic's instructions. She knew he was right, that capturing and handing in the murderer would not result in justice. She indicated the tall man to Ral with a flick of her tail.

The barman acknowledged her signal as he wiped the counter and replaced the cloth underneath. The room dimmed, leaving only the bar and the group illuminated. Kat paraded past the leader where he sat on a stool, the bar girl now pulled onto his lap. He bellowed for another drink, then began nuzzling the woman's cleavage.

Kat froze. His scent came in waves. She tensed to attack while he was unprepared, grip his head with her needle claws, and rip his throat out with her canine teeth. *No. Not that way.* She panted to control her racing heart. She had to follow Mystic Nivlac's plan or she'd never leave the waystation alive.

She brushed past several of the men, allowing them to caress her flank or shoulder, enough to make her frenine musk send signals to any male in the vicinity. She had no doubt she stood out among the other women. Not only was she a frenine with silky brown fur, feline ears and a long tail, but her short skirt, waistcoat and matching thigh boots in soft, red-and-black zeena suede, and the sparkling stone choker, drew attention.

The leader of the men at the bar looked up and blinked. He let the bar girl slip from his lap. "A frenine, here?"

She threw a coy look over her shoulder at him, giving him the eye.

"Never had it with a frenine before." His voice was as coarse as his smell. "Come here, you."

Kat hesitated under his gaze. Now the moment was upon her, doubts raged war with her determination. But then she saw Tar again, his body bleeding and limp, slung on the vehicle, disappearing from her. Taking away not only her future, but the future of all frenines.

Her ears flattened. She hissed. Her claws erupted from her paws in a flash. She crouched into position to spring.

"Hey." The big man's hand reached for his holstered laser gun. "Don't you go getting snaky on me."

Kat retracted her claws with a click, paws reverting to hands, and straightened up. *She must control herself!* "Sorry, I'd heard men think our claws provide extra stimulation. Some like it rough."

He laughed harshly. "I don't need no help to get it up. Wanna drink with me, then?" He turned to the barman. "Where's that drink I ordered? And another for my sexy friend here."

Kat slinked closer, purring.

He patted his leg and she slipped onto the recently vacated lap, the warmth of the previous girl giving her pause. She wasn't a pro like them, she hadn't even mated, despite her regular off-planet trips to inhale the nectar of the lassivar flower, an aid to increasing her fertility for when she came of age. Frenines had great difficulty conceiving, but their culture forbade the use of genetic manipulation or artificial means of conception.

The memory of how close she and Tar had come to consummating their mateship drove her will as strong as the armour of an r-drive all-terrain vehicle. She relaxed her jaw and snuggled closer to his killer.

The man gave a loose smile and leered down at her barely-clad body.

Kat's purr increased, even as she tried to ignore his hand rubbing up and down her thigh.

He licked his large lips before taking a quick swig of the fizzing drink that Ral plonked in front of him.

"Frigging hell!" He glared at the barman. "What do you call this? It's damn well burnt my tongue."

Ral kept a straight face. "Speciality of The Grotto, sir. Everyone has one on arrival. It contains locally enviro-grown chilbean—hot stuff, good for performance, if you know what I mean."

The tall man tipped Kat off his lap as he leant across the bar and grabbed the dineeth by the throat with a muscular hand.

His angry words were lost on Kat as she gave a quick nod of thanks to Ral. This was her opportunity. She scratched at her choker as if it were too tight, slipping the emerald gem into her fingers. The round stone nestled between her fingertips as she moved her hand across the tall man's drink, a dribble of liquid trickling in with a burst of fizz, hidden by the action of her picking up the glass.

"Here, big man," Kat purred, "surely the local drink doesn't put you off? I like my lovers to be strong and tough."

His coarse face looked down at her, nostrils flaring as her scents rose. His eyes narrowed as he understood Kat's invitation. "You're right, what's a little spice between friends?"

He accepted the glass and guzzled it down, his face reddening as he struggled not to choke. Having finished, he rose from the stool.

"I think it's time for you and me to go into a private alcove. It's been a long while between planets."

Kat gasped as he grabbed the loose skin at the nape of her neck and bent his face towards hers. She leant back, worried the choker would come off.

"Wait." With a twist of her lithe body, she pulled away.

He looked at her, brow furrowed, eyes unfocused. "Hey," he growled, "where're you going?"

She leaned forward and hissed into his ear, "Leaving you to your fate. For Tar." Despite all her self-control, a tear slipped down her furred face.

As Kat backed away, the man's face turned rubbery, eyes rolling inwards. He staggered. The crash of the man's body hitting the ground stopped all other sound, including the off-key band. Two of his friends crouched, pulling out their lasers in reaction, waving them around as if not sure where to aim. Another bent over his twitching form, yelling into his face.

"Rast! Rast! You alright? Baden-Hauf! What's the matter?" He shook his friend by the shoulder but received no response.

Kat watched the drool pouring from the side of the hunter's gaping mouth. He'd never respond, never be able to form the words to answer. The poison had done its work before breaking down into untraceable constituent parts.

"Call security!" "Send for a medic!" "Did anyone see anything?" The friends shouted and milled in confusion.

Kat didn't need to act to look horrified. She had killed. She had wanted Tar's murderer dead and now he was. *She was no better than him.* She shivered uncontrollably as she backed towards her alcove.

The man who had shaken the hunter's shoulder stood and grabbed one of his compatriots. "He's dead! What'll we tell Lord Baden-Hauf when he comes back from his hunting trip?"

Kat froze. *Lord Baden-Hauf? Had the man who had been on Crofta, with Gorind, been someone else? If so, they had near-identical scents.* Her mind grappled with the possibility she had made a mistake.

She crept quietly towards the door.

"Hey! You! Frenine!" One of the victim's friends pointed her way.

She ducked around a group of stunned revellers and hastened to the exit. She had to get out before the authorities arrived.

A soft knock on the door alerted her. Already in hunting form, she drew in a large breath. A familiar scent eased her tension. She slowly reverted to her upright stance. "Come in, Ral."

The flimsy door shuddered open and the dineeth squeezed through, activating the lights as he passed the control panel. The glow lit up the sparse room.

Kat sat on the edge of her cot and smiled with trepidation at his worried expression. "What can you tell me?"

"I didn't know how important your target was. That was Lord Baden-Hauf's son you killed."

Kat flinched at the confirmation of her mistake. Now she really was a murderer.

Ral didn't give her time to think more about that. "The authorities here have called in the Lead Enforcer from Crofta with a team to investigate."

"Gorind!" Kat snarled, thinking of the blocky, self-important man. She might have known they'd want someone familiar with frenines since the notice had gone out about her being a person of interest.

Ral perched on the cot next to her. "You can no longer stay here until I can get you off the asteroid. The bargirls knew you were different. In return for favours, any of them could accuse me of being involved. They're not the most trustworthy lot."

Kat had no idea how to escape notice on the barren, rocky waystation. It wasn't as if she could blend into the grassy plains as she would back on Crofta. "What do you suggest?"

Ral scrubbed at his hairy jowl. "For Mystic Nivlac to send you to me, whatever you're involved in must be important. I have another room. It's rough, but you can stay there at a pinch." He lifted a small bag. "Here. Some supplies and clothing for you. I'll lead you there, then come back and sanitise this room to erase your presence."

Chapter 4

Kat, dressed in trousers with boots and waistcoat, crouched in the alleyway, her heart racing. She eyed the dishevelled hideaway Ral had provided, putting himself in real danger to help her. Earlier that morning she had snuck out to wash and to use a public comfort station. Now her tiny room's warped door hung ajar, its furniture overturned, fitting right in with the clutter of cast-off space junk and building off-cuts in the slums of K-Astar3. She'd only stayed one night, but it was no longer a sanctuary, no matter how dilapidated.

The hunt for her had caught up.

Gorind was on her trail, backed up by a lot of muscle. Not only did he know a lot about frenines and their habits, he knew her. The hair along her spine rose as she remembered meeting him the first time. She had been at his mercy, a cub on a school excursion to the orphanage near Sensuna. A well-meaning teacher had thought the pupils should see how the less-advantaged children lived. She had naively gone to the orphanage believing the authorities—enforcers were to be respected and to be obeyed—and had followed the enforcer's directives. She hadn't understood until too late that the lessons he had in mind were nothing to do with philanthropy.

The teacher had told her she had too much imagination and to hold her tongue, so she said nothing to the pride about the hands and tongue that had invaded her body in the dark of a cupboard, a black secret that had always lived with her.

She hissed as she peered around the corner of a dilapidated shack, spotting the sheen of light off Gorind's shaved head, his blocky figure swaggering self-importantly as he led his enforcers through the knocked-together buildings in the outlying regions around the central hub.

A faint crackle came over the noise of the waystation waking up, clattering metal and incoherent groans. Her ears swivelled and her breathing stilled as she tried to locate the sound. *Was it an inhabitant of the sprawling slum, someone who had either given up hope of transiting from the high grav asteroid, or had a reason to hide?* Typically, they were unfriendly, unhelpful, and unscrupulous. She didn't need to be caught between the locals and Gorind's crew.

The desire to flee swelled in her. After several deep, shuddering breaths, she filled her lungs, quelling the flight reflex. Her almond-shaped eyes flicked rapidly, assessing the surroundings, reviewing her options.

She couldn't risk capture, not with the latest interrogation techniques, and long-term hiding was now out. She had to get off the asteroid and Ral, if he was still able to help her, was her lifeline. With all the news screens flashing rewards for information about her, she couldn't trust anyone else.

Kat had to leave the search party chasing its tail to give her time. She spied another dark alley between two precariously leaning, biliously-coloured buildings. In two bounds she was in the space, conscious that each step left an infinitesimal part of her spoor behind, enough to track. She removed her boots and rolled them up before slipping them into her pack, then extended claws on all four paws. A spring of powerful leg muscles put her near the top of the building. She gripped the hard surface and landed on the roof with a lithe twist and little sound.

Kat flattened, slipping off the pack to reduce her profile. With her rounded ears flattened against her skull, she peered towards the tower in the distance that marked the central hub. A hint of movement from a street two blocks back showed how close her pursuers were. Her neck fur bristled at a clatter from below. *No time*, it said. *No time.*

But Kat was a frenine—a species who could conceal themselves and change defence into attack. She crouched down to wait and plot.

The roofs, looking like the aftermath of wild storms, spread haphazardly in all directions. Chunks of sheeting projected at an infinite number of angles, giving many hiding places—deep pools of shadow from the artificial lighting of the terraformed asteroid added to the opportunities. It should be simple for her to settle down in one spot and allow the pursuit to go past. *But would she have enough time to get back to The Hub and seek out Ral for a ride off the asteroid?*

Kat blew heavily through her slitted nose as a thought came to mind. If Lord Baden-Hauf came to collect his son, she might still be able to satisfy her revenge. It would be risky—he'd have his bodyguards on alert and would be closely involved with the enforcers—but life without Tar held little meaning. She'd willingly risk her life to see his murderer get what he deserved.

Booted footsteps pounding at a run along the street one block away drew Kat's attention. Among the group of men, a whiff of Gorind's odour turned her stomach.

They moved past. She had time to consider her next actions. There was no point moving until the succeeding spacecraft came in. Then she would check to see if the elder Baden-Hauf was onboard. *But could she kill again?* Seeing the man die from poison, delivered by her hand, had made her want to vomit. She couldn't deny the remorse at killing a human, a sapient species, not an animal for food. Mesat was right that it went against the natural laws of evolved frenines.

But again, the memory of Tar's lifeless body slung over the vehicle reinforced her resolve. Lord or not, sapient species or not, she would kill the older Baden-Hauf. She had nothing left to lose.

While she waited, Kat dreamt of playing with cubs, suckling them, and teaching them to hunt tiny rodents. A rattle, infinitesimal but picked up by her acute senses, had her on high alert. Someone was sneaking across the rooftops on silent shoes, probably grip-pads designed for those without natural stealth abilities.

Well, they didn't know frenines. She purred aloud at the thought. *Time to go fully native.*

She slipped off her trousers and waistcoat, and unclipped the choker. After bundling the clothing into her pack, she took a quick gulp from a capsule of Energ+ and headed towards a spot she had picked out earlier a few shacks across.

Kat knew whoever was approaching would follow; there was no way she could eliminate her spoor altogether. A vertical spar with a bulbous top stood above the roofs. She reached the base in a loping stride, shimmied up, and placed the pack among the few scattered aerials set at the high point. A quick push flattened it, making it inconspicuous.

She dropped down and glanced back. "Not following my spoor yet?" she murmured. "I'll have to initiate some misdirection."

She marked a corner of the nearby building with her cheek gland. "They won't know what to make of that." The territorial musk of her species was extremely powerful and likely to cause the sensitive equipment of the enforcers to overload. Instead of finding a molecule or two of odour, they would receive millions in one hit.

Her claws dug into the sheeting as she ran flat out, leaping in long strides in the lower gravity, touching down on the haphazardly placed material with a light tap and then bounding on, too fast for anyone looking across the roofs to see much against the darkness of space. Her destination wasn't for the squeamish, but that wasn't a consideration when the life at stake was hers.

Like all societies in the galaxy, there remained one taboo subject that no one raised yet all had to address: sewage. The waystation on K-Astar3 solved the problem at little cost by diverting it away from civilised parts to the outlying areas where most of the unrecyclable waste ended up. Kat headed on, guided by her nose. It didn't need to be super-sensitive to find the cesspits.

She dropped to the ground, taking advantage of the shadows of increasingly decrepit structures as she neared the settling tanks. Senses alert, Kat watched for the inhabitants who eked out a living from any by-products of the waystation's waste. Anyone here wouldn't hesitate to turn her in for the smallest reward. The stench was soon so overpowering that her senses threatened to close down. As she turned a corner, a slum dweller in ragged overalls almost bumped into her. He looked up as she hissed in surprise.

"Who?" He pulled off a broken hat and peered into the darkness. He squeaked in alarm. "What was that?"

Kat's fur flattened and took on the colour of the grey wall as she melded against it, closing her eyes to slits so they wouldn't reflect golden in the vague light.

He came closer. "I could'a sworn I saw somethin'." He scratched at his scalp, peering into the shadows.

Kat kept still, willing him not to see her. She had no doubt she could overcome him but it was not in her interests to do so. She slowed her breathing.

"Must be seein' things," the human mumbled as he jammed his hat back on. "Bin too long on this rock." He turned and shuffled off.

Kat waited, furious at allowing a close encounter with a vagrant in these slums, not even one of her pursuers. She closed off her nostrils and, breathing through her mouth, moved on, maintaining the grey colour of her fur.

She entered a wide dirt area dotted with large holes in the ground, hard rims outlining their rectangular shape. Pipes, some oozing trickles of a rank black liquid, snaked their way from the direction of the waystation. The odour was so strong she imagined seeing a black cloud hovering over the eroded sides of the slums surrounding the foul place.

Kat stretched out lengthways, as thin as possible, against a junction where a corrosion-etched wall met the grimy surface of the asteroid. Again she changed the colour of her fur, letting it lose its lustre and darken to become one with her surroundings. Her ribs barely moved as she sank into the torpor of a prime hunter, the top of the food chain.

And waited.

A squad of black-clad men confidently stalked onto the ground around the septic tanks like a rush of scummy oil. Their scent rose above the putrid waste, hot from anticipation.

Kat flinched. This close to her, Gorind's odour overcame even the worst of the smell.

Through slitted eyes, she watched his familiar shape, gloved hand covering his long nose, followed by his men. If he knew it was her he was pursuing, he would stop at nothing to get her. The death of his influential client's son was the real incentive, but he would remember Kat from when she scarred his manhood with her claws as she fought back against his assault all those years ago.

Being caught by Gorind didn't bear thinking about. Kat swallowed the bile that rose in her throat.

"This place stinks worse than a whore's crotch!" Gorind pinched his nose closed and muffled his mouth with the rest of his hand. "Check around. See if the pussy isn't trying another trick, then let's get outta this cesspit. But find her spoor."

"Chief," said a slim, black-clad figure tapping the screen of a hand-held tracking device, "the sensor is too overloaded to work here. There's too much stink to pick up even a trace of the frenine."

"You're ferking useless, all of you," Gorind growled. "Why do I get the dregs of law enforcement when I come to K-Astar3? Couldn't catch a cold, you lot. Check the area thoroughly and move on, unless you enjoy breathing shit."

The squad spread across the open space, some holding gloved hands across their noses as they investigated the shadows cast by the decrepit structures surrounding the tanks.

Gorind watched for a moment, then grunted and hurried past several tanks of foul-smelling liquid to stand at the entrance to another alleyway. "Keep up and focus. We can't lose her, not now."

One by one, they shuffled past their chief.

Kat watched them go. Several had almost stepped on her, but her camouflage and the odour overload had served her well. She growled in relief.

Instead of leaving, the last enforcer looked around.

Had he heard her?

The enforcer watched his detector for a moment, looked back to Gorind and motioned towards her location.

"What, Moraint?"

"Maybe something, chief." His words came indistinctly to her.

Kat's tail twitched, a hunting reflex she couldn't control.

Moraint froze at the movement and grabbed for the squat laser gun on his hip, Gorind glancing down at his own detector.

With no clear way back, she sprang from immobility to full speed in less than a heartbeat. Body extending like a coiled spring, she was on the enforcer in a moment, her claws extended, slashing his weapon away and knocking him to the ground. A sudden swerve brought her onto Gorind in an instant.

He reached for his gun.

She smashed into his gut, knocking him into a spillage of sewage.

With both men on the ground and sounds of the other enforcers returning, Kat had little time to escape. She swung around and raced towards a dark space.

In the brief time she had taken to deal with Gorind, Moraint had regained his feet. Now he blocked her way.

With no time to think, she took a huge leap, trying to clear the enforcer.

Gorind fired.

The laser blast singed Kat's belly. She clipped Moraint's head with a hind leg, feeling his neck snap, and then landed past one of the tanks, almost slipping on the malodorous liquid spilling from the sides.

Another blast melted a hole through the metal sheeting near her head. She tore down the dark passage.

"Moraint!" An angry bellow reverberated among the buildings, followed by a moment of quiet. "You, frenine! You've broken his neck! His death is on your head!"

Kat had little time to consider the implications as she ran for safety. Making a huge leap onto the roof, she left only a scratch on the edge where she scrabbled over, then bounded across the roofs. Keeping low, she headed towards the spar. Without taking time to see if she was still being pursued, she climbed, retrieved her pack, and sprinted silently across the precarious roofs.

With Gorind busy dealing with the dead man, she should have time to get away. She couldn't wait for Lord Baden-Hauf now, not with a dead enforcer linked to her.

Chapter 5

The massive bubble of The Hub reminded Kat of the plexiglass dome of the all-terrain vehicle with Tar on its luggage rack. No doubt a leftover from the days before the asteroid had been terraformed, its diamond-hard clear panels, supported by criss-crossing beams, glinted in the artificial light and accentuated the glowing news screens.

A variety of species of presenters from planets across the galaxy barked out news in a wide range of tongues. The rolling text in the universal language at the bottom of each giant holo revealed coverage of the same story—the furore surrounding the tragic death of the up-and-coming entrepreneur Rast Baden-Hauf on the waystation. A holo of his famous father, the mega-rich, renowned Lord Baden-Hauf, accompanied news of his imminent arrival on K-Astar3. A female frenine was wanted for questioning. The image showed a frenine in hunting form, racing across the plains of Crofta, making her homesick but relieved they didn't have her true likeness. She couldn't risk being recognised.

Space travellers milled around the vast area, buying tickets, towing luggage, or greeting friends. Kat kept well out of the way, leaning against the wall of a unisex relief station and trying not to stand out. With her camouflage ability useless in genoid form, she wore a long, dark coat that hid her tail, with a high collar folded up around the dineeth choker. With all the activity concerning the deaths of Rast and the enforcer, there was no way she would be able to get near Tar's murderer. She needed to get home and rethink her strategy for revenge.

As a graphic scene on the holos grabbed the attention of most onlookers, Kat took the opportunity to slink into a cubicle. Her nerves tingled as she scanned the concourse. Even with her disguise it wouldn't be long before one of the enforcers flitting through the crowds asked for identification.

She'd left a note behind the bar, along with the ancient dineeth tooth Ral had returned to her, to tell him when she'd be here. Had the police found it? Had he been arrested for helping her? Maybe even now he was being questioned by Gorind. The tip of her tail flicked at the thought. She pushed back against the wall to still the rebellious appendage as she waited.

Kat gathered her resolve—she really couldn't stay here much longer—and was about to sidle from her hiding place when she caught sight of Ral. The dineeth sauntered across the large space in her direction, but was doing a good job of concealing the fact that he was looking for her. As a member of staff, he attracted no particular attention from anyone, his presence inconspicuous due to his right to be here. He tipped his head towards a nearby auto-drink dispenser.

Kat found a seat nearby, hoping to go unnoticed, until his order of a steaming beverage appeared, then approached the same machine. A second steaming container emerged. Ral reached for them both, then grabbed the second, leaving the first behind. He walked away, ostentatiously sipping his drink.

Kat picked up the first drink and felt underneath. Something was stuck to the base. This must be the false identity that Ral had promised her should her plan go awry, as it had. As she strolled towards an automated ticket booth, she prised the chip off, gulping at the beverage before disposing of the remainder in a waste recycler. Having already removed her true ID chip from her wrist with a sharp claw and wrapped it in a protective shield in her pack, she held the new one under the scanner. Despite her trust in the mystic's agent, her stomach churned. With ears pricked to pick up any alarms, she tapped in her destination.

The machine spat out a boarding chip and a mechanical voice told her the time and port number of her departure, before wishing her a comfortable journey. Doing her best to appear nonchalant despite her tense muscles, she wandered through the departure gate, knowing the security robot would find nothing incriminating on her. Even so, it felt as if every eye in The Hub followed her.

The orange disk of Crofta came into view on the shuttle's observation screen. Kat warmed at the familiar sight of her home planet, the sandy shades of the plains broken by the dark ridges of the mountains. From this approach, none of the larger lakes were visible. Unlike some inhabited planets, Crofta didn't have vast oceans. Whatever rainfall that wasn't soaked up by the thirsty plants settled in small ponds, the streams gone as soon as the clouds disappeared, the pools themselves ephemeral. Even so, there was always enough to drink, except in Sensuna where humans wasted the precious resource to immerse their bodies. Kat shivered at the thought.

The shuttle descended and docked with automated ease. Kat disembarked, her legs shaking with exhaustion as she stood on the travellator to reach the exit of the terminal. She had removed her coat and scarf—Crofta was warm and she would have looked out of place—and let her fur assume its natural beige colouring. She had to appear as normal as possible now that she was home. Deciding against replacing her true ID chip into her wrist, she had taped the new one on during her flight.

Expecting someone to accost her, Kat twitched her nose and cast her eyes from side to side without moving her head. It took all her concentration to carry her tail aloft rather than letting it flick in fear.

She relaxed. Nothing looked suspicious.

As she passed through the double doors of the last security lock, the sweet air of Crofta greeted her. Never had she been so glad to be home. She glanced around automatically, as if expecting someone to meet her. Normally one of the pride, particularly Tar, would have been there, engaging an autocart for her luggage or calling a flitter to take them out past the city.

Tar. Never again would he greet her, arms wrapping her with his musky smell strong in her face. Never again would he tempt her to mate when she smelt so strongly after the infusion of the lassivar nectar. Never again would he whisper promises in her ear of places they'd go together with their cubs, or for romantic getaways. A single tear streaked her face. She swiped it away. She couldn't let herself be weak, not with Tar's death still unavenged.

But now she was a murderer. She had been responsible for the deaths of two men, one the son of a killer and another seeking her capture. *Would the pride still welcome her?*

Stop that! Her future didn't matter at the moment. She tightened her resolve to seek vengeance. Neither of the men she'd killed had been innocent, one an enforcer who no doubt used dubious methods, another the arrogant son of a super-rich man who probably enjoyed hunting sapient species as much as his father.

No. If anyone was to blame in this, it was Mystic Nivlac. He'd sent her to the wrong place and had her kill the wrong man. She ripped off the choker and stuffed it in her pack.

As much as she wanted to go home, she had to confront the dineeth first.

Having left her pack at the bottom of the cliff, wedged out of sight between two boulders, Kat climbed the rocky track to the mystic's den. This time she didn't need to look for landmarks, her memory of every handhold secure in her mind from her first visit, her speed driven by anger.

As before, Mystic Nivlac appeared to expect her, with two steaming cups of some aromatic concoction she didn't recognise on his stone bench. He waved for her to sit and drink.

"I'll stand. I won't be here long." Kat glowered at the dineeth from near the den entrance.

Mystic Nivlac casually sipped at his tea. "I'm surprised you're back on Crofta. You haven't finished your mission."

The fur on Kat's neck and spine stood erect. "No. No thanks to you. You sent me to the wrong place. I broke my custom of not killing except for food with the wrong person! How can I continue now?"

The mystic flicked an imaginary speck of something from his knee. "You were impatient. You should have checked your target more carefully. Obviously a frenine's sense of smell is not as sensitive as a dineeth's."

The slight to her skills did nothing to assuage Kat's guilt or fury. Her claws clicked out and she stepped forward into a crouch. "Your directions were flawed. You said if I waited, Tar's killer would come to me. Well, the real killer wasn't even on K-Astar3. He was off hunting somewhere, murdering more sapient species, slaughtering us for trophies."

"Actually, he was heading to K-Astar3. You should have been more patient. I told you he would come to you there."

Kat growled and tensed, ready to spring. "He's only there now because of what I did! I killed the wrong man!"

Mystic Nivlac stood and motioned for her to settle with a wave of his paws. "Please, let me explain. I understand your impetuousness. It is my fault for not taking into account your age and inexperience on these ventures. Forgive me."

He indicated again for her to sit. "He was going to K-Astar3 anyway. That's why his son was there, to meet him."

Not sure if she wanted to be pacified but feeling guilty at her rashness, Kat reluctantly sat, more to quell her trembling limbs and stop herself from doing something crazy like attacking the mystic. "So what am I supposed to do now?" she asked, picking up and playing with her cup without drinking.

"For one, you must be careful, especially here on Crofta." Mystic Nivlac topped up his tea from a small pot and took a long slurp.

Kat fidgeted on the seat. "But no one paid me any attention at the spaceport on K-Astar3, nor when I arrived. I'll be safe here."

The dineeth raised a furry eyebrow. "You think so? I would be more worried because they didn't show any interest in you. This, being Lead Enforcer Gorind's home base—" He raised a hand to stop questions about how he knew Gorind had chased her, "means he is powerful. Add to that the importance of Lord Baden-Hauf and you have a dangerous combination. Now his son is dead, he is alerted. He won't have any trouble linking a "frenine of interest" with his recent hunting."

Kat shrugged. "I've looked after myself so far. I didn't deliberately kill the enforcer at the cesspits, but I had no trouble fooling them. I can still look after myself."

"Do you still want to seek revenge for your partner's death?"

"Of course! I just don't know what to do next." Kat leapt up. "You've been no help—in fact, quite the opposite. I'll work something out."

As she stomped out, his words followed her. "You're welcome to come back whenever you're ready to continue your quest. I have more that can be of use to you."

When she reached the base of the cliff, Kat sniffed the air. The scents of soft herbs, grasses and small herbivores came from a long way off. Several frenine prides were near, including distant cousins of Tar. The scent brought fresh tears to her eyes.

She pushed down the emotion, determined to pursue his killer, with or without help. After removing and folding her clothing into her pack, she shrugged it onto her shoulders and fastened the clips. Having dropped to all fours, she dug her clawed paws into the soil and sprinted off, stretching out with feline grace. No matter what came next, it was good to be back on Crofta where she belonged. She raced the wind, assailed by the smells of home, the ground springy beneath her feet.

She reached the low hills that pushed into the grasslands surrounding her home, following a track worn from generations of frenines going to and from the capital. The dry winds increased as evening fell and the red moon rose, tickling the back of her nostrils even as it rippled through her fur, flattening her ears against her head, her tail streaming behind her.

Her blood pumped fast and the thrill of speed coursed through her body, washing away her fears and hurts. She ran on through a scattered clump of bushes, revelling in the primeval joy, crashing through the long grasses rather than following the track.

A pack of dineeth, their mottled coats indistinct across the plains, spread out in hunting form far to her right. They must be stalking tek-tek, as the Council would never have granted permission for them to hunt zeena at this time of year. The alpha female yelped and the pack surged forward, tongues lolling and ears forward.

A pair of zeena bounded high.

In outrage, Kat veered towards them, down a well-worn track where she could make more speed and still watch ahead. Mystic Nivlac's words about frenines not being as sensitive as dineeth pierced her mind. Anger at a pack hunting zeena without authority drove her faster. She intended to give the alpha female and male a piece of her—

Sprannnggg!

Her breath cut short as heat sliced into her belly. Her hind legs flipped over her back as she crashed to the edge of the track, then she doubled over as she fell against a needle tree, the thorns digging into her flesh. She heaved air into her lungs, her body and belly on fire, the pain intense.

Writhing in agony, she rolled to gain her feet, without luck. A taut wire tangled around her midriff. Her mind whirled.

The stench of unwashed human assailed her before a sharp blow hit her head.

Chapter 6

Water dripped down Kat's furred brow, ran alongside her nose, and paused on her thin lips. The tip of her pink tongue touched it and drew it in. Another drop followed.

She opened her eyes, gasped, and closed them. A blinding light added more pain to her already pounding head. Her belly stung and heat seared through her body. She tried to pull into a ball but her legs and arms wouldn't move.

"Want a drink, pussy?" asked a masculine voice. "You must be thirsty."

Kat knew that voice. Her eyes flashed open and she squinted into the bright light.

"Remember me, Kat?" His stench reached her before his florid face and small eyes moved into view. "I hope you do, 'cause I certainly remember you. And now you've cost me a good man."

She snarled and attempted to swing a clawed paw at the hated face.

"No, no, pussy. You won't be able to do that. I took the precaution of tying you down. Wouldn't want you to hurt any more of my men, would I?"

Kat hissed.

"You've led me a long and expensive chase." Gorind's head blocked the light as his foul reek gusted over her.

She held her breath.

"You might consider yourself a mighty hunter, but you're just a frenine. I would've caught you on K-Astar3, but Moraint's death dictated the end of that chase. You were lucky then, but let's face it, you're no match for a human."

He moved back, the light again blinding. "There's a huge bounty on you alive; even dead you're worth something. Killing Lord Baden-Hauf's son has massive consequences. You've really pissed off the authorities, and hurting his Lordship means you've hurt me."

Kat lay unmoving, saving her energy. "What makes you think I had anything to do with his son's death? I only saw it on the news screens. Let me go!"

Gorind broke wind and patted his belly. "Do you really think I'm stupid, Kat? I know frenines, how they think. I've studied your species a long time. I even remember a succulent cub on a school excursion—very tasty. But to business. Hunting safaris aren't put together overnight, you know."

Kat flinched.

The enforcer sniggered, the sound at odds with his powerful body. "It was you, I know it now, following us after we'd taken that big male. A friend of yours, was he?"

"He was my mate!" Kat couldn't help answering.

"Ah," he said, barking a laugh, "no wonder you came to the asteroid to kill Lord Baden-Hauf's son. I was a hair's breadth away from taking you before you killed Moraint. Not much of a pacifist, are you? Now, because of you, I'm no longer Lead Enforcer on Crofta and I've lost the main contract with the Sensuna Policing Corporation. But they've allocated me to 'special projects', the first of which is to bring Rast Baden-Hauf's killer to justice."

Gorind's head moved back into view and he wagged a finger in her face. "But I won't be handing you over any time soon. I have an extraction to make first."

Kat squirmed in reaction, her bonds cutting deeper into her wrists and ankles. *How could she have been caught? A poor hunter to be distracted by the dineeth hunting pack and not sense the wire, or the humans. Mystic Nivlac was right—danger had followed her to Crofta.*

A painful prod in her wounded belly caused her to yowl.

Gorind's eyes glistened. "Stop crying, my lovely pussy, "cause no one cares about frenines. Humans are far more important. We're the ones who made space what it is today. You lot just fiddled around, doing nothing."

He poked her stomach wound again.

A wave of pain forced a moan through her clenched teeth. She panted in an attempt to control the agony, shutting off the hated voice.

A machine whirred near her ear. She jerked her arms, but the bonds held firm.

The harsh light withdrew, leaving a softer glow. Kat subtly assessed her surroundings. Cargo fasteners stretching each limb to the corner of a table exposed her unclothed body to three men in the room. Gorind still wore a black uniform like the one he had worn on the asteroid waystation, but his men's uniforms didn't have star-shaped decorations on the chest. Each had an equipment belt holding a gun and comm unit.

The whirr came nearer.

"That got your attention, pussy." He waved a buzzing tool above her. "Know what these clippers are for?"

She heaved at her bonds.

Gorind laughed, spittle landing on Kat's face. "While I know I'll be re-instated when I hand you in, I thought I'd have some fun beforehand. Firstly, for Lord Baden-Hauf and his unfortunate son but, more importantly, this is for what you did to me in the past'—he glanced over his shoulder at the two dark-clad men, eyes fixed on her exposed body—"and for Moraint."

He brought the device close to her eyes for a moment, before jamming his other hand under her chin and painfully arching her neck. The blades nicked her skin as the shaver began to move down her body. The whirring intensified. She shuddered as the vibration moved down between her breasts along her stomach to her crotch.

If all he was going to do was shave her, she could cope with the embarrassment. Once she was formally arrested, she could seek legal help. The pride had powerful contacts she could use, if they didn't disown her. Or maybe the mystic could help. Gorind and his partners wouldn't want the hunting of sapient species brought out in the courts.

But the need for personal revenge still roiled within Kat.

Gorind lifted a handful of her light brown fur. "This is so fine I could use it to stuff a pillow. What do you reckon, Wreith? Jekar?"

The laughter of the three men broke through Kat's pain, strengthening her resolve.

As the men fingered her shaved pelt, Kat tested the bindings, trying to cut into the material with a dew claw. She shivered as a coarse hand ran down her freshly shorn skin.

"Smooth and pale, pussy. Could be as good as a woman's skin. Now we can have the real fun."

"Hey, boss. They reckon frenines have unusually tight…you know," said Wreith, licking his lips.

A hiss broke from Kat's clenched mouth. She tensed, resolving to make it as difficult as possible for them, whatever they tried. No way could she stomach Gorind's groping again.

"Yeah, Wreith." Gorind smiled at Kat's despair. "You rarely get frenines in The Grotto on K-Astar3, but no doubt you've heard they're alright. Well, I know they are," he guffawed.

Horrific memories flushed Kat's face with blood.

Wreith's voice interrupted her thoughts, his mouth at her ear as his hand moved down her body."You'd like to give us a good time, pussy, wouldn't you? I've heard what you were wearing in the sleaze pit. Asking for it, you were."

Kat twisted her head away.

Gorind stood up straight. "No, Wreith. That's not what I had in mind, not this time. I want to ensure she can never breed. Filthy genoids should be exterminated, but I want the larger reward for her being alive. Stand back."

"But I thought we'd have some fun, chief," growled the other enforcer. "It's a long time since I've had sex."

"No!" Gorind shoved both men away from the table.

A vague hope grew in Kat's mind. Maybe they'd fight, give her a chance to get free.

"I see I've gotta explain it to you two. If all three of us have her, especially with what I'm going to do to her, she's likely to bleed to death. We can't risk that."

Wreith and Jekar looked glum.

Gorind picked up a vibro-knife. "We keep her alive, but we extract a bit of flesh first."

He shoved a calloused finger hard into Kat's belly, opening the wound where the wire had caught her. "About here."

She screamed, her body arching in agony.

"Sounds good, doesn't it?" He pressed harder. "Right here."

"So?" asked Wreith.

"She'll never attract another mate without the ability to breed. "Course, in the prison hellhole on X-Astar9 it won't matter."

The mention of a mate tore into Kat's guts more than the threats. She gritted her teeth and concentrated on finding a way to get free. She'd kill these men if she could, frenine laws or not.

Gorind placed the knife against her lower ribs. "We'll cut her from here'—his finger drew down to below her navel to her crotch—"to here."

Kat panted, pulling with her arms, stabbing into her bonds with her dew claw.

His foetid breath rolled over her. "It won't hurt a bit. Not me, any-way," he roared.

She tensed as he moved the small instrument into her view.

He chuckled. "Now, relax. I have it on slow, as I want to take my time, but I don't want you to die on me."

Worse than a poisoned beezle thorn driving into her flesh, hot pain lanced Kat's torn belly. She screamed, a long wail that echoed around the room. Another erupted from her throat, ringing in her ears so she wasn't even sure it came from her. And another.

"Blast the beast. Gag her, Wreith, or someone could hear."

A foul rag was shoved under her canine teeth and partially down her throat. Kat hardly noticed as she worked frantically at the bonds binding her arms.

"Where was I?" growled Gorind. "Ah, yes, starting to cut her belly. Look, her blood's the same colour as ours. Would you credit that?"

The pain continued, deep and sharp. Kat pulled with all her might, stretching every sinew, every joint in a snapping motion of her well-toned body.

A binding parted with a bang, releasing one arm.

She arced over in an instant and swiped across Gorind's throat.

He gurgled, stumbling backwards, clutching his neck, before falling and writhing on the floor.

Kat snatched up the knife, bringing it down on the binding hold-ing her other arm.

Wreith and Jekar backed off, reaching for their guns while Gorind writhed and choked on the floor, blood pulsing from his wound.

Kat twisted her body, slashing at the bindings holding her legs. The table crashed onto its side. A spray of laser fire hit the protective barrier of the table, melting holes in the thick metal.

Kat ripped at the gag and spat it to the ground. Crouching lower, she ignored the pain and flow of blood from her belly to scan the room for opportunities.

She flipped her only weapon, the knife, at the light above. Its housing cracked, throwing the room into darkness. With her frenine sight she had an immediate advantage.

The men kept firing at the table, slowly reducing it to a melted mess.

Kat backed away, blinking rapidly, adjusting her eyes to the dimness. The flash of the lasers revealed the men's positions.

She stalked them.

The surroundings were not what she was used to when hunting, and she wasn't normally wounded or facing armed opponents. Nevertheless, her primal instincts kicked in.

"Is she dead? Did we get her?"

"Don't know, Wreith. Save our charges. Get some ferking light!"

Kat crept closer. Time wasn't on her side. Blood dribbled from her wound, even though she held her skin together with the claws of her left hand. Her enemies were close. She could smell them, hear their breathing where they crouched.

One chance while I have strength. She drew her legs beneath her like springs, getting a grip on the moulded floor with her long claws. She could vaguely see the shorter enforcer, Jekar, pointing his gun in her direction.

She leapt.

Her free arm hit him across the chest. They rolled together as she burrowed her head beneath his chin, ripping at his throat with her fangs extended to their maximum. When it came to her life or his, she had no hesitation at killing. *Eat or be eaten,* that was the law of nature.

Flashes of light from Wreith's gun lit the room. A blast singed Kat's rump as she slid from Jekar's spasming body and hit the wall.

"Get away! Get away!" Wreith scrambled on all fours towards the door.

Kat pushed off the wall, hit him in the legs with her chest, and flattened him on the floor. She twisted, biting back a scream as her stomach wound tore further. She swung her legs across Wreith's chest and, with a quick downward jerk of her hind claws, slashed his throat. Blood spurted.

A pain sizzled across her head. She twisted off the dead man, rolling into a corner. The laser flashed again.

"You ferking pussy," Gorind croaked, "you've killed my men."

Beams of laser fire sprayed the wall, roasting Wreith's body, edging across to where she stretched flat against the floor. Gorind's blocky shape lumbered across the room. He tripped against the table she'd been strapped on and cracked his head against an instrument trolley.

His croaking ceased.

She needed to escape while she had a chance. She grabbed at the latch and pulled the door open, hunched over to protect her stomach.

Smoke filled the next room.

She coughed. Flames licked up the walls, growing higher as she watched. Her eyes stung. Acrid air filled her lungs. She coughed again, drew in a shuddering breath, and hacked out a dirty glob of phlegm. Her body hunched further in reflex, driving a sharp pain through her insides. She mewled, gripping at her torn belly. Her claws punctured the skin, curling over, holding her slippery skin tight. Blood seeped through her fingers.

The crackle of flames punctuated her consciousness as heat licked her body. She retched and scrambled along the floor to get to cleaner air, away from the increasing heat and fumes.

As she struggled to keep moving, Kat's hind claws splintered on the hard surface. The agony in her belly threatened to overwhelm her. Her energy drained away. Thick, oily smoke billowed over her, choking her, blinding her.

Her senses closed down. She collapsed on the hard floor.

Chapter 7

oren, in worn jeans and a sloppy shirt, headed to an abandoned warehouse on the outskirts of the slums, keeping to the shadows and grumbling under his breath, "Looking for creds is ferking never-ending."

After escaping the orphanage, he and his friend Hana had agreed that once he'd gained sellable skills, he'd get them out of the slums and into a better future. But in the meantime, ever since their escape, there'd been the continual quest to earn money to keep their tiny house. The so-called landlords in Sensuna's slum still required their take. He wasn't in a position to ignore their demands.

He looked around before fiddling at the base of a large fibro door with corroded hinges. He eased it open before sneaking through in his worn, rubber-soled boots, and closed the door behind him. Flicking on his head torch, he stepped with the assurance of routine to open several skylights by pulling on their dangling chains. Satisfied he could see without being seen, he hastened to a long workbench that ran the full length of the vast, otherwise empty space.

Miscellaneous bits and pieces lined the back of the bench, some in old tins, some in glass jars, others in buckets, depending on their volatility. Scraps of metal, electronics and polycarbonate were arranged according to size and function at one end. In the centre, a small device that looked like a cross between a knuckleduster and a robotic animal sat in a clear space.

Coren unloaded his pack and extracted a small jar of crystals. Using a spatula and wearing gloves, he counted out half a dozen pink, sugar-like grains and funnelled them into the mouselike contraption. He gently shook the device and screwed on an old bottle top to keep the contents firmly inside, then carried it across to the middle of the warehouse.

Taking a deep breath, he flicked on the switch from a room heater protruding from one side of the device, then raced back to the bench where he crouched facing the wall.

Nothing happened.

Gingerly, he peered over his shoulder. The device remained exactly as he had left it.

"Ferking stupid thing. That should have—"

Whoomph!

The device exploded, sending fragments pinging against the ceiling and walls.

Coren ducked, then yipped with glee, punching the air. "It worked! Maybe not so many grains next time."

With satisfaction, he jotted down a few notes in his personal device and swept up the mess in the hope that at least a few of the parts would be re-usable.

Excited to tell Hana of his success, Coren hurried to pack up. All Hana wanted was to set up a real home, with him. It wasn't much to ask for, but so far away from what they could achieve at the moment. He eased the door open and looked carefully along the sides of the warehouse. Nothing moved. No one had noticed; not that there would be much activity in this wasteland. Satisfied, he forced the door shut and jammed it with his home-made locking device.

"Done," he muttered, and pulled his backpack firmly onto his shoulders before heading down the alley. He hadn't gone far when he detected an oily smoke over the foul smells usual in this area. Deciding to investigate, he moved into another rubbish-filled walkway, squeezed past some rubble, and scanned the sky. A curling black cloud rose into the air a short distance away.

"Better see what it is before other scavengers come," he muttered to himself. "I might score something of value."

Someone grabbed the scruff of Kat's neck and pulled. She bumped over legs blocking her escape, agony suffusing her belly. She struggled, but the fight had gone out of her. She gasped. The grip on her neck released. Sweet oxygen flooded her lungs.

Safe. Safe from the fire. The pain burned in her stomach as she panted shallowly.

"What're we going to do with you?" a voice asked.

She peered through slitted eyes to a pair of scuffed boots only centimetres away. *Another enforcer?* She shut her eyes, waiting for the searing heat of a laser.

A hand caressed her remaining fur. "What's a frenine doing here?"

So, not an enforcer. Who, then?

"Stay there for a moment. The authorities will be crawling all over the place soon and there's stuff here worth a few creds."

Kat lay still as the owner of the boots hurried off. Then she attempted to sit up, clutching her bleeding stomach. She fell back with a thud, suppressing a groan.

The boots came back. He leant over her; a whiff of fear overlaid by desperation entering her nostrils. And youth. A young human male.

"You're in a bad way, aren't you? I don't know what you had to do with this fire, but I'd better take you with me before the authorities arrive. We might be competitors, but against the enforcers, we're in this together."

As she was hefted onto strong shoulders, Kat choked back a mewl of pain. The jiggling as the young man hurried from the building, plus all that had happened since the wire snagged her, proved too much. She blacked out.

As Coren heaved the limp, battered body of the frenine onto his shoulders, he tried not to react to the soft contours of a breast pressing into his cheek. She was heavy for a lithe creature, and though he was young and strong, her weight stretched his abilities. But no way was he going to leave her, especially as there would be more enforcers coming to collect the bodies of their own. She wouldn't stand a chance, even if she hadn't killed them.

His memories of a drastic fire affecting those he felt responsible for came flooding back from his time at the orphanage. He'd done his best to save the children from the flames, despite the lack of action from those in charge. And this was another such event, where a vulnerable person needed his help.

Fluids seeped under his collar and down his back, the wetness infiltrating his clothing and sticking his shirt to his back. He shifted the frenine to ease his shoulders as he followed a dark laneway, mindful of the noise and flare of firelight he'd left behind, the combination of the frenine's body and packs almost too much to bear, but he hadn't far to go.

He was compelled to save the frenine, but at the same time he couldn't bear to leave anything for other scavengers to find

The familiar waft of sewage told him he was nearing his small house, crammed into a small space between two decrepit buildings. Accessed by a narrow laneway, it was ideal for his comings and goings, particularly when he didn't want to be noticed by the authorities or the gangs that operated in these less desirable parts of the city.

I hope Hana is home, he thought, the breast against his chin making him think of her soft roundness and dark skin. Not only was she beautiful, she was a moderating influence on him ever since they had come together in the orphanage. She was never unreasonable—well, not often. His face warmed at memories of their fights, the making up worth the screaming and thrown objects. But against anyone else, she always backed him up, even when he was in the wrong. Although he'd never admit it to her, she was the real brains of their partnership. She'd know what to do with the frenine.

A soothing stroke over Kat's belly brought her to a slow awareness. Her befuddled mind fought to make sense of her surroundings, her brain numbed, presumably by a sedative. But the clean air and the soft surface beneath her gave her comfort.

She closed her eyes and listened, taking in the scents around her. A background smell of mould, rotting wood, and astringent antiseptic almost overpowered the scent of a female human, newly mature judging by the mixed aroma of hormones. A hand smoothed a cream onto Kat's belly. She tried to remain still but her lungs spasmed. She bent up into a great, hacking cough.

"Here!"

A basin was thrust under her mouth as she heaved up black sputum. The effort left her weak, and the throbbing in her belly and hands returned. She mewled and curled up on her side.

"I'll give you something more for the pain," the young woman's voice whispered in her ear.

Kat closed her eyes at a prick in her shoulder. She abandoned herself to the effects of the drug, her pain and images of Tar being shot underlying the sleep.

Chapter 8

Kat woke to a quiet, dimly-lit room, no one near, pain throbbing dully in her belly and hands. She gently raised her arms. Smooth med dressings had been sprayed over the fingers of both hands. The bandaging tightened across her abdomen as she lifted her head and cautiously moved her legs. Gritting her teeth against the searing pain, she eased each leg over the side of the small bed.

The sedative had worn off. When her feet touched the floor, she stood, shakily stooped over her belly, but alert.

A buzz of conversation came from another room. She smelt two people, the one who had taken her from the burning room and the female who had treated her. Nearby, a tray on a small table held a number of curled, black objects. She gingerly pushed them with one bandaged hand and drew a sharp breath. They were claws, ripped from her fingers.

No wonder her hands stung. She had assumed the bandages were because of the burns. *Who would do such a thing? A trophy hunter? Mercenaries looking for credits?* She'd heard frenine claws sold on the black market as aphrodisiacs, but never expected they'd be taken from someone alive. She crept across the room, thankful her feet remained unharmed, and edged to the door. Her keen hearing discerned the occupants arguing.

The young woman was pleading with the man. "She's wanted, worth 50,000 creds, any condition. That's enough to get us out of here."

"But Hana, from what that bulletin said, she's been through a lot; and against the authorities. No way we'd hand her in, despite the reward, not after what they've done to us. Why'd you even think of it?"

"We have to think of ourselves. This is our big chance! She might be dangerous, even to us. Remember, the bulletin claims she's a killer."

"Do you believe that? Frenines are a passive race. They don't go around murdering people. As soon as she's healed, we can take her back to her own kind, so it's just the two of us again. I'm not suggesting she stays with us forever."

"But if we do that, we won't get the creds! They can buy us a new start, even off-planet, away from Sensuna."

"Maybe, but I'm sure there's more behind this than we know, Hana. If we claim the creds, it'll expose us. Do you want to risk that after all we've been through? Besides, we're older now. They won't hesitate to lock us up with the worst scum on the planet. Then where would we be? We've got this far avoiding the law. We don't need to stick our fingers up their noses for any reason, least of all creds."

"I know, Coren, but I want a real home, one where we don't have to sneak around, where we can have friends visit. One without the stench of this place."

Kat heard a loud sigh.

"Let's see if she gets better first, then we'll talk about it. If she dies, we'll take the reward."

"Coren, I—"

"Come here, Hana."

Kat heard them move, then quiet. She tried the door but it was locked. She drank water from a container on a small table and lay back on the bed, resting her painful belly, her mind buzzing with how she could get away. At least she was still on Crofta.

The click of the door made her sit up, arms raised. Her hands stung as she moved her fingers, the sudden vulnerability of not having her prime weapons adding to her tenseness.

A tall young woman dressed in a loose smock stood in the doorway, her striking brown face framed with long straight black hair. "You're awake, then? I've found clothes for you, in your pack."

She held out a bundle. "I'm Hana, and my partner who rescued you is Coren."

Kat's ears flattened as she stared past Hana to the open door.

"I wouldn't if I were you. You're not well enough. We're in the city and the word's out for you. But we're not exactly best friends with the authorities, so you're safe for the moment."

Kat forced herself to relax as Hana closed the door.

The woman tentatively approached the bed. "Lie back so I can check the dressings. Kat, isn't it?"

"You know my name?" Kat lay back, ready to spring up if necessary.

"Yes," said Hana, as she ran her hands over the med dressings. "It was on the bulletin. But that's not my concern. You had a vicious cut down your stomach. Thankfully, you held it together with your broken claws. I had trouble prying them open. I'm sorry I had to remove them, but they were too damaged and likely to get infected. You can grow them back, can't you? Those crims deserved what they got. If Coren hadn't found you when he did—"

Kat let Hana ramble on, probably in nervousness. Relieved that her claws hadn't been harvested to sell, she would have believed the woman genuinely cared if she hadn't overheard the earlier conversation. She pondered more about her situation. The ambient scents told her she was in the seedier side of Sensuna. Very likely she'd be turned in for the reward when she had healed.

She had to get away.

She flinched when she heard a word in Hana's ramblings. "Gorind? Did you say Gorind?"

"What?" Hana's eyes narrowed to slits. "Damn, I swore never to say that evil creature's name again. But Coren thinks that may be who did this to you. We've heard he takes delight in torturing genoids."

"What do you know about him? Is he dead?"

"Let's leave it for the moment," Hana mumbled, rubbing more soothing cream into Kat's belly. "You need to heal."

She stepped back towards the door. "Sorry, that's the best I can do. You'll need to rest for a time. I'll let Coren know you're awake."

With Hana gone from the tiny room, Kat gingerly pulled on her black trousers, slit for her tail, a string vest, and a dark overjacket, before pacing the room, stretching her limbs carefully, testing the limits of her fitness. Whoever young Hana was, her healing was effective. The pain burned in the background but she could function.

A knock startled her. She backed to the wall as the door edged open. Coren, the one who had carried her, came in, gun in hand.

"Sorry about this," he said lifting the weapon, a nervous smile on his broad, high-cheek-boned face, "but I've seen what you did to those enforcers who were torturing you."

Kat growled, assessing the young man in front of her, working out his most vulnerable parts to give her the best chance of taking him. "Hana didn't need that. Let me go. I'm no threat to you."

"Look, we saved your life," —the gun barrel drifted lower— "Relax. If I'd wanted you dead, I'd have left you in the fire, with the bodies."

"So put down the gun. Or are you afraid? You just want your reward." Kat spat and stepped away from the wall.

"Stop!" The barrel rose. "Get better first and then we'll talk."

"No, we'll talk now." Kat thought for a moment. "I know what you're thinking. I heard you and Hana talking. 50,000 credits is a lot of incentive. I can't match that. But they're after me for killing a killer."

"Yeah," Coren agreed, "I saw what you can do."

"It was me or them!" Kat snarled and poised to pounce.

"Don't! Wait! We've no problem with you killing enforcers," Coren added, "but now we've got to decide what to do about you. You're at the top of the authorities' 'Most Wanted' list. We'll be blamed too if we're found hiding you."

He relaxed and propped himself on the end of the bed, motioning for her to sit near him. "If it were just me, I'd take the risk, but Hana's my responsibility. I'll need to work it through with her. We're partners, in every sense. Any decisions have to be made by both of us."

Kat dropped her arms and eased her tense muscles, remaining with her back to the wall. "I'll stand, thank you. I don't trust human men, especially when they have a gun in their hands."

Coren leant over and placed the gun between his feet. "Better? Let me tell you a bit about us so you understand more. We met at a kids' home. I'd been there for years, abandoned at birth. They told me my mum was a prostitute."

Kat waited for him to go on, thinking of her pride. Cubs would never be abandoned to be raised by unknown frenines, even if the mother died.

"Hana had only been at the home a few weeks when we met. She's the one who encouraged me to leave. She had creds, see, and contacts. She's really bright. I'd never have left without her."

Kat could hear the love in his voice as he spoke about Hana. "So how did you survive?"

Coren shrugged. "Who knows? Maybe we've got a guardian angel." He laughed as if such a thing existed. "By our wits, and stealth, and keeping out of the authorities' notice. That's why we need to decide what to do about you."

Kat flinched. "I'm sorry you've been put in danger through rescuing me. I promise I won't tell anyone about you. Let me go, and you can forget you ever met me."

The expression on Coren's face was full of regret. "Too late for that. Anyway, get some rest. I'll find you some food—meat's best, right?"

Kat shrugged, accepting she was in no condition to fight past both of them, and not sure she wanted to anyway. She sat back on the bed as the door closed behind him, considering her options. For now, food and rest to help her get well seemed like the best thing. But 50,000 credits was a lot of temptation. She needed to keep sharp and watch for a change in their mood. She was confident Hana was a healer so wouldn't hurt her, but that didn't mean they wouldn't hand her in.

She understood. The youngsters of a pride were a close-knit team too, regardless of who their mothers were. The males eventually left to set up their own pride, but when they were young, male and female frenines all lived in the pride house, ruled by the alpha female. Had she had cubs, she and Tar would have been the leaders of their pride, not just in charge of hunting.

A pang of jealousy surprised her. How come Hana and Coren had each other, and she no longer had Tar? Tar, her best friend and lifemate. Now she had nobody to make decisions with, or confide in, or enjoy raising cubs with.

The door to Kat's room opened a crack. The point of a gun came through, along with a nervous scent.

She quickly slid off the bed and crouched to the floor.

Hana's face peered around the door. "Kat?"

"What are you doing? You didn't need a gun last time," she hissed, crouching even lower.

"I know. But you were drugged then. But it's not what it seems," she whispered, straightening her slender body as she entered the room. "I've come to get you out. Coren's not here. He doesn't know."

"Why? For the credits?" Kat stood up, knowing she could take out the young woman, gun or no gun. She doubted Hana had ever fired a weapon from the way she held it.

"No, not that. We've had enough trouble with the law without them working out we've got you. We don't want to get their attention, even that way. I just want you gone. You'll bring trouble down on us."

Kat hesitated, breathing Hana's pheromones, searching for the hint of a trap. All she could smell was the stink of fear. *Why? What had brought on this change of heart?*

She itched to go, though she was afraid to trust Hana. But she had to take the chance. She stepped forward.

Hana stood to one side, holding the door open, gun still pointed at her.

Kat stared at her without blinking. "Put that laser down and I'll come."

Hana's eyes flickered, sweat beading on her forehead, but she lowered the gun. "Come on then."

Kat slipped through the door into a small deserted kitchen. "Where to now?"

Hana followed close behind. "We're off a back alley. Follow it along to the markets. If you're clever, no one will see you. Then you're out of our lives."

Kat checked her again for tell-tale signs of treachery, but fear still dominated Hana's body language and scent.

The young woman slid the gun into a drawer and moved to the outside door, cracked it open and looked out. "All clear," she whispered.

Kat stretched her head past and peered along the rubbish-strewn alley. The dark end drew her, offering shadows in which to blend, but Hana pointed the other way.

"It's where the market begins. The dark way leads to the sewers. You'd better get going before Coren comes back." Hana stepped back as Kat headed off into the alley.

She hissed and drew in the air. Many smells hit her, too many to discern any danger. *Maybe Hana was genuinely concerned that Coren would want to take her back to the pride, risking being caught with her. But why not convince him to let her go in the city? Why sneak her out while he was away?*

Kat's hackles rose in suspicion. Nothing about this felt right, but she had to move with Hana still waiting in the doorway. She could find her way out of the city and home, her sense of direction strong. She hadn't been in this part of Sensuna before, but it wouldn't take her long to recognise the skyline when she could see it. Then all she had to do was avoid the authorities and head off across the plains.

Although her injuries still restricted her, she could use her camouflage and ability to walk unseen. Ignoring the dull throb of her hands and the stabbing pain in her belly, she crept towards the lighter end of the alley. A quick glimpse of market booths reassured her that Hana hadn't lied. People mingled among them, purchasing produce, inspecting homewares, and trying on second-hand clothing. The nearer she approached, the more the aromas changed to stale vegetables and cooking meat.

Her stomach rumbled. She didn't dare risk using the credits associated with her identity chip. She edged towards the end of the alleyway. On her left, a dilapidated warehouse stood with broken windows, the inside dark and silent. She stood still, considering her options. Better to hide until dark when the market would be deserted. Perhaps by then she would have a better idea where she was, without the overpowering scents. She doubted that Coren would search for her, or suspect she was still so close to their home.

Still, Hana's nervousness had rung alarm bells in Kat's head. *Why hadn't she just told Kat to leave? Why the fear, and her watching from the doorway?*

Listening for any sound of being followed, Kat stared around her for a possible trap. The alleyway remained deserted. Nothing moved. The enticing aroma of cooking meat teased her nose and moistened her mouth, but she swallowed back her saliva. She couldn't be distracted. After a few more moments, confident she was alone, Kat eased the door to the warehouse further ajar.

Whooosh!

A heavy net fell across her, pushing her to her knees. She lashed out with her bandaged hands and clawed feet but they tangled in the mesh. She writhed as if scalded, her stomach wound shrieking.

Heavy boots ran towards her, thudding into the alleyway from around the corner.

Enforcers! How could she not have detected them? If she didn't hurt so much already, she would have smacked herself for being a fool. The stink of her surroundings must have overridden her senses. She should have listened to her instincts, warning her of danger. Distracted by the market, she hadn't thought to look above her.

"Hold still you ferking pussy!" a gruff voice bellowed close to her head, followed by a hard blow. She snapped her jaws in his direction, canines extended to tear at his throat if need be.

His companion wrestled with her legs, trying to tie them together. She wriggled and lashed out, kicking at anything solid. Something sliced into her shoulder and pain shot through her belly, but her need to flee overcame her instinct to protect her wounds. She yowled and tore at the net, ripping a hole large enough to get her legs through.

A familiar voice accompanied a patter of light feet running toward her. "Don't hurt her! That wasn't the bargain!" Hana's shrill tones rang in Kat's ears, confirming her earlier fears.

The first man stepped away from Kat's gnashing jaws. "Get lost! This is our business now. You'll get your reward when the captive is safely locked up. Get out of the way!"

"You said you'd look after her! I only came to you because I saw the way my partner looked at her! She'd have split us up." Hana's wheedling had no effect on the men.

They continued to try to truss Kat up, grabbing at her limbs. She ripped them away, hind claws and teeth slashing at random.

Hana forced her way between the men and Kat. "Stop it! I did as you asked and let you catch her. Treat her well. And give me my creds!"

The men refused to be intimidated by Hana until she pulled out her gun. Even though her hand shook, the safety was off and she pointed it at the first enforcer's midriff.

Kat stopped listening to their arguing. With both men distracted, she wriggled through the hole in the net. As soon as her head came free, she sprinted towards the market, hoping she could find safety among the mass of people. Shouts followed her. Some people tried to grab at her arms as she fled past, others held out their hands for her to stop, claiming they could help.

She no longer trusted anyone. Almost doubled over from the pain in her belly, dodging left and right through the stalls while doing her best not to knock anything over, she searched desperately for a quieter location. Her eyes blurred from pain, her mind numbed from loss of blood, her tongue stuck like cardboard between her teeth.

Ahead, a dineeth came into view. He didn't try to stop her, only held his furry head to one side, his ears pointed alert.

She had to take the chance. She staggered to him, grasping her belly wound. "Enforcers…after me. Can you help? Mystic Nivlac—"

Without a word, he shed his jacket, wrapped it around her, then scooped her up in strong, hairy arms.

She lost consciousness.

Chapter 9

Kat's eyes snapped open, head clear, instantly aware. Disinfectant filled her nostrils, her pain a distant ache, arms and legs tethered by soft fasteners to a bolted-down seat. A black couch against a wall and a matching chair a distance in front of her broke the monotony of the otherwise white room.

"Not again," she muttered as she heaved at her bonds, snarling in frustration, scratching her hind claws on the hard floor.

A smell of lightly cooked meat permeated the room a moment before the door opened behind her. She twisted her head.

A plate clunked onto a hard surface. A tall figure with the myopic look of someone with corrected vision, dressed in an immaculate grey suit, stepped into view. He shifted a small table near to her and let the aromas waft over. "Sorry about the bonds. I didn't want you to hurt yourself even more when you woke up. Also, I thought you might be hungry."

Kat's stomach, despite its soreness, growled in response. She watched him through narrowed eyes, squashing down her traitorous gut, her tail flicking behind her.

"If you'll calm down and listen for a moment," he said in a soft, modulated voice, his lined face giving a hint of a smile, "you can be released."

Kat growled.

"I'm informed you're an effective fighter, even for a young frenine. The trouble on K-Astar3 and here on Crofta, plus the unfortunate deaths, have brought you much attention, even if for acceptable reasons. Need I go on?"

Kat's ears flattened. "I've never —"

"I'm not here to go over old ground." He walked to the table and ran a fingertip through the gravy on the plate, then slowly licked it, back half turned. "I'm here to ask for your help."

"What?" Kat leant forward.

"Yes, you heard right, Katerina Ellana Schlorati. I know all about you. I'll release one of your hands so you can eat while I explain, if you agree to behave."

She froze for a moment, wondering how he knew so much about her, before giving a curt nod. She had nothing to lose and was hungry.

He moved the table to her side and deftly released her right hand before seating himself on the black chair.

Kat kept one eye on him while she ate the food, slowly at first, awkward in swathed bandages, a spoon stuck between sausage-fat fingers. When the delicious tastes of roast zeena and crispy skin met her tongue, she couldn't help but ignore the discomfort and gulp the food down. Her stomach warmed and gurgled in appreciation.

The man let her satiate her initial hunger before clearing his throat and raising a slim hand in the air. "I represent a small but well-resourced organisation in this section of space that has links through much of the explored galaxy, one that works deeper than normal law enforcement and uses various means to achieve desirable ends. I don't need to tell you much except that we keep ourselves out of the public view and take no credit for what we do."

Kat swallowed and her ears pricked up. "I at least want to know your name. And what sort of organisation? What does it do?"

He ran his fingers through his thinning hair as if to keep every single strand in place, then smoothed his creased trousers. "You can call me Ardan. The Agency is the best way to refer to our organisation. One of The Agency's prime focuses is to prevent the exploitation of sapient species on all worlds."

He smiled tightly. "Because of the vast areas we cover, we often utilise others to assist us. Here, our resources play a significant part. We are offering you a way forward, to help make those who slaughter sapient species, such as your mate Tar, pay for their crimes."

"How do you know about Tar?" She snarled to prevent herself from crying at the renewed memory of him callously tossed on the luggage rack of the hunters' vehicle.

"I told you. I know everything about you, including your visits for lassivar flower therapy. I know what drives you. We have vast resources and extensive databanks. We know more than you could ever dream, Kat. I also know that now you have killed people, your pride is likely to turn against you."

He pushed at his wispy black hair again. Kat couldn't help thinking it must be dyed, a vanity at odds with its sparseness. *Why didn't he get it regenerated?*

"If you know so much, why was I attacked in the alley? Why not meet me in a civilised manner?"

"I told you we have few people on any one planet and, while keen to contact you, I knew nothing about the attack. It was fortunate you met up with one of our…sympathisers. It was through him that you are here now. We're not your enemy."

Kat resumed eating while she thought it through. Her last memory was pleading with a dineeth to contact Nivlac, so it stood to reason that the mystic had a link to Ardan's organisation if what this man said was true.

He coughed to get her attention. "While I have every confidence you'll accept my offer, you should know what you're getting yourself into."

His slight smile faded. "We want you to be part of finding out who is enabling the slaughter of sapient species on this and other worlds. You're to report your findings back to me or my agents, and you may be required to eliminate certain threats in order to break up the network of corruption. You will have total autonomy with how you go about your task, and I'll ensure the authorities are no longer interested in you. We will provide resources, but with our very limited manpower, I expect you to develop your own contacts, too."

Kat struggled to take in this change of circumstance. "If your reach is so extensive, why do you need me, an insignificant nobody?"

He blinked a few times. "You're hardly an 'insignificant nobody', Kat. In return for your co-operation, we'll protect you, to the best of our ability at least. And as I said, we need to remain unacknowledged. Anonymous. I'll pull strings where I can to ensure you can pursue your mission, but we'll always operate in the background. If you get caught in illegal activities, The Agency can't be openly involved. It'll do you no good to mention it, or me, in an attempt to explain your situation."

Kat's meal sat like an acidic lump in her guts as she considered her options. *Would this secretive organisation really help her, or were they setting her up to do their dirty work, to let her take the blame later on?* "I still don't see why you need me. You must have access to other individuals who would be far more skilled and experienced."

Ardan crossed his legs and straightened the creases of his trousers. "I admit you'll essentially be a resource, a 'gun for hire' in Earth parlance. As to why you, it's your very lack of experience in the field that'll make it easier for you to undertake this task. Our other resources are limited, could even be compromised. You've proven to be an effective fighter and I believe your motivation, after the death of your partner, gives you a great incentive."

Kat ignored the pain from her stomach wounds as she leant back from her plate and watched the man in front of her. "You mean to turn me into a mercenary. But I'm not a natural killer. Frenines only kill for food, and while I was forced to kill to save my life, it goes against our ethics."

"Even Rast Baden-Hauf? I think not."

She eyed Ardan on the chair. "If you know so much, you'll know the reasoning behind that. I thought you were above that sort of thinking."

Ardan shook his head. "Sorry, you're right." He leant forward. "If you'll accept the task, I'll do everything in my power to support you, even remove your 'wanted' status."

"Really? How?"

"I've told you, I can pull strings. You'll have to trust me on that."

"But only if I become your investigator? A mercenary? What about my injuries?" She held up her free hand. "I need time to heal. I can't fight without claws."

He waved a dismissive hand. "I told you, we have resources. You'll be given the best treatment. We can increase the speed of claw regeneration. You don't need to start until you're fit and able."

Kat's mind whirled. The proposition was almost too good to be true. She knew what awaited her if the authorities caught her. Yet a niggle still remained, tapping at her intuition. "How do I start looking for this corruption that you talked about? Is Lord Baden-Hauf involved? What resources will I have access to?"

Ardan's smile widened, exposing perfect white teeth. "All in good time. If you agree, you will be briefed and provided with what you need."

Kat breathed deeply a few times, trying to quell the hope rising in her heart that she might yet escape the attention of the Sensuna Policing Corporation. "I guess I have little choice but to accept. What now?"

Ardan leant over and began removing the last of her restraints. "I'll introduce you to my second-in-charge on Crofta. I think you'll like her."

Ardan led Kat from the room out into a white, non-descript corridor, the ambient odours indicating she was somewhere near the centre of Sensuna. The ever-present smells of antiseptic indicated The Agency had medical facilities. A door hissed open to reveal the bent, white-coated back of a grey-haired woman sitting at a desk. She looked up as they entered.

"Relina, meet Kat, our new recruit." He gestured towards the skeletally-thin woman who greeted them. A few steps away, a young man glanced at them from behind a vid screen, eyebrows raised.

"And Chaz," he pointed, "the sum of our people on Crofta."

Kat narrowed her eyes before acknowledging the introductions. Still unsure of the extent and veracity of Ardan's operations, she intended to remain wary until they'd gained her trust.

"Kat." The thin woman smiled and stretched out her hand in a distinctly human greeting.

Kat hissed and drew back.

"Sorry! I forgot you're hurt. Let me see." Relina reached with open palms for Kat's bandaged hands.

Ardan inclined his head. "Do what you can for Kat's injuries, please, Relina. We need her to recover as quickly as possible."

"We've good facilities here," the woman said, looking Kat in the eyes. "If you'll come with me, I'm sure I can fix all your wounds in quick time. We can easily regrow your claws and repair any skin damage. Our technology is the best."

The woman smiled at Ardan, still hovering in the doorway. "Leave her with me. We'll have her back to normal in no time."

Ardan returned the smile and disappeared through the doorway.

"Come with me," she said to Kat. "The sooner we get started the better. Chaz, stop fiddling around with your electronics and give me a hand, would you, please?"

Still in a bemused state, Kat let herself be led into a small room with a long, flat bench. Keen to be healed, she shoved aside her concerns for the moment. Her instincts and their scents rang no alarms. The sooner she was fully recovered the better.

Once Relina and Chaz started work, Kat had little time to reflect on her miraculous healing. Even while she underwent rapid claw and fur regeneration, she learnt much about The Agency and what it faced. Once the medical processes were complete, Relina returned her to Ardan.

The briefing she had received filled her with concern while strengthening her resolve. The man she was pursuing was part of an illegal subsidiary of the Interplanetary Hunters Organisation, a group named Hunters Extreme, or HuX. She now knew she had no choice but to accept the deal Ardan had offered; otherwise, she would always be looking over her shoulder for Gorind or other people like him.

She didn't bother sitting in the proffered chair. "Thank you for healing me. I'm in. What happens next?"

Ardan nodded. "I suggest you gather a small team, two or three perhaps, and bring them back here. You'll need to be fully briefed, trained, and provided equipment."

Still unable to fathom her position, but grateful for the support, Kat headed out of the room. First, she had return to the pride and face their reaction to her activities.

Chapter 10

Kat jogged along the grassy path through her village towards the haphazard structure of the pride's home. Sunlight glinted off the small windows between vine-clad walls, the vertical maze a welcome sight to her racing mind. Memories of chasing Tar through the tunnels between rooms and sliding down the chutes between floors flashed with the sunbeams.

Kat choked back a sob. She had no time for self-pity.

The palm print of her left hand opened the front door as she shrugged her pack from the opposite shoulder. She dropped it inside the welcoming entryway and called out to announce her arrival.

With a shriek, Sashyr ran along the twisting corridor, her bare feet barely making a sound. "Kat! Thank the sun and moon! You're home!"

Almost strangled by her friend's embrace, Kat rubbed her face against Sashyr's fur, their colouring almost identical except for Sashyr's golden tufts behind her ears. "I'm alright! I'm alright!"

Tears streaming down both their faces, they hugged one more time before heading into the sitting room. With their legs curled up beneath them on the sofa, a hot tea in their hands, Kat reassured her friend that the authorities weren't chasing her, despite what she might have seen on the newsfeeds. "I'm sorry I haven't contacted you earlier, but it wasn't possible where I was."

Mesat, the elder frenine, strode into the room with a frown wrinkling her normally smooth face. "And where was that? Somewhere artificial, as your scents clearly show. From what I hear, you have a lot of explaining to do."

Kat growled, bracing herself for a confrontation. "I saw the mystic as you advised and did as he suggested, going to K-Astar3. I was there when Lord Baden-Hauf's son was killed so the place was mayhem. I came back, and was approached by someone in a special organisation—"

Mesat held up a hand. "I think you've missed a few points out. The newsfeeds say you are the one who killed not only Baden-Hauf's son, but an enforcer too. We're not aware of any other frenines being off-planet."

With her guts in turmoil from guilt, Kat couldn't lie. "It's true, but I only killed the enforcer by accident, to save my life. He—"

"And the other one? The man in the bar?" Even Sashyr looked grim as Mesat questioned Kat.

"I did exactly what Mystic Nivlac said. You sent me to him! Are you saying I shouldn't have followed his instructions?" Anger rose in Kat's throat as she stood up.

The frenine elder glared at Kat. "So you admit you poisoned this man. Killed two humans. Not for food, but for revenge."

Kat faced the angry elder. "Yes, but—"

"No buts. As a member of the Frenine Council, I pronounce you exiled from frenine society. You will leave this house immediately. You will be sent formal notification once the Council have ratified this order." Mesat stood. "Sashyr, you will help Katerina pack her things and ensure she leaves within the hour."

To stunned silence, she left the room.

Kat turned to her friend. "This can't be happening! I knew the Council might eventually decide this, but Mesat?"

Sashyr gave her a gentle squeeze. "You must have known it was possible, Kat. All our lives we've been told only to kill for food. Come on, I'll help you pack, or I'll be going with you."

When they reached Kat's room, Kat looked around her, stunned. "Sashyr, I need help, not just because of being ostracised, but to track down the organisation behind Tar's murder. We'll be given special training, and resources. The people who rescued me fixed my injuries with amazing technology. They can help—"

Sashyr frowned. "Kat, I agreed to help you pack, but I'm not going against your exile order, and I'm certainly not going with you. I'm sorry, but you need to prove to the Council your reasons for killing without need if you want to come back."

Stunned by her friend's rejection, Kat shoved clothes and her other important possessions into an empty pack. "Fine, I'll do this alone. Without Tar there's no point being here anyway."

She finished and stalked out of the house without another word to anyone. If she could bring down the organisation behind the illegal hunting, maybe the Frenine Council would allow her to return. Until then, she would track down whoever was responsible for Tar's death and make them pay.

Hana poked her head out of the door in the twilight, checked the alleyway was clear, and darted out. Running quietly on long, slender legs, she headed towards the dark end of the passageway, accustomed to navigating the rougher side of Sensuna.

She breathed heavily, still annoyed at Coren shouting at her for letting the frenine out, but even more because she hadn't been able to find any trace of where Kat had gone. The authorities she'd originally contacted and organised the trap with had denied all knowledge of being involved. Now she and Coren had no frenine, and no reward.

She mumbled to herself as she hurried to the sewer end of the alley. "Someone's taken the creds for themselves. No hope for a young woman like me. Now the word's out that I can't be trusted. Why did Coren get involved and rescue her? Aren't I enough for him?"

Slipping along a narrow path lined by broken-down walls on one side and an odorous, scummy wasteland on the other, guilt riddled Hana, knowing she'd lied to the frenine when she'd told her the best way out was to go into the marketplace—this way was less obvious and safer. But of course, that wouldn't have led Kat into the trap.

Hana again cursed herself for being stupid, knowing her jealousy had been the cause, but her earlier life of wealth and ease, then the short time she'd spent in the orphanage, followed by living off the streets with Coren, had made her rash. She eased past a tumble of bricks with her head down, still mumbling to herself when a band of iron gripped her throat. She twisted, hand dropping to the gun she'd carried ever since being duped by the enforcers, then froze as a familiar voice hissed hotly into her ear.

"You turned me in, Hana."

A brush of fur accompanied a golden-brown arm under her chin.

She tensed, not even breathing. "I… I'm sorry… *gurk*."

The arm squeezed tighter. She yelped at a sharp pain in her ear.

"No words, Hana. They'd be lies anyway. Should I rip your throat out here? In this sewer? A fitting place for your life to end," Kat purred in her ear.

Hana's guts churned as if she were about to throw up. She dry-heaved a couple of times.

The arm withdrew.

Hana dropped painfully onto a pile of broken bricks and wheezed in air before looking up.

Kat wore black, form-fitting trousers and a shiny grey shirt with a black over-vest. Her left hand, with no sign of injuries, hovered over a bulging equipment belt fastened above her hips. *Was this really her, the same frenine? Could claws regrow so quickly?*

"Kat! You scared me!" Her heart slowed as she took a deep breath, grateful to be alive. "Let me expl—"

Kat's hind claws scratched the ground as she dragged Hana to her feet by her arm.

"Yes, Hana. I'm here. Alive. Free. And very angry at being betrayed."

Blood dripped down Hana's wrist. The thought of reaching for her gun flitted through her mind but she was no match for the quick reflexes of a frenine. "Kat, I'm sorry. But people like Coren and I never get that amount of creds. We want to get away from here and make a home together. I couldn't let that pass. The people I contacted said they wouldn't hurt you, only wanted to talk."

"Just you, Hana?" Kat pulled her closer, their chests almost touching. "Not Coren too?"

Hana stared at her feet and shifted on the bricks. "No, just me," she sighed. "Coren wouldn't have agreed. He thought we should hide you until you were well enough to leave. He's really upset with me, and I didn't get the creds either."

"No, you didn't." Kat extended her long canines. "Did you really think you would? A slum dweller? The authorities don't deal with people like you."

"They're swindlers, all of them." Hana looked up at Kat, relieved she appeared less on edge. "I'm sorry, I really am. At least you look well now. Can we leave, please? We're vulnerable out in the open."

Kat released her neck. "We'll go to your home. I need to talk to you and Coren. Give me your gun."

Hana extracted her weapon and placed it in Kat's hand, exhaled, and straightened. "At least seeing you well and free might make Coren forgive me now."

They walked side by side along the quiet alley, a supposedly friendly arm around Hana's waist, though sharp claws stuck through her shirt. Once at the battered door of her home, Hana fiddled with the lock.

"I knew the dark end would be better," Kat whispered, "unlike where you sent me. I should have trusted my instincts."

"I've said I'm sorry," Hana mumbled as she shoved the door open. "I had to, I—"

A table crashed onto its side. A body dropped out of sight and a laser barrel appeared over the edge of the table.

Hana shrieked. "It's me, Coren! It's alright!"

"What's she doing back here? Blast you, Hana!" said Coren, head just visible, his weapon unsteady. "First you risk our exposure by dobbing her in, now you bring her back! What are you thinking? We're in big trouble."

Kat slid an arm around Hana's neck as she attempted to slip sideways. "She had no choice. I wanted to face who betrayed me and know why."

"Shit! Shit! Shit!" Coren banged his gun on the table. "Life goes from crappy to crappier."

Hana cringed at the trouble she had caused. Even if Kat let them go, they would have to find another home now, never easy with few creds and dodgy backgrounds. She wished Coren had never saved Kat.

The frenine stood with her free hand on her hip, clicking her claws in and out.

Coren sighed. "You're obviously alright now. Can't you just forget you ever saw us and go? We've got enough problems just staying alive. The word's out we were involved with you. Now everyone we ever crossed is on our backs. All we were trying to achieve has been for nothing."

Kat tightened her grip on Hana's neck. "You have problems? Well, I'm another, and the most pressing. Drop. Your. Gun!"

"Pleeaasse," squeaked Hana.

"Shit!" Coren flung the gun to the floor and slowly rose from behind the table.

Sweat dripped down Hana's face, despite the coolness of the dark interior. "Don't blame me. You were the one who rescued her in the first place. And you would've been happy if I'd got the creds. Then we could've left this fetid hole and made a new home, somewhere clean and decent."

Kat banged on the table. "Shut up, the pair of you. I didn't come here to listen to you argue. We need to talk. As uncomfortable as it makes me feel, you're my only option now. I'm sorry I had to play heavy-handed in getting back here, but I had to ensure you were who you pretended to be. You both helped me before, and I'm hoping you can help again."

Kat picked up Coren's weapon and placed it on the righted table along with Hana's before sitting in the most comfortable seat, an old armchair with torn upholstery.

Coren dragged over a chair for Hana before straddling a three-legged stool. "What do you want with us?"

After Hana seated herself, combing fingers through her bedraggled hair, she gave Kat a meek smile. "Despite everything, I'm glad to see you. You seem to have recovered quickly. Is that something frenines can do?"

Kat resettled her equipment belt. "I've had an interesting adventure."

Coren held up both hands. "I'm sure she isn't here to talk about frenine healing, Hana. What do you want, Kat, since you presumably aren't going to kill us?"

Kat pushed her tail to one side, crossed her slender legs, and released the fastenings on her over-jacket. "Kill you, Coren? After you rescued me from the fire? Why would I do that?"

She did her best to give Hana a quick smile. "And thank you, Hana, for your first aid. I'm fully recovered."

She looked between the two. "What I need to know is, can I trust you? You've already let me down once. If it happens again, we won't be sitting quietly talking."

Coren's eyes tightened in his strong face and he clenched his fist. "I know you feel betrayed, Kat, but you've got to know Hana's reasons. It wasn't personal. The thought of all those creds was too much for her. I haven't been able to give her the home she deserves'—he threw Hana a loving glance—"and I scared her when I rescued you. What I did means we'll have to be on the move to keep out of the authorities' attention."

Kat smiled with her lips only. "Relax, the authorities you're concerned about don't know where I am. But you're right, you're probably wise to move on. I would have said that's not my problem. However, we might be able to help each other."

Coren baulked. "What do you mean?"

Kat drummed her claws on the tabletop. "I have to check first, but if what I'm thinking works out, you'll have a way to get out of this place to somewhere far better. I'll come back when I've sorted a few things out."

"You want us to stay here? After you agreed it isn't safe? You must be addled." Coren rolled his eyes.

"I'm sure you know how to look after yourselves," said Kat. "If you can wait a few more days I'll be back with a proposition, a way for you to be safe without needing to betray me."

"We need more than promises," grumbled Coren. "Things have livened up already."

"I'm sorry, but believe me, I need you and it'll be well worth your while." Kat didn't give him time to argue, heading out the way she had come.

Chapter II

Night had fallen, the scarred red moon low on the horizon providing poor light, as Kat headed east, beyond the shadier parts of Sensuna. She avoided dislodging any stones with her feet as she trekked up the red-tinged track to the mystic. Stepping over cracks, she took special care on the crumbling edges despite her excellent night vision. She wondered why he had to live in such a desolate place, especially since she was making a habit of visiting him here. All she knew was that he was a creature of significant power who had resided in this place for as long as anyone could remember, isolated from his pack and his people.

Kat's claws flicked in and out as she climbed, the fur rising on the back of her neck. A trickle of gravel from above warned her there was someone or something ahead of her. *Should she wait?* She didn't want to encounter others consulting him.

The track wound to the right, away from where the movement had originated, the flash of a ground squirrel reassuring her. She crept on, steeling herself for a confrontation after her abrupt exit last visit. She'd originally had no intention of returning, but Ardan had insisted she use her own contacts. No longer able to involve her pride, she knew of no-one else who could help apart from the mystic and her two rescuers.

At least the mystic was a genoid, like her, their two species having centuries of close ties. She hadn't mentioned him to Ardan, wanting to keep things close, not sure if she could fully trust The Agency. For now, she would find out all she could and then make up her mind what to do.

She called out a tentative hello as she approached the mystic's den.

He asked her to enter.

The room had changed little from last time. Mystic Nivlac looked like he hadn't moved, sitting among matted vegetation emitting a strong smell of humus. She lowered herself onto the stone bench where she had sat before between two lengths of intricately woven wall hangings.

She removed the jewel-studded choker from her neck, amazed she still had it after all she had been through, and held it out. "I'm sorry I left in such a rush last time. I forgot to return this. In fact I wish I had—I may as well have been wearing a tracker beacon."

Mystic Nivlac accepted the black tek-tek leather choker. "It wouldn't have been this that gave away your presence. No technology can track this, and when you use your camouflage ability, it blends in too. They must have had other means." He turned it over in his hands. "It still has much power and I attuned it to you. Are you sure you don't want to keep it?"

Kat fidgeted on her seat. "I'm not sure. I don't know where I'll be going next, or what I'll be doing."

"All the more reason to retain it, then." The mystic handed it back.

"You haven't told me yet what I owe you for your help. I may be able to pay you, but I'd rather know up front what my obligations are." She didn't want to add that she no longer had access to the communal pride funds, only her savings.

The dineeth shook his head. "I've no need for credits. A time will come when you will fulfil what I require of you. For now, be calm while I read your aura."

Kat squirmed, unhappy with the open-ended agreement. *What if she couldn't, or wouldn't, do what he required of her later?*

Mystic Nivlac sat as still as the rock of his home, not even his chest rising and falling with his breath. He held his hands out in front of him, eyes vacant.

As time passed, Kat did her best to sit still, conscious of an energy wrapping around her body as before. Warmth permeated her skin, not unpleasant, more like the sun moving across her fur but not as hot. The feeling spread around her back, over her head, and down her legs.

When the heat had completely enveloped her, the mystic sighed. "I recall advising you that taking the path of vengeance might have unexpected consequences. It seems it has."

He cleared his throat and leant forward, eyes barely visible under the brim of his hood. "Your aura is full of pain, not that of merely losing your mate, but of more recent events, physical and emotional."

He sat back and moments passed, the vague whisper of wind along the cliff face and the gentle inhalation of Kat's breath the only sounds. She remained still, not knowing how to respond.

The mystic eventually spoke, his voice soft like skittering leaves. "You need to continue your journey."

Kat wriggled on the hard seat, using her hand to still her flicking tail. "I had hoped I was finished, but I failed. Now I'm caught in a situation where I'm uncertain what to do." She hesitated, "You know what's happened, don't you? I've been exiled from my pride, and been asked to seek information about a certain organisation."

The mystic turned in a rustle of dry vegetation and reached into a small hollow. "I think we'll have tea. We may be here for a while."

Kat suppressed an urge to leave. She hadn't come for tea or polite conversation. She wanted answers. Instead, she felt beholden to him. *Was he, like Ardan, using her? Who knew what powers he had?*

"Here, my young friend." The scrape of pottery on stone drew her attention. The mystic lifted a cup to his lips.

Kat sighed and picked up a similar cup. A waft of herbs hit her nostrils as she took a sip of the clear liquid, grimacing at the muddy taste, about to put it down.

"It is best to drink it all in one go," he murmured.

She hesitated, ears flattening before she drank it down. She needed to keep him on side if she were to get any more information from him.

"Good, Kat. Now we wait for it to take effect as we discuss your situation." He pushed his hood back and leant forward.

Kat blinked. "Take effect? What do you mean?"

"Relax. You can rely on me as frenines have for generations. You wouldn't be here if you didn't trust me."

The features of the mystic became clearer to Kat, the brown teardrop mark on his bristly patterned face focussing her attention away from his protruding snout and the small pointed ears on the top of his head. She could see the signs of age in this venerable dineeth but was unprepared for the obvious concern in his golden-brown eyes. If she could, she would have fled back to the comfort and security of her pride, yet that was no longer an option.

Though her body felt glued to the stone seat, her brain remained sharp. She had no choice but accept what he had in store for her. "What now?"

Mystic Nivlac placed his hands, palms down, on his knees. "Assume I know little. Tell me all you can about events since I first saw you, especially your encounters with the authorities and other people you have met along the way, such as the two youngsters and your benefactor."

Kat's senses pricked at the extensive knowledge the mystic had. *How did he get his information while living in a cave on this isolated mountain? Perhaps from the dineeth packs living in the region. And what did he know of Ardan and The Agency?*

Before she could ask, the roof blurred, becoming vague and insubstantial. The room glowed, picking up and amplifying the sparse light. She could no longer feel her body, or the cold hard stone beneath her, but her sense of fear had dissipated. Warm and content, she outlined her story, from her flight from K-Astar3, to her capture after leaving the mystic last time, her torture by Gorind and his thugs, then her rescue by Coren and Hana. By the time she reached Hana's betrayal, Ardan's proposition, and her exile, her throat was parched.

The mystic maintained a relaxed posture until she had finished, then handed her a mug of water.

She guzzled it down, washing away the horrors of recent events and the taint of the muddy tea. Relieved to get the story off her chest, she waited in contentment for the mystic's response, unburdened. She could never have so clearly told anyone else all that had happened.

The mystic sat up and coughed deep within his chest. "As I said before, I had a premonition you were a catalyst for change, but nothing prepared me for the extent of that change. I believe you have a crucial role to play in saving all genoids, not just frenines and dineeth, but those across the galaxy."

He fetched a large mauve crystal from a recess in the cave wall and placed it on a table in front of him, keeping his hands wrapped around it. "You are young, have natural abilities, and will need them all if you are to survive. You are the hope for Crofta and our various species, but it will come at great personal cost."

"Personal cost? What could be worse than losing Tar? I'm prepared to die. I have nothing left, other than my revenge, to live for." Images swam before Kat's eyes of Tar being shot, Rast Baden-Hauf crumpling to the ground, the enforcer's neck cracking beneath her foot.

The mystic's figure broke apart into shards of colour. Kat's eyes flickered closed, not wanting to know more. A floating sensation fill her, and her dread dissipated.

The mystic's voice took on the singsong tone of a chant. "Though you prefer to work alone, you will need reliable associates. You have already made such contacts. Your two young companions have complementary talents, and will prove effective and loyal."

Kat grimaced at the memory of Coren and Hana. *Loyal. Yes, like Hana trading me in for the reward. Loyal to each other maybe, not to me.*

"You will need to be skilled. Develop your attributes, learn new ones, and keep your nerve. Above all, use your instincts. They are one of the elements that raise dineeth and frenines above humans."

Time passed in a blur. Kat felt the mystic's valuable influence infiltrating her brain, information flowing, settling in unfamiliar areas. She became a sponge, absorbing the dineeth master's instructions without understanding all of them, awed at what he was and how he operated. No wonder the genoids of Crofta treated him with respect.

While it principally centred on the choker, a catalyst for situations she might encounter, it seemed her wide range of skills as a prime hunter became enhanced, matured. She would be able to recognise and call on her skills more intuitively in diverse situations. In effect she had grown up, as if she were now five years older and an established elder of the pride.

Movement brought her back to full awareness of her surroundings. Nivlac had left the cave. She panicked, but when she attempted to rise, she slumped back down. Again, her fear dissipated and comfort wafted over her.

A short time later, a waft of lightly grilled zeena meat with cooked tubers and okka nuts, her favourite, made her salivate. She looked up into the mystic's eyes.

He held a plate towards her. "Eat this, Kat. You need it."

She pushed herself up with a groan and took the plate with trembling hands, her arms stiff, her legs numb, and her belly hollow.

"How long have I been here?"

"The sun will rise soon." He held up a hand. "Don't be shocked. Much had to be done. I have taken steps to ready you for your quest."

Kat stopped with a sizzling strip of zeena close to her lips. "What have you done to me? Don't you think it would have been appropriate to discuss these things with me before you started?"

Mystic Nivlac sat down. "Relax. I've done nothing to harm you, only to help. Your permission was given the moment you stepped through my doorway."

Kat shook her head. "But we still haven't discussed what you want from me."

The dineeth waved away her concerns. "Should you achieve your quest, then that will be my reward."

"And I'm supposed to be satisfied with that? My instincts warn me you haven't told me everything." Kat's tail tip flicked in agitation.

"I have told you everything, though you may not recall it. Not yet. Not until the time is right. Have faith, I wouldn't do you any harm." His face remained enigmatic. "When you have eaten and washed'—he pointed to a shadowy gap in the rock face from where Kat could smell water—"you will need to leave. Time is of the essence now. My lessons are within you. Be true to yourself. Refuse to let the anger of revenge drive you."

Kat headed down the narrow track in the crispness of a new morning, her mind buzzing with what had happened. She squashed down her feelings of mistrust at Hana's betrayal and headed towards where she and Coren were staying, determined to draw them into her cause.

Coren opened the door the moment she placed her foot on the step, waving her in and signing for her to be quiet.

As soon as the door shut behind her, he joined Kat and Hana at the centre table. "We don't have much time. Enforcers were seen in the alley this morning, peering through windows and any gaps in the walls. We'll hear what you have to say, then we're getting out of here."

Their eyes followed Kat as she paced the small kitchen, outlining her proposal for them to work with her, with support from The

Agency, to bring down the Interplanetary Hunters Organisation subsidiary, HuX. "Ardan is confident that we have advantages over his usual agents, and will support us in any way he can."

Coren mumbled under his breath. "You've not said what's in it for us."

Kat halted. "Whatever you want, within reason. Creds, weapons, transport. I can arrange for you to get off Crofta, too."

Coren sat up straighter. "Where d'ya get access to that sort of stuff then? How come you need us?" Before she could respond, he added, "And we've gotta be alive to spend it. Sounds ferking dangerous to me."

"Coren," pleaded Hana, "think. We can get off-planet! We've little or no option now, especially since I tried to get creds for Kat. I'm sorry about that, but anything that gets us out of here has got to be good."

Coren grimaced. "I suppose you're right. If we let Kat organise this, we have little to lose. As you say, we have to get away."

Hana watched Kat through lidded eyes. "I'm not going to let her organise everything. We still have to remain in charge of our lives."

Kat restrained a snarl. "And I can't have you acting like a rabid enforcer with a laser. There can only be one person in charge, and that's me."

Coren held up both hands. "Calm down, Kat. Hana didn't mean we weren't going to listen to you. But we need to be consulted on things that affect us. That's only fair."

Releasing the tension in her shoulders, Kat agreed. She couldn't afford to lose the support of the only people she could call on.

"So, run through it again, Kat," said Hana, "so we're clear before we make a final decision."

Hana settled back in her seat watching the sleek, purposeful figure of Kat pacing in front of her. The frenine had come into their ordered existence like a storm, shattering their uneasy peace and pushing them into another stage of their lives.

Somehow, she knew Kat would get them involved in a just cause and give them purpose. If she really thought about it, the timing couldn't be better. She and Coren were almost always at each other's throats on what to do next, whose ideas to follow, and how to keep ahead of the authorities. The stress of living on the streets was getting to them both, as much as they loved each other. The way Coren looked at Kat didn't help either, but deep down she couldn't really believe he'd leave her for a frenine, not with all they'd been through together.

When she'd met him at the orphanage, she'd been surprised to discover Coren was only six months older than her. Since then, they'd looked out for each other, protecting and supporting whichever one got into trouble. After a life of luxury, she found the constricting circumstances unbearable. It hadn't been hard to convince him to escape the confines of care and set up on their own. She was often the one with the ideas, as well as having a small number of regular creds from her relatives to make it feasible.

Their skills combined well, Coren good with vehicles and a fixer of any gadget or device, and her organisational ability and contacts. Sufficient creds had been difficult after a while until she had persuaded her relatives that being out of the orphanage was best for her. She'd learnt not to ask questions about where Coren found what he brought home. A number of their enterprises had been risky, but as their talents developed, they were able to earn more than they stole and move into better premises.

They had ended up in this small, less squalid shack, finding work where possible and generally making a living. Recently Hana had suspected Coren of going further outside the law—she had been horrified when he'd come home with guns and other enforcer equipment after rescuing Kat from the fire. He'd claimed he'd found them in an abandoned building and hadn't hurt anyone, but Hana's suspicions lingered. Someone must have fed him information on where to go. She didn't want to be on the wrong side of the law more than they already were—dodging community service and squatting were minor infractions.

Whatever Kat was proposing, Hana was almost convinced that they had to go with it, or she and Coren would be irrevocably torn apart. And it offered them a chance to get off-planet, create new identities for themselves and start again where they weren't known, where they wouldn't be looking over their shoulders all the time.

Hana continued to watch and listen as Coren argued about the risks and rewards, and questioned the real purpose of Ardan getting untrained youngsters to seek HuX when The Agency's resources should allow him to put together a much more effective team.

There's more to this, thought Hana. *On the surface Kat makes sense, but she's hiding something.* "What's the real reason you're approaching us, Kat? I mean, we've limited talents, although Coren has enough skills to operate just about anything, including a spacecraft. I have skills too, but there's something else, isn't there?"

Kat's face tightened. "Yes, there is. I'm not only jumping into this because my mate was killed and I was being sought by the local authorities. It's more to do with what we're about. What right has someone to kill others for sport? Because they can? The influential people, groups or organisations can show they're trying to fix things and we'll know no better. But we have a chance, an opportunity to do something to help our people, our planet. And it's something I need to do."

Hana considered the impassioned plea. "And you'd like us to help?"

"Yes, Hana, I would. I've no one else I can call on who I'd trust as much with a mission like this." She paused. "I've been ostracised and exiled by my community."

Coren laughed. "So that's why you're gonna trust us now. I knew there was more to it than you let on before."

Hana glared at him. "Shut up, Coren. It sounds like a good motive to me, and if it means we can leave here, it's worth trying, isn't it?"

She hoped that was the truth, and that this offer wasn't some convoluted plot to bring them down. "I think we should give it a go."

Coren shrugged. "Me too, I suppose. I only hope the risks aren't as bad as they seem."

Chapter 12

Kat and Coren sat at one of the eateries set around Founder Square to catch the office traffic, inappropriately named Al Fresco in a bid to attract the space traffic and the well-heeled travellers, particularly from Earth. Its popular brew was based on various ground beans, including the native catner bush, while meals varied from local snacks to exotic foods—grazier's steak was big on the menu, especially at this time of the evening.

Coren fiddled with his spoon. "I can't believe we're doing this. It'll only get worse for us. And make Hana and me even more of a target."

Kat took a sip of catner tea and leant back on the bench. "Stop moaning, Coren. We need to do this, to make certain. You'll get to assess her too, which should make you more comfortable about what we're in for. We'll catch her away from the office, when she's more relaxed. I'll point her out when I see her." She wore a black cap pushed low to help disguise her frenine look, despite her form-fitting black trousers and jacket—and her tail—being dead giveaways.

Coren, cup in hand, watched her as the office workers flooded out from the buildings.

Kat spotted their target and nudged Coren. Relina wore a business suit, unlike the last time Kat had seen her, her thin build standing out from the more well-fed individuals in the crowd. Her flickering glance passed straight over them, seated a distance away among the other patrons of Al Fresco.

"She's heading towards the long-term flitter ranks," Coren said, his voice low and urgent. "If we're going to get to her, we'll have to move."

"Hold on," said Kat, unsheathing a claw and snagging his arm. "You'd never make a hunter." She waited until Relina disappeared from the square. "Right, come on." She slid to her feet and left the eatery with Coren close behind.

The vehicle they'd rented was parked in a short-term bay in a public zone just off the square. Kat slid in as Coren activated the drive. The flitter rose and he swung it in the direction of the ranks.

They arrived as a similar vehicle, their target aboard, pulled out of its park to head straight down the thoroughfare towards the northern suburbs of Sensuna. They followed at a discrete distance. Against the darkening sky, their flitter lights picked out a line of multi-storey houses, most finished in a local, expensive green marble. Some of the well-presented entrances had automatic sliding gates, and all had the latest spyware security.

Figures, thought Kat, as Coren kept the vehicle far enough back from being noticeable.

"Ferking hell. This is where the rich live. We never go here. Even Hana can't get through their state-of-the-art security."

The homes didn't look anywhere near as appealing as her own to Kat, but compared to Coren's shack they would appear to be palaces. "Enjoy the atmosphere while you can. We won't be here long."

Coren slowed the flitter as they neared an apartment complex set between two large houses. A dark opening appeared for Relina's vehicle to move through, then quickly closed.

"Pull in here." Kat said, indicating a kerb space some distance back from where the flitter had disappeared.

"Don't come until I signal you," she warned as she slipped out of the vehicle and into the dimness.

The dark spaces between the pools of light from the street poles enabled Kat to move unobtrusively to the central door of the apartment complex. She watched carefully until a light showed on the second floor, then looked at the activation pad set near the doorway.

She then beckoned to Coren.

He raced along the street to her. "Shit, I hardly saw you. You move like a…well, a cat."

"Come close. I think Relina will open up for me, as long as she doesn't see you first," Kat urged.

She placed a hand on the comms pad. "Hello? Relina?"

"Kat? Is that you?" a disembodied voice sounded.

"Yes. I need to talk with you. Can I come in?"

"What's so urgent? What's wrong with the office tomorrow?" Relina's voice showed her concern.

"Please, I'd rather not wait." Kat responded, signalling Coren to stay back.

The door hissed open and Kat hurried through into a lobby. She strode up the dark carpeted ramp to the second floor with Coren close behind, by which time Relina had her apartment door ajar.

"I thought you were alone," stated Relina, holding a gun in a steady hand.

"This is one of my colleagues, Coren," said Kat, as she gave the woman a pleasant smile. "Please put that laser away. If I wanted to hurt you, I wouldn't have waited until you were safely home."

"Of course, I'm sorry. Habit." Relina slid the laser into a pocket. "You'd better come through."

She turned and headed into a large room decorated with souvenirs from distant planets. Glass cabinets and tables in subdued hues melded with a range of artefacts on the walls and floor. She gestured towards a powder-blue memory-foam couch set under a 4D scape of the Crofta plains.

Kat's gaze fixed on the projection, feeling pulled into the familiarity of her home, her opinion of Relina rising a notch, though her curiosity piqued at how she could afford such a luxurious home.

"Drinks? Kat? Coren?" Relina waited until they had sat down.

Kat shook her head. "No. This isn't really a social call."

"Well, I'm having a drink. It's been a hard day and I was looking forward to relaxing. On my own." She took a small container from a wall cabinet and activated it. The hiss sounded as the gas cooled the liquid before she took a sip.

"I'll have one," said Coren.

Relina opened another and handed it to him. "So?"

"Call this insurance, if you will," began Kat. "We're about to undertake a significant and risky operation at the request of your boss, Ardan. I've had to take him at his word, just as Coren here has had to take me at my word. I want him to be assured by you that what we're doing is real and above board."

She sat up straighter on the edge of the comfortable sofa. "I've come to you particularly, away from your office, because you've been nice to me and helped me when I needed it."

"Yes," added Coren, his eyes on Relina. "The last dealings we had with any form of authority weren't good. But she says you're on the right side. That you'll back us, provide everything we need to get the job done and so on. I'm still not convinced."

Kat watched the thin woman lean back, cross her legs and take a sip of her drink.

"What Ardan told Kat was totally accurate. While we are an extensive organisation, we are stretched for operational resources across the galaxy. The situation that Kat stumbled into is part of a much bigger picture, one The Agency has been working on for some time. We see the opportunity presented by this—sorry, Kat, the killing of your mate—as an event to be pursued. Financial resources aren't a problem, but people are."

"What about the authorities? They've always been a thorn in our side. How can your limited organisation stop them from ferking getting us?" asked Coren.

"All the more reason for you to help us. Kat vouches for you and… Hana, isn't it? So that's good enough for us."

Coren shook his head. "It's been hard to trust, especially after the run-ins we've had with the authorities over the years."

Relina smiled at him, then glanced at Kat. "I understand why you've come here, away from anything official, but I'll be there for you. I'll make sure you have as much help as you need. That's my job. Can the rest wait until tomorrow?"

"Sure." Coren grunted as he stood, shook her hand and walked to the door.

Relina trailed after them. "Thanks for coming, Kat. I'm sorry I wasn't welcoming at first. I didn't expect you and it's been a trying day, but I understand your need for reassurance, particularly for your friend. I'll meet Hana when the three of you come in for your intensive training."

Kat followed Coren to the door. *How had Relina known Hana's name?* Kat hadn't mentioned the people she had chosen to bring on board. The Agency must have her under surveillance and probably knew more about Coren and Hana than she did. The fur on the back of her neck tingled in wariness.

As planned, the three of them arrived at The Agency's offices early. Kat had slept on Coren and Hana's battered sofa, not wanting to risk booking a hotel until she was sure the authorities were no longer pursuing her. Her back ached from lying on protruding springs and her muscles had complained until after she'd performed her morning stretches. She'd cut her exercises short when she'd realised Coren was watching her, but by then there was only time for a quick breakfast anyway.

Relina met them at the office door and handed them temporary security passes. "You'll need these for getting between the various rooms. I'll fit you with permanent chips later in the day." She pointed to a small meeting room. "If you wait in there, Ardan will be with you soon."

Kat took a seat at a round table, facing the door. Coren and Hana sat to her left.

Moments later, Ardan arrived and introduced himself to Coren and Hana. "Thank you for coming so early. I have to go off-planet today but wanted to greet you all formally. Welcome to The Agency. The next few days will be hard, but should give you all you need to know to conduct your mission."

Coren raised his hand from the table, palm towards Ardan. "Before we start the briefing, I'd like to confirm what's in it for us. So far, we've only had promises, but no specifics."

"Of course." Ardan smiled, his face transforming from worry to reassurance. "I believe you want to move off-planet, be free of pursuit from any authorities, and have sufficient resources to start a new life."

Hana's eyes lit up. "Can you really do that for us?"

"Yes, and I will. Whether or not your mission is successful, providing you see it through as far as we can go." Ardan turned to Kat. "What about you?"

Kat hadn't thought further than getting her revenge on Tar's murderer. But there was something she needed. "You can't help with what I want. I've been exiled from my pride. Only the Frenine Council can overturn that, and you have no authority there."

Sadness swamped Ardan's features. "I'm sorry. You're right, I have no influence in frenine society, but I will back you whatever you need for you to regain their trust. Tell me, and if it's at all possible for me to provide, you shall have it."

"Thank you. But I doubt there's anything you can do." Nausea roiled in Kat's belly at the thought of never returning to her home, resuming her friendship with Sashyr, or hunting with the pride.

Ardan coughed. "Let me start by giving you an overview of what you face. The Interplanetary Hunters Organisation, IHO, is a legal entity that provides hunting safaris across the galaxy, to those who can afford it. They target feral species, food animals, and help keep down the numbers of problem creatures. There is nothing we can do about that—in fact we wouldn't want to—as they provide a necessary service to keep life in balance."

Kat nodded, knowing how the frenines and dineeth managed the herds of zeena and tek-tek.

"However"—Ardan looked at each of them in turn—"they have a secret subsidiary, Hunters Extreme, or HuX as they refer to themselves, who specialise in hunting sapient races, a practice which is both illegal and, in many eyes, immoral."

Coren sat up straighter. "Is that who killed Kat's mate?"

"Yes. And many other intelligent, not to mention rare, genoids. Not only here on Crofta, but wherever these hunters consider there to be a thrill of pitting their technology against natives of various planets."

Hana shook her head. "Are all members of HuX human?"

"As far as we know, yes. We have a false ID account on their dark net, but we haven't been able to penetrate the actual organisation as yet. That's where you three come in." Ardan went on to describe what The Agency did know about HuX's operations.

Kat's eyes widened at learning the extent of abuse that went far beyond her own grief of losing her partner and the resulting threat to the frenine species. It seemed that everywhere in the galaxy there were humans trading off the misery of other species, thinking they were better or more entitled, profiting on hunting and slaughtering any species considered 'game'.

One question lingered in her mind that she didn't dare raise. *How did Mystic Nivlac fit in? The dineeths must be affected too. Was that really why he was helping her?* Unease at the price he might extract from her still bubbled at the back of her mind.

"Now, let's take a break. I'm sorry I have to leave, but Relina will oversee your training. You'll all get experience with our communication methods and the weapons we will provide. Kat, Relina will provide you with access to credits, identities and details of where we think you should start. Hana, Relina will show you around our system so you can research whatever you wish. Coren, I gather you have experience with various vehicles and technology. You'll be given advanced training in land and space vehicles, and anything else you think you might need that we can provide." He stood up and led them out to where food and drinks had been laid out. "Good luck, and thank you all again for agreeing to participate in bringing down HuX."

After Ardan left, Kat collected a plate of nibbles. Coren and Hana buzzed with what the future might bring, but she didn't share the excitement. However, while she didn't fully understand Ardan's motives in utilising inexperienced operatives such as herself, Coren and Hana, she wasn't about to throw away the chance to bring down any part of HuX's operations. And if she could track down the hunters responsible for Tar's murder, so much the better, Lord Baden-Hauf especially. One way or another, she would have her revenge.

The three days of intensive training left Coren exhausted but exhilarated. Back at their home in the slums, he looked around at the odd pieces of furniture they'd scraped together. He would miss nothing, especially not the overriding stench and fear every time they walked out the door. It all sounded too good to be true, but so far, The Agency had delivered on its promises.

He handed Kat a plate of rehydrated rations that Hana had cooked. "K-Astar3? I can't go to that hell-hole again. I nearly had my backside fried last time, and for once I hadn't done anything wrong."

Kat's tail twitched. "If that's the case, you've nothing to worry about. But our enemy has an operations centre there. At least that's what Relina told us, remember? It's got to be Lord Baden-Hauf from all I've put together." She leant back in her chair. "You're not going to pull out, are you? I doubt Ardan would be happy with that after what you both know about The Agency. Isn't your word worth anything?"

Coren thumped onto his chair, knowing he had no choice. "Of

course it is. More'n you know. I've never let anyone down, human or genoid. Don't worry, if that's where we have to go, that's where we'll go. But I hate the place."

Hana kept a strained smile on her face.

They had shared what they'd learnt in their individual training, but Hana had expressed her fear to him about what they were expected to do on their own. While Coren hoped that participating in this mission would ease her concerns about their future, he wasn't worried about their capabilities. He'd rather operate without supervision anyway. "We said we'd help, and we will. Besides, this place is no longer safe," he sighed, "or profitable. We need to leave our old lives behind."

"Good," Kat agreed, her tail stilling.

Coren had never had much to do with the frenines of Crofta before. They lived far out of the city, across the endless plains. He hated the thought of so much open space. Anything could get you out there. If he had been a genoid, he'd rather have been a dineeth, safe with his pack in a mountain den, or prowling the city streets at night. Give him a dark alley and secret spaces any day, or the emptiness surrounding a spaceship.

His fingers drummed the table. "So, we have to get to the way-station?"

Hana nodded. "That's where we'll find Baden-Hauf, apparently. We'll get more instructions when we arrive."

Already Coren's head buzzed with planning. That was what he was good at, why he intended to be the leader of the three of them. Kat may think this was her mission, but she had already got herself into trouble. "I'm wondering if we should go openly or covertly. Any suggestions?"

Kat shrugged. "No point in advertising."

"The waystation is usually first stop before leaving this section of space, so that works out. Hana can arrange passage for us on a freighter for tomorrow now that you have access to funds for the mission." He smiled at Hana. "Not just a pretty face, are you, Hana?"

She remained serious. "No, I'm not. If it wasn't for me, you would have starved to death the first cycle of the moon after we left the kids' home. And probably been knifed in an alley somewhere by now, too."

Coren puffed up. "I would've coped."

Hana smacked him on the arm. "You're too bold for your own good. You need me to keep you sensible. Not to mention my extensive contacts."

Coren grinned. "You're right. That's why we make such a good team."

Kat cocked her head at Hana. "Talking of team, I need to make it clear that I have the final authority if we disagree on anything."

Coren leapt up. "No way! What do you know of illicit operations? I've been keeping Hana and I safe since we escaped the orphanage."

Kat snarled. "Ardan made me the leader by giving me control of the credits. It's my mate they killed, and I have natural hunting abilities that neither of you could match, weapons or not. And remember, I recruited you. I'm happy to listen to your advice, but final decisions rest with me."

Miffed, but seeing he had no option, Coren agreed.

Hana nodded as if there had never been any question, which surprised Coren. She'd normally want more say in what they did.

Kat placed a hand on Hana's arm. "If you can organise transport for tomorrow, your contacts are even better than you let on. Did you tell Relina?"

Hana smirked. "Not fully. We girls have to have some secrets, don't we?"

Her eyes narrowed as she looked at Kat. "I know you're questioning our abilities, but we're very capable at surviving. We've had to be. You won't be sorry, even if you're used to working alone. I'm more concerned we'll regret joining you."

Kat paused before she answered. "Although frenines work in prides, unmated females often roam alone. But it's really not too late if you want to back out. I can smooth it with Ardan, I'm sure."

Coren wondered whether Kat wanted them to go back on their word. *Would she be better alone?* But they couldn't stay where they were any longer. Too many things were against them. "We're in. We told you that and we meant it." The truth was, the thought of this mission excited him. A chance to not only get away, but having the support of a secret agency, access to creds and who knew what else. His heart pumped.

Passenger accommodation on the freighter was basic, preferential space given to the cargo. Kat could have used The Agency's credits to upgrade to something better but preferred they kept a low profile. The three of them sat in sagging temporary seats along the side of a narrow corridor lit by luminescent strips, no windows, only uncoloured sheeting lining the walls. Several other passengers occupied seats further along, while small pallets of cargo occupied any spare space.

Coren slung an arm over the back of his seat, his hand brushing Kat's shoulder. "If I ever get creds like we should've got for the reward, I'd never travel this way."

"Travelling premium class would make us stand out. If this doesn't suit you, you could go in stasis if the flight was any longer than a Crofta day. But as it isn't, you'll have to put up with it like the rest of us." Kat flicked her claws across his wandering hand.

He sat back, hard. "I thought we'd be travelling in style with the backing of The Agency."

A dark-faced, rough-clad man two seats across looked up briefly before returning to his comgame.

"Coren," Hana whispered, leaning forward, "were you born without brains?"

Kat softly growled at them. "If we have to go further, we'll travel differently. Other destinations will need a sequence of jumps to go the distance."

Coren inhaled deeply. "You got that right, and that's if their drives have the latest technology. Some of the earlier ships took months to get anywhere."

Kat turned towards Hana. "Let's take our flight time to prepare how we're going to proceed once we arrive. Who knows what we'll find?"

Chapter 13

The crete landing pad cooled quickly once the ship had settled. A flurry of hoverbots approached the hatchway and began the process of unloading. Coren groaned as he stood and stretched his back, dragged on his pack, and watched Kat as she bent to lift hers, the black skintight leather pulling tight across her bottom. He shrugged at Hana's frown and hoisted his own pack across his shoulders before following her to the ship's hatchway.

The three of them waited while the other passengers pushed past, a rough-clad man giving Kat a quick glance as he went by, before he stomped down the gangway to the crete surface. Maybe he wasn't used to seeing frenines, especially when travelling in space, or maybe it was the fact she was travelling cargo—frenines were renowned for their love of comfort. Kat didn't seem fazed by the man's stare. She led them after him, striding out with confidence.

Coren paused on the gangway, looking around. "This is the best part of the asteroid." The other planets of the Crofta system didn't require a jump-off point, and certainly not a terraformed asteroid. The bright lights of the spaceport couldn't dim the mass of stars studding the blackness overhead, stretching into infinity. The buildings appeared insignificant and artificial in comparison. The hum of the vast machinery sustaining gravity and air echoed across the expanse of rock. He would have loved to visit the control centre and investigate the equipment. All his knowledge of mechanics had been picked up by experience, tampering with gadgets he could find. To work on something as big as an atmosphere creator would be his ultimate dream job. No more sneaking around for parts to make a generator to sell on the streets, or repairing gear for a few creds; he'd be a real engineer. The additional training he had with the Agency only skimmed the surface of what he desired to know.

Kat scanned the area around the visitor clearance checkpoint. The central hub and the massive bubble covering the large concourse, with its curved white polycarbonate walls and rows of dark seats, hadn't altered. Even the vending machines looked the same. In-going and out-going passengers of various species dotted around pre-grav airlocked entrances, each designed for different beings.

No sign of security other than the usual officers checking passengers raised her interest. Glowing news screens blaring out recent galactic events in a variety of languages to the throng of space travellers moving to and from the exits still dominated the whole area. *At least the news is no longer about me,* she thought with relief.

She remained motionless, outwardly calm but ready to react, while the detector travelled over her, its blinking lights yellow. It beeped once as they changed to green to signal she could pass through. She tried not to sigh. The others followed in silence, with that edge of nervousness of people with something to hide. The detector flashed yellow then green for each of them, finally enabling Kat to relax a fraction. Ardan had smoothed the way as he had promised.

They lugged their packs towards the exit, threading past knots of humans, genoids and various other creatures, but none paid them any attention. Kat extended all her senses, ready for the slightest anomaly, the scent of unease, of recognition, or unusual sounds. All seemed normal, or as normal as such a place could be.

Then she recognised the suspicious passenger from their freighter heading towards a side door. He glanced around before slipping through. Her hackles rose. She wished she could follow him and discover what he was up to, but now wasn't the time to draw attention.

Before she could tell Coren and Hana, she caught sight of a familiar figure. Ral, the barman from The Grotto, wandered past in an employee uniform, exhibiting a keen interest in a vendor machine across the concourse. Kat held up a hand to keep her companions from banging into her. "This way," she whispered.

"What?" asked Hana, looking at the dineeth ahead of them. "Is that who I think it is?"

"Yes, he'll have something arranged for us."

Ral was already grabbing a steaming cup from the dispenser by the time they approached him. He jerked his head towards a nearby booth before sliding in.

"Coren, could you get us all drinks please?" asked Kat, handing him a cred chip before following the dineeth into the booth.

She shifted along a low bench to give Hana room before looking towards Ral. He kept his eyes on his cup for a long moment, only lifting his head at Coren's arrival with three steaming cups.

"I even got you catner tea, Kat," said Coren, keeping his eyes on the dineeth as he sat.

"Ral, I'm happy to see you again," she said. "I've been wanting to thank you for all you did for me."

"No time for that, Kat." His voice was husky. "Your friends?"

"Hana and Coren. We're working as a team."

"Fine. I've got you accommodation, at the Star View, without names. Keep a low profile and you should be fine, although…'—he paused to rub a hand across his bristly chin—"there's a bit happening here. Too many different people around. Too many interests."

"Do you know anything about a character on the same freighter as us? A man was checking us out," interrupted Coren.

"I did keep an eye on offloading passengers, and I think I know who you're talking about. I'm not sure of him, but he's not one of the people we need to avoid as far as I know. My contact is…well, you know, Kat. And I'm not fully in the loop with your sponsor."

"That makes it all the more dangerous," said Hana.

"Shouldn't we be going then?" asked Coren.

The dineeth growled. "Yes, the less I'm seen with you the better. Here, you'll need this for your transport." He passed over a chip, which Coren snatched. "I'll endeavour to find out more but my position here is already tenuous."

As he slid out from the booth, he added, "Wait a while after I leave."

Kat scanned the concourse. "If that suspicious person from the freighter is gone, we should be safe enough to finish our drinks."

After they did so, and threw the cups down the recyclables chute, Coren rose from the seat and did another sweep of the room. "All clear."

They headed towards a blue-coloured, moulded structure set into a white-panelled wall near the exit. "This is the hire portal," said Coren. "If Ral is good, the vehicle will be garaged outside." He extended his hand into a slot marked with a shooting star logo. A beep acknowledged the chip and a small remote dropped into his hand. "Let's go."

Kat's heart raced as they ventured outside The Hub, still on high alert despite the ease of negotiating the clearance checkpoint. A nearby flitter, its kaleidoscopic paintwork matching the remote to identify it, opened its doors as they approached. Once they were seated, it silently glided through the narrow streets. With the route set in advance, none of them needed to touch the controls. No amount of using auto travel had inured Kat to being under the control of a machine, especially in a foreign place. She'd rather have been running on four paws, but that would draw suspicion and her human friends would never keep up.

Despite her misgivings, they slipped into a garaging space at the Star View without incident, the flitter automatically slotting into a recharge socket. The long, squat building hugged the eroded surface of the asteroid.

"So much for Star View," grunted Coren, scratching at his chin as they alighted the flitter. "Ferking poor ports. No view at all."

"Hopefully we won't be here long," commented Kat as she led the way along a narrow corridor lined with doors, some faintly glowing to indicate they were occupied. They reached one with their allocated number, the outline of the door lit to show it was booked. She touched the wall with her fingerpads below the glowing number. The door slid aside with a hiss. "I'll check the room."

Crouching slightly, ready to react, she entered and sniffed the air. Only the stringent smell of cleaning fluids lingered. Her ears twitched but detected nothing. "All clear."

The room contained three single beds, one against each wall, with a bathroom door in the fourth. A table and three chairs in the centre completed the basic furnishings. For once, the ever-present white panelling had been modified by streaks of blue and grey sprayed across the surface, done by someone with a modicum of artistic talent.

Kat ducked into the bathroom and retrieved the weapons Ral had hidden among the plumbing, then threw her pack onto the nearest bed. She sat, swiped off her cap, and dragged off her high boots. She stretched out on the bed, arms under her head, and sighed. "This will do. We shouldn't be here long. Settle in and relax for a bit, then we'll head back to The Grotto."

"She's not telling us much," whispered Coren to Hana as they entered.

"Better that way," said Hana, "until we know what we're in for. Best to get some rest and acclimatise—the grav's a touch less than Crofta."

Kat grinned. "Yes, Coren, and don't forget I have great hearing."

Coren had the decency to look embarrassed as he claimed a bed, while Hana lay down on the remaining one. The lights dimmed as if night had fallen. Although there was no diurnal rhythm on the asteroid, the room recognised its occupants were resting.

A rhythmic creak brought Coren slowly awake. He opened one eye. Across from him, Kat stretched into an impossible curve on her bed, her backbone looking like it would snap. One muscular, furred leg raised towards the ceiling, claws unsheathed, then the other. She repeated the exercise. The bed groaned in complaint. Then her torso whipped forward, her arms wound around her legs, squashing her small breasts as she eased up towards her feet. After holding the pose for a few seconds, she relaxed and slid sideways onto the floor on all fours.

Her slitted eyes caught his and she smiled, straight-lipped, before standing and slipping into loose trousers and baggy top.

Shit, he thought, *still sexy and dangerous no matter what she wears.*

"Time to find food and information," she announced.

Coren looked over to where Hana lay on her side, head propped up on an arm, wide awake. A flash of embarrassment surged through him. He cleared his throat to cover it up. "I could do with a feed. Are you coming, Hana?"

The Grotto hummed with people. A light and sound show sent kaleidoscopic images pulsing across the room in time to the loud music, hiding the people drinking and eating in the small alcoves set around the curved walls.

Kat's eyes immediately slid to the bar and the set of stools spaced along it, noting that Ral wasn't on shift. A memory of Rast Baden-Hauf dying near that very spot threatened to ruin her appetite. The whole scene replayed in her head: watching his body fall, his sudden death from the poison, then finding out he was the wrong victim. She shivered and vowed she wouldn't make that mistake again.

The usual bar girls hovered, seeking drinks and credits from the wealthier patrons. Kat hoped her change of dress prevented them from recognising her and flinched at the memory of pretending to be one of them, albeit seeking a different outcome. She moved across to a vacant alcove and sat, watching for anything out of the ordinary. The others joined her and scanned the menu on the partition, scrolling through different languages, some of them recognisable words, others only symbols or pictures of an array of foodstuffs.

"Want anything, Kat?" asked Hana.

Nothing appealed, but she had to eat to ensure she had reserves in case of an emergency. "A Crofta special and blue juice, please," she answered, without taking her eyes off several groups near the bar.

Coren grimaced. "That's raw, and expensive. I like my food well and truly dead. A beer, star burger and frits'll do me."

Kat shrugged at his preference for reconstituted protein instead of real meat. Maybe he didn't know how they made it. She was happy to pay extra for imported food. Hana ordered a spicy vegetarian dish. At least that had the chance of being hydroponically grown on the asteroid. Their order arrived via an automated trolley, the cost already deducted from Kat's expense account when she confirmed their choices with The Agency credit chip.

They ate in silence. Like her, Coren surveyed the room, assessing the occupants, mostly of human extraction though several frenine and dineeth genoids highlighted the relatively close proximity of Crofta. Spacers and transiting passengers were in the majority, but small groups of uniformed regulars came and went as their work shifts changed.

She stiffened as she saw the passenger from their freighter join several people in a far alcove while studiously avoiding looking in their direction. His companions wore expensive looking suits and had an air of authority, their self-importance portrayed in every gesture.

Her heart raced.

One of the men casually looked over, saw Kat watching, and stared back at her before turning away.

She hissed. "They know we're here. I suggest we move."

"No time for another beer?" asked Coren.

"Keep a clear head," warned Hana. "If you'd been observant, you'd know why."

They left the remainder of their food, the plates almost empty, and slid off the bench seat. Before they could leave, a knot of dark-clad enforcers pushed through the crowded room, their leader a Gorind look-alike, though taller. His head half turned as he strode past.

"Go!" hissed Kat.

They hurried outside and into their flitter waiting in The Grotto's bay.

"We've been noticed. Not a bad thing in itself," said Kat.

"Is it? I thought we wanted to observe without being seen." Coren tapped the console. A glowing representation of K-Astar3's buildings and transport links emerged. "Where to?"

Kat shook her head. "Don't go to the Star View. Let's see who's interested in us. Head to the outer districts. If those people are undercover enforcers, they'll be able to track the flitter's locator. And it's not only the authorities who have that technology. This is why we came, remember?"

Coren set the flitter in motion, floating above the poorly graded surface.

The road narrowed as they left the better-used tracks, an occasional ping as rocks hit the underside of the vehicle making Coren jump. "Reminds me of the road at home. I won't be sorry to leave that place."

Hana agreed.

Coren navigated the flitter between increasingly dilapidated buildings. "Say when you want to stop, Kat."

"Reverse into the next side alley."

Coren deftly parked the vehicle and they exited the sliding doors before the flitter locked with a click. "Now what?"

A maze of flimsy buildings stretched in all directions, most poorly fitted-out and sloped for convenience, not architectural integrity. The main road leading back to the central hub loomed in darkness where the artificial lights failed to penetrate. No sign of activity broke the shadows. No one but the down-on-their-luck or destitute would live here. A faint stink of refuse permeated the air.

"You wait," murmured Kat, "and have your lasers ready, just in case."

The faint whirr of a flitter came to her ears. She drew back under the overhang of the building and waited until it stopped a short distance away.

Footsteps crunched on gravel.

Kat slipped away without a sound, hugging the darker sections. After sliding off and stashing her boots, she transformed to hunting form, her hands and feet changing to paws and her hips and shoulders swivelling to enable her to run easily on all fours. Moments later she sprang along an angled wall to a flat roof. The structure sagged as she slithered over it. With her ears flat, she peered over the edge, listening and smelling, like when she and her friends had played cat and mouse as cubs. She shoved away the memory of the pride.

The footsteps continued, more hesitantly than before. A human shape edged below her, hand on laser, his scent that of the suspicious passenger on the freighter. She dropped soundlessly onto him and wrapped all four limbs around his torso, pinning his arms and legs, one hand over his mouth. He struggled as he fell, then stilled as Kat's teeth closed on his throat. "Why should you live?" she hissed in his ear.

"Ardan," he mumbled between her fingers. "I'm with Ardan."

She released her grip and rolled off him.

His hand went to his throat, rubbing it as he sat up. "It's been hard to find you alone, though I don't appreciate the welcome."

"Who were those men you were with at The Hub? I didn't think Ardan had operatives here," she growled.

"Don't worry about them, they're concerned with another project. I was using them as a cover."

Kat still wasn't totally convinced. "Is that why you didn't make contact with me at the Hub?"

"Yes. And on the ship. Too dangerous," the dark-faced man said. "Didn't you see the enforcers? They're on to you. Baden-Hauf has left. He flew out after you arrived." He rose to his feet as Hana and Coren crept around the side of a building, lasers drawn.

Kat held up her hand to stop them. "Where's he gone?"

"We suspect Earth. Relina knows IHO have major operations there, and suspects HuX do too."

Finally satisfied that this man was truly from Ardan, Kat looked at Coren. "Do we have transport?"

"Shouldn't take long to arrange. Unless he can help?" He waved toward the man. "Whoever he is."

"My name's Baltane. I was tasked to keep an eye out for you and help with whatever I could. We have a small, ex-military ship here that you can use. I won't leave with you, though."

"Sounds good," exclaimed Coren. "I've always wanted to fly a military vessel."

Kat shrivelled him with a look. "This isn't some great adventure game that—"

Hana interrupted by speaking to Baltane. "Do you have details, type, ratings?"

Baltane handed her a chip. "Everything you need is on here."

"We'll head back to the Star View and collect our gear. The sooner we get off this rock the better," said Kat."

Baltane dusted off his trousers. "I'll meet you away from The Hub, at the Primal Field. The place can be confusing with abandoned ships all over the place. Do you know it?"

"We'll find it," she said.

Chapter 14

Baltane was gone from Kat's mind as they entered their flitter and headed back to the Star View. If anyone thought to stop them leaving the waystation it would most likely be there.

"Bring up the grid," she said. "See where the Primal Field is."

Hana touched the vid screen. "Opposite side of the asteroid to our accommodation, over the horizon."

"Right, Coren, we'll need to snatch our gear from the Star View and head there quickly. From what Baltane said, someone out there doesn't like us too much."

They pulled up a block away from the Star View. "Best you come with me, Hana, but you stay with the flitter, Coren," said Kat. "We have to make this quick, so be ready for a fast departure. If anything happens, we'll meet at the airfield."

Kat and Hana slipped past open-doored buildings where people were working. More traffic was on the road than earlier so they waited until it lessened before crossing to the building. Kat kept her senses open. She felt nothing, saw no one suspicious, even though the fur rose on the back of her neck. "Anything?" she whispered.

Hana shook her head.

They entered the Star View and Kat placed her hand below the number of their door as she had before. The door opened. When it automatically began to close, she stopped it with her foot. They dashed in.

Everything was as they had left it. Hana started tidying the bed-linen and towels.

"Just grab the bags," ordered Kat, as she snatched hers.

Hana did as asked, then followed Kat out the door and back

down the corridor.

"Still no one?" pondered Kat. Her hackles tingled, her instinct raising alarms. "It doesn't seem right."

"Be glad," said Hana, looking both ways as they reached the exit from the building.

Kat stepped into the street, still looking around her, wishing Hana would hurry. A flitter bore straight at them, wind hissing with the speed of its passage. They leapt at the same time, Hana going one way, Kat the other. The wind of the flitter pushed Kat as she dived out of the way. The whine was almost deafening as it carried on past her. With a resounding crash, it smashed headlong into their waiting vehicle a short distance away.

Boooom!

Both vehicles burst into flame.

The shockwave flattened and rolled Kat over, hot debris and gravel splattering her body. Pieces of flitter fizzed overhead, crashing into buildings, rattling down around her as she lay on the roadway. The boom echoed around her.

Silence slowly returned.

Kat staggered to her feet and looked to where their flitter had been before seeing Hana. She lay face down on the other side of the road, struggling to push up with her arms. Kat rushed to help her.

"Wha… what just happened?" she gasped. "Coren?"

"Someone tried to kill us!" Kat cried. "Coren! Hana, I don't know what to say, I think he must've been in there!"

Hana wailed and then choked, coughing as she scrambled to her feet. "No! He can't be dead!" She flung off the two packs and limped across the road, pushing past the burning debris. Shouts rang out. People, some carrying extinguishers, converged on the scene.

Kat hurried after Hana and grabbed her elbow. "Stop!" she hissed. "You don't want to see. He can't have survived. We have to get out of here."

Hana pulled away and kept heading towards the burning vehicles, her fists clenched. "He's my partner! I can't leave him. What if it had been Tar?"

Kat flinched. She wouldn't have left Tar in a burning vehicle, no matter whether he was alive or not. Just as she couldn't leave his murderer out there somewhere without seeking retribution. But they needed to escape, not risk their lives.

"Hana, I'm sorry, but we can't do anything." Kat pulled at her, partly to protect her from seeing any grisly remains, partly due to the urgency to get away.

Adrenalin fizzed within her body, the need to move driving her. She couldn't process Coren's death yet, not on top of Tar's. "We must get away. Coren wouldn't want us to risk our lives too. Come on!"

Hana gulped and sniffed. "But what if—"

"If he's around, we'll have to find him later. We can't do that if we're caught or killed. Hurry!"

Hana glared at Kat, mouth tight. "I wish we'd got the reward and never seen you again."

"Please, Hana," Kat implored, gripping her shoulder, "we have to go. We can't avenge him if we're held by the authorities, even if they see we're innocent."

Hana shrugged off Kat's hand before looking to the wreckage. Several official-looking vehicles pulled up, people in dark uniforms scrambling out even before the flitters halted. "I'm not going without his things."

She rushed back to the discarded packs and dragged them up onto her shoulders. Kat took one from her. Hana's face cleared fractionally, tears barely noticeable as they streamed runnels down her soot covered face, her long hair peppered with flakes of ash. "I'll get who did this, I will."

They hurried away, dodging the crowd descending on the scene. As the sound of the explosion had reverberated loudly, everyone would know about it. Kat steadied her nerves with deep breaths and hung on to Hana's arm to make sure she didn't change her mind and bolt back. "We've got to head to the Primal Field and find Baltane."

Hana's eyes remained glazed, her limbs working like an automaton. "How do we know he isn't in on it?"

"What other choice do we have? At least he knew Ardan's and Relina's names," gasped Kat, as she tried to balance the two heavy packs she was carrying. She hesitated, uncertain which would be the best way to go. "We'll need to find transport."

Hana stood up straighter, frowning as she concentrated. "The Hub will be in lockdown, any flitter'll be monitored. We'll have to walk."

Kat flicked her a look, relieved she was back in control of herself, for now at least. Grief would come later. "How far is it? Can you make it?"

Hana staggered even under the weight of one pack, still limping "You're right, too far for me to hobble. But Coren taught me a thing or two. I might be able to bypass a flitter's security."

They spotted a vacant flitter near a small shed, its door still open from the occupant's hurried rush to the scene of the explosion. Hana looked in at the instrument panel. Her fingers trembled, whether from fear, pain, or grief, Kat wasn't sure. After taking a deep breath, Hana crouched down and fiddled underneath the controls. "I guess we can borrow this while the owners are gawking."

The lights flickered on. "Got it. Let's get out of here."

Kat gave Hana's shoulder a quick squeeze and then dumped the packs on the cargo tray. They scrambled inside, Hana driving. "To the Primal Field!" she snapped, as she accelerated away.

"Yes. And keep your eyes open. We're not out of this yet." Kat's claws pulsed in and out as she sought to keep calm.

Hana didn't turn her head, her eyes focused forward. "You're right about that. Someone is going to pay for this."

The flitter moved out against the flow of traffic, racing away from the scene of the explosion. "Keep it steady. Don't risk an accident." Kat kept a wary eye out while trying to rationalise how quickly their enemies had acted.

"I'll get us there. You keep a lookout for more trouble," Hana snapped at her.

Hana's loss renewed the pain of Tar's death for Kat. She would also miss Coren, his quick wit and capable hands. She only hoped Hana's grief would keep her focussed like she was and not closed down. She couldn't tackle this alone. Not anymore. Had the enemy's flitter been on auto or had they sacrificed their own people? "This really isn't good."

"Not good? It couldn't get worse. Coren's dead! My only real friend! Now I'm stuck with you, who caused it all." Hana flung an angry glance at Kat.

"Keep driving, Hana," growled Kat. "Deal with the present for now. We've got to get the people behind this. It's what Coren would've wanted. I hope Baltane has a backup plan, because neither of us can fly that ex-military ship."

"Shit! I hadn't thought that far ahead." Hana hunched over the controls and sped up.

The road led away from the conglomeration of buildings that sprawled around The Hub into unformed parts of the asteroid, jagged and rough. Occasional side roads led to shacks and warehouses, but little else broke the scene. A scatter of old, derelict spaceships appeared, clustered around a well-used landing field. The odd light showed some activity but in the main it was dark.

"This looks bad," whispered Hana, as she slowed the flitter.

"Try going to the far side, where the smaller ships are."

Some of the spaceships looked complete, despite signs of wear on their hulls, others were clearly used for spare parts, with sections of their fuselages missing. "Just how I feel," moaned Hana, "parts missing."

"It can't be far," warned Kat. "Be ready to get out of here if we're spotted."

Hana slowed the flitter and pulled in under a derelict ship with old-style tail fins, the dark bulk screening them. She indicated a group of ships with military insignia, two on their sides, one upright on its tail. "Do you think it's one of those three?"

Kat watched for a moment and began to undress, dropping her top on her pack.

Hana's eyes bulged. "What are you doing?"

"Don't worry, I'm going hunting. Stay here." Kat threw her a commanding look as she removed her boots, equipment belt, and trousers before slipping out of the door and into the shadow.

She edged around a tail fin and onto the eroded crete surface on her belly. Her fur began a rapid transition from light brown to off-white, similar to the surface she lay on. When she was satisfied, she raised herself to all fours, her hands and feet transformed to paws, and eased away from the tail fin in a circuitous route towards her quarry. She had noticed a small patch of shadow moving near the upright ship, her target. Ears pricked forward, nostrils flaring and eyes wide, she stalked her prey in a crouching shuffle.

A figure stood rigidly in front of a hatch at the top of a set of steps, with a second lying on the ground, a flitter nearby. The stench of fuel overrode their scent, hiding their emotions and intents. The standing person's gaze swept the area where she crept but didn't react to her approach.

Good, she thought, *I should be able to take them out*. Surprised at her coldness, she pushed aside the fact that these were people and considered them as if they were merely food animals. A quick, clean kill. She could do that. She manoeuvred around the side of the ship, keeping its bulk between her and her target. She wriggled closer, gauged the distance and, hunching her legs, sprang. One giant leap, body extended and limbs stretched, aiming to come down on the standing figure.

A familiar scent assailed her nostrils. She twisted in mid leap and dropped, coming down as the figure whipped around.

"Kat?"

"Coren!" She picked herself up and, retracting her claws, grabbed the man in a hug. "You're alive!" Sobs of relief choked her from saying more.

Coren briefly returned the hug, then tried pushing her away. "Easy Kat, you're crushing me."

"We thought you were dead," she replied.

"Where's Hana?" asked Coren, a catch in his voice.

Kat pointed to where their flitter was hidden. "Over there, waiting. Why weren't you caught in the explosion? We thought you were in the flitter."

"I would've been, except for poor Baltane here," said Coren, crouching down next to the body at their feet. "He didn't make it. He was shot when you and Hana went into the Star View," said Coren. "He came by, said he knew something was wrong. We ducked into his flitter to talk, then they came. Shots were flying, so we took off. We thought you'd be safe inside and make your own way here as agreed."

"Poor man," murmured Kat, looking at Baltane's body. "I'd better get Hana. She's devastated at losing you. And I need the packs so I can dress." Before she could move, the sound of running feet and a keening noise startled her. She spun around.

Hana rushed up, dragging all three packs. After dropping them, she flung herself at Coren, huge sobs wracking her body.

Coren embraced her tightly then, peeled her arm off his shoulder, "Enough of that. You can't get rid of me that easily. But we've got to get going. These crims seem to have a lot of influence. The sooner we're away, the better."

Kat's spirits lifted. "I hope Baltane arranged everything with this ship so we can continue to Earth. And with you alive, we have a pilot." She shook her head at the strange turn of events.

"I think so. Baltane gave me the chip. This is the *ScarthepD2*," said Coren, reaching across to close Baltane's dead eyes. "At least we know he was on our side, so it should be safe."

"Yes," said Kat, "he's another reason to end these people and their network."

"We'll have to leave his body in his flitter. Let's hope we're not pinned with his murder."

Hana waited, still unable to fathom that Coren had survived, as he inserted Baltane's chip into the slot situated beneath a small panel next to the *ScarthepD2*'s hatch. After a row of lights flicked on in sequence, he removed the chip, and handed it to her. The hatch opened with a satisfying hiss of the airlock, releasing the stale smell of sweat, oil, and hot metal. As much as she loved Coren, she didn't understand how he could enjoy the stench. She squeezed into a narrow corridor packed with bulkheads, panels, and tubing. Handholds presumably led down to crews' quarters, storage, and engines, while above was most likely the flight deck.

"Get the gear stowed," said Kat, as she climbed in behind her. "We'll take off as soon as Coren's ready."

Hana dropped her pack before following Coren as he hummed the theme from his favourite spaceflight vid. He'd spent a lot of time playing vid games, including flying simulations of modern and antique spacecraft. She'd preferred to use her time to hack into networks to see what her relatives were up to, leaving them cryptic messages to prove she could. She grinned at what she'd be able to do now since The Agency's training.

The flight deck was a revelation, out of keeping with the outside appearance of the craft. Four state-of-the-art seats lined a narrow port sweeping in a semi-circle across the nose of the ship. Kat dropped into a seat and clipped in her restraints. "Time to stop singing and get moving, Coren. If you look past the field, towards The Hub, you'll see lights coming our way. I don't want to be here when they arrive."

"It's not responding! It must need something else!" Coren pushed at buttons and flicked switches, sweat beading on his forehead.

"Hurry! They're almost here!" Hana leant across and ran her fingers over the controls.

Kat bent forward. "Maybe there's a slot for the chip. Can you see it?" She spotted a hinged flap and raised it. "Here!"

Hana pressed the chip into the slot. "Try now!"

The instrument panel lit up, lights flashing in sequence, readying itself for take-off.

Coren braced. "Right. Kat, do we need clearance or can we just go?"

"Go, go, go! I'll send a verification as we leave." She opened the communicator.

"Hold on, everyone." Coren flicked the switches as the first of the approaching lights reached their craft.

Shots flashed across their line of flight, deflected by a power field over the innocuous exterior. As they shot skyward, Coren stroked the control panel. "That was close! I didn't know these old ships had this technology."

"Wouldn't The Agency have upgraded them?" asked Hana.

"You're right. If I remember from the training, that panel is activating a weapons system, while the navigation pod has the latest in jump drive technology." Coren touched a console next to him. "This is all we could ask for, and more. Even the fuel cells are full."

G-forces thrust Hana back in her seat as the *ScarthepD2* accelerated. She didn't particularly like space travel, but she'd go anywhere for Coren. She turned to Kat. "Will they follow us, do you think?"

Kat shrugged. "That depends where the enemy's ship is, here or at the main spaceport. But if they know we've found out Lord Baden-Hauf is on his way to Earth, they're likely to follow."

"How would they know we'd know? Do you think The Agency has been breached?" Hana didn't like the thought of being chased all over space. She wondered how long it would be before they could go back to Crofta. Then the thought that they could never return to their familiar surroundings hit her. They'd have to make a new place somewhere, probably on another planet.

Would her relatives still help her out when needed? What if she couldn't contact them anymore? She'd always thought of herself as independent, but maybe she had relied on them more than she realised. She pushed the thought aside and concentrated on keeping her stomach from erupting. She had Coren, and he was all that mattered.

"Great galley back here," said Kat, from behind her. "I'm starving. How about you two?"

"I think we all need something after what we've been through," Kat said, glad that the tension in the air had lessened.

"It'll probably be half an hour before we're clear for our first jump," said Coren. "I can't wait to do this for real! Keep an eye out for other ships on that screen, both of you."

Kat took her eyes away from the vast display of stars through the port. "Hana can watch. Best we eat before we settle into the drive and get used to the grav setting for Earth."

Once she had organised food for them, they sat around an extruded table eating various food concentrates. Hana brought up information on a viewer from the chip Baltane had provided and scrolled through instructions. "It's almost as if he knew he wouldn't be coming," she said, her face dropping.

"Don't think like that." Coren squeezed her hand. "He wasn't coming with us anyway, remember? What does Baltane's chip say about where we've got to go, Hana?"

"There's some info here. It seems that Lord Baden-Hauf was definitely an Earther and the ship he took, *The Celestial Hunter*, is a day ahead of us. Baden-Hauf is out of Cape Town, Africa, so we can assume that's where he'll go. He won't know that their men have failed to kill us yet."

"So, do we go straight in, do what we have to, and then get out?" asked Coren.

Kat grimaced. "I think we'll need to be more subtle than that. We'll have to see who and what Ardan has in place on Earth, if anything. If the *ScarthepD2* is an example, then we should have some help there. At any rate, we have a lead."

The navigation pod chimed.

"Finish up, everyone," said Kat. "We've got company."

"Can't we jump yet?" asked Hana.

Coren checked the instruments. "Nearly."

Kat leant over the screen. "They're closing! Get us out of here!"

A look of determination settled on Coren's face. "Hold on! Jumping in 3, 2, 1—"

Chapter 15

Time travelled slowly between jumps. Each segment of their travel to Earth had to be set and precisely calculated—an error could send them way off course and unable to easily return to charted space.

Kat relaxed whenever she could, an advantage of being a hunter conditioned to long waits for prey, but her mind remained active, planning and thinking through every eventuality. When not discussing tactics with her, Coren and Hana slept or researched Earth on the chip Baltane had provided.

They took it in turns to check whether their enemies followed them, using the sophisticated technology they'd been trained in. Kat was glad The Agency had separated them to hone their different skills; her brain felt overloaded with information just from what she'd learnt. However, they'd all studied communications and the tracking equipment. So far, space was quiet and empty, distant suns barely a glint in the blackness. After a while, Coren dimmed the flight deck window and relied purely on the console views.

They planned to land at Ysterplaat, an outlying spaceport near Cape Town on the African continent. Using the on-board data banks, they'd assessed the conditions they would encounter and obtained background on their targets. The great game parks of the 20th and 21st centuries had shrunk substantially—many game species had been wiped out by population pressure and poaching, despite all attempts to secure the gene pools.

Kat mulled over her future and that of frenines, and all other sapient beings. She had known since being a cub that those from Earth considered species like hers less than human, even though they were genoid. She half dozed, lost in her thoughts, with Coren's exclamations from his vid game punctuating the air. Hana sat strapped in reclining bunks to her left, patiently ignoring her partner.

How could she and two young humans stop the might of HuX? None of them had experience at this, nor visited Earth before. She had shocked herself how easily she had been prepared to kill the person guarding their spaceship until she'd realised it was Coren. *Was she as bad as those she hunted?*

But thinking of this hardened her resolve. Even if she died in the attempt, she had vowed revenge for Tar's murder. She couldn't be responsible for leading Coren and Hana into further danger, though. The attack on K-Astar3 had woken her to the reality of what they faced. She sat up higher in her seat. "When we get to Earth, I don't expect you both to dive into danger with me. Be there to help me if I get in trouble, and keep the ship ready to go, but you don't have to confront the hunters."

Hana glanced at Coren before shaking her head. "No, Kat. We agreed to join you. We're a team."

Kat wasn't surprised, but suspected they didn't fully appreciate the dangers. "You have your lives in front of you. Don't get tangled up in what might end with you being killed, or incarcerated on X-Astar9 for life."

Coren stared at her. "We're in this as deep as you are. There were two of us, now we're three. We're not only a team, we're family."

The sentiment moved Kat beyond anything she'd felt since Tar's death, especially having been exiled from the pride. "Thank you. You're true friends." She let the subject drop, silently vowing to not put them in danger's way if she could avoid it.

As they travelled nearer to Earth, Kat's doubts continued to plague her. The three of them were insignificant in the scheme of things, yet that very insignificance might help them achieve their goal. She grimaced at the recollection of how Ardan had manipulated her into taking on an almost impossible task, though perhaps the fact they had been targeted on K-Astar3 meant the enemy was concerned about them. *Maybe they did have a chance to at least disrupt the hunting.*

With no evidence of pursuit on their equipment, and her hunter instincts at ease, she allowed herself to stretch and relax in the confines of her form-fitting bunk, the stillness before a hunt triggering ancient responses in her DNA.

Earth hung before them, a part cerulean and part verdant sphere, such a contrast to sterile space. White clouds whirled over the equator and shining ice fields covered the poles. Greens, browns, yellows, blues and oranges blended over the land masses cut by snaking rivers, their deltas leaking colours into the oceans.

Hana had never seen so much water. She gasped. "It's beautiful! Even better than the images I've seen. I know they call it the blue planet, but I'd never imagined it to be so varied. No wonder only the rich and famous are permitted to live here."

Maybe if they had to find a new home, they could do it here. The idea dissipated like mist as soon as she thought it. Even if they had the creds to buy a residency permit, they'd never be accepted, not a pair of orphanage escapees. And no doubt whatever they did while on the planet would have them on a 'most wanted' list, too. The thought of running for the rest of her life scared Hana more than the thought of being caught.

She pushed away her negativity and stared again at the orb growing larger through the flight deck window. The others also took a moment to enjoy the view before the navigation pod lit up. Coren changed the controls to manual.

Hana tweaked her earpiece. "Contact from Earth Central, Kat," she said. "They say we have pre-arranged clearance to enter the atmosphere but want to know our point of landing. Do we tell them?"

"Yes, why not? At this stage no one should suspect us, so we go with the plan. There's no point upsetting the local authorities unless we have to."

Coren locked the co-ordinates in and the *ScarthepD2* dropped into the queue of spacecraft orbiting Earth.

After gaining clearance at the Ysterplaat port the *ScarthepD2* had a straight run onto the landing apron. From there they were directed to a small hangar where a gantry lowered the ship to the horizontal before moving the vessel inside. The large door rumbled shut behind them and a blaze of lights lit the surroundings.

"Let's see if Baltane's information was right and someone friendly is waiting for us," said Kat, adjusting her belt, preparing for any eventuality. She unlatched the airlock, her nerves on edge.

A puff of hot, dry, tangy air burst in. Kat immediately assessed it, nostrils flaring, ignoring the background scent peculiar to the area and taking in the minute traces of people standing a short distance away. She smelt uniforms, weapons and stale food, but no anxiety, fear or anger. She stretched before walking down the set of steps to the crete floor, then kept her back to the craft while watching a small group of people approach as the others joined her.

"Welcome," a hard-faced, middle-aged woman in a green uniform said as she approached, a smile barely making it to her eyes. She focussed on Kat. "So you're the infamous frenine."

Kat growled softly, ears flattening, hand hovering near her hip.

"Ardan said you were a hunter." She stopped and looked beyond Kat to Hana and Coren. "Though you all seem too young to be experienced in this type of work. But he vouches for you. I'm Director Trushaw"—she turned back to her companions—"and these are Velhker and Kreltes. We're the leaders of The Agency's Earth base. We'll do all we can to facilitate your mission."

Velhker smiled warmly, his eyes alight in a round face accentuated by his lack of hair. He was shorter than his thinner companion, with a gaunt face and cropped grey hair. Both wore similar green uniforms to Trushaw. "Welcome to Earth," they chorused.

"Let's get moving. As you can see," she waved an arm towards the closed hangar door, "we made your arrival as discrete as possible. But don't go anywhere unaccompanied as our facilities are quite extensive." She ushered them through a narrow door into a descending tunnel that smelt of people. It ended in a grey-painted room simply furnished with a table, chairs, vid screens, and a food dispenser. "I'll let you freshen up and eat before we debrief."

Kat twitched. Everything seemed too smooth. *With these facilities, why hadn't The Agency fixed the problem itself?* She paced the room, ignoring the refreshments, noting the camaraderie of their hosts and the ease with which the others accepted the conditions. Coren was checking out the electronics while Hana, nursing a hot drink, spoke with Velhker.

Kat strode to the wall composed of a large vid screen displaying a game park scene. A herd of what she believed were wildebeest ran across a dry grassy plain. Something had spooked them. Her heart raced as she made out a brown, indistinct shape. *How Tar would have loved to have been here, racing across the plains by her side.* She blinked away her emotions and turned away.

The crack of an ion rifle shattered the stillness of the room.

Kat ducked, her claws extended, tail lashing.

"Sorry, Kat." The Director's voice was harsh. "It wasn't meant to startle you. It's relevant to why you're here. It's a recent vid, unfortunately."

Kat turned back to the screen. The wildebeest swung as one, something crashed through the undergrowth behind them, kicking as it went, the image too blurred to see clearly. An r-drive all-terrain vehicle pushed into the picture, bringing back more painful memories of Tar's murder. She growled. "Start talking!"

Coren sat with his back to the wall where he could see the vid screen, plus everyone else. He watched their body language. Director Trushaw oozed confidence as she directed proceedings and her two companions exuded professionalism. He relaxed, all the while noting Kat's difficulty in settling down, her tail lashing and neck fur bristling.

The leader remained standing. "What you're seeing is a spy-vid of a private game park in this part of the world. It's one of a number owned by reputable corporations which are really fronts for the people we're dealing with. The wildebeest"—Trushaw indicated the running herd—"are worth more than two million credits each. Although the pics are distorted by the park's security interference, we think the animal shot by the hunter was a big cat, worth many more credits as they're nearly extinct."

Coren couldn't stop himself reacting as he totalled up the sums involved. "That's a lot of creds. What I couldn't do with that."

"You're right, Coren," she continued. "With credits comes power and influence over which The Agency has little control. We can't enter their private domains. Even the strength of each solar system's animal welfare organisation can't help us here."

Kat grimaced. "We realise The Agency has its resources stretched across the galaxy, but can't you even stop them here? Isn't this your main base of operations?"

Trushaw shook her head. "We could, but what good would it do? We don't want to expose our hand for a small gain. These are ruthless people and they move about, people are bought or disappear. The destruction of animal species goes on. Now 'pleasure hunting' has its tentacles right through known space, as evidenced by what happened to your mate on Crofta."

Hana laid a gentle hand on Kat's arm. "So how can we influence anything?"

Kat blinked back tears and swallowed, for once stuck for words. Trushaw faced Hana. "We need to go outside the norm to influence anything. We use any opportunity and allow our operatives a degree of autonomy. Ardan is in charge of the Crofta system and recruited you despite your age. As I'm sure he told you, we can't acknowledge or openly support you, although all our resources are at your disposal."

"You mean we're on our own?" added Coren looking around the room. It seemed that people were resigned to taking small steps for the greater good. Knowing Kat as he had come to, if he and Hana could do something to help stop this evil spreading then they should, no matter the benefits to them. *But no support?* That wasn't what he'd expected. He glanced at his two friends and grimaced.

"So, if we're caught, there's no help?" asked Hana, eyebrows raised.

"We'll assist where we can, but we can't jeopardise our whole operation for anyone."

Kat cleared her throat. "We knew all this before we came. Let's get on with what we can do, not what you can't."

"You're talking about threatened species which are being hunted for pleasure and profit," said Hana. "Are there any exotic species in these parks? I mean, do the hunters have to go to the home world of their prey, as happened in Crofta? Or are they relocating species to game parks such as these in Africa?"

"Good question. As far as we know, they go to the home worlds to hunt. Here, they breed up stocks of endemic species, but there are inklings of something else occurring. What I mean is" —Trushaw looked at Kat—"we have suspicions that they've upped their game and are manipulating genetic material."

"They're not trying to create new races from frenines and other species, are they?" Kat blurted. "If they are, they don't deserve to live. It's against every moral and legal value in the galaxy."

The Director shook her head. "We don't know. That's why it's even more important for you to find out what's happening as part of your mission."

"Which is the best park to approach?" interrupted Coren, looking up to the screen resolving into a selection of maps superimposed on the outline of South Africa. "There are a lot to choose from. Do you know where Baden-Hauf is?"

Velhker wiped his bald head with his free hand. "We can't be certain, but our best guess is Mokala, near Greater Bloemfontein, where the vid was taken. It's where Baden-Hauf seems to be based, and recent information is that he is there, returned from space yesterday."

Kat held up a hand to interrupt him. "And you're certain that Lord Baden-Hauf is the man who shot Tar?"

Kreltes answered. "He boasted on the HuX network. We've recently discovered he uses the name Riddenhof, his wife's maiden name, when hunting. She's the one with all the credits and how he bought his seat on the Intergalactic Council. He arrives on Earth under his true identity when he comes on official business. It's one of the reasons it took us longer to discover who was the main player behind the hunting here."

Velhker fiddled with the tabletop. The tri-D maps expanded, showing greater detail. "This is the region where several of the game parks are. Our location is the fixed star at the bottom corner. The parks are flat, eroded washes where flood waters escape, with drought-tolerant plants. Watering and food points to keep the animals alive are marked by an icon."

He looked at Kat. "I'll download this to your personal device, if you're agreeable to having the latest technology in your skull, linked to your optics."

"What does that involve?" Kat asked.

Velhker leant away, quickly refocusing on the screen. "We have the latest equipment which can painlessly insert a nano-receptor via your nasal cavity and link it to the optic nerve."

"No way I'd do that, Kat," stated Coren, horrified at the thought of someone fiddling with his brain.

"I don't like the sound of it either," murmured Kat. Then louder, "I didn't think I could take my personal device in with me."

Velhker agreed. "But the receptor can upload data you require beforehand and enhance your vision. More importantly, it allows us to be in communication via your thoughts, provided there's no jamming."

"How do I use that?"

"Select a word that you're unlikely to think about normally. I'll set it up as a keyword to activate the comms."

"Great idea, Kat'—Coren raised both hands, impressed, despite the implications—"but what if someone else can tap into your thoughts?"

Kat grimaced. "I'll have to take that risk. If this aids my mission, then I'll do it, providing it can be removed afterwards."

"Good, it can, easily." Velker relaxed and then continued. "Natural features are few, primarily to aid in keeping track of the animals. They're valuable commodities, so once you're in the park you have little cover. Plus, there're sky trackers and rapid response units. Poachers have little chance anymore."

Velhker zoomed in further, bringing the image area into greater detail. Vents on the table emitted a waft of the dry, harsh climate. Sounds emitted too—the rustle of dried grasses and thorn bushes, the whine of mosquitoes and buzz of flies, the occasional cry of a bird.

"Take us even closer. There." Kat pointed out long rows of rocky outcrops, the orange-brown contrasting with dark shadows. Scrub with outriders of taller trees lined their slopes. "That's good hunting ground, good cover. I can use that."

"Zoom back, Velhker," said Coren. "Follow the perimeter. We'll need to see the security. What does it entail?"

"I can answer that," said Kreltes. "For a start, state-of-the-art force fields. Anything trying to enter will be fried. Conversely for anything trying to leave, though the force field is less intense."

"How do we get in then?" asked Hana.

"Any assault will have an almost immediate reaction, although there might be a way. Getting out will be the problem." Kreltes paused as the scan showed man-made structures forming part of the perimeter.

"And that building?" asked Coren, pointing to a solid complex in one corner of the Mokala game park.

Velhker zoomed in the view. The structure resolved into solid warehouse-like brown and grey buildings. They merged into the surroundings where bare rock, dotted by skeletal acacias, predominated. One warehouse of huge dimensions butted into the park. A vague blur surrounded it.

"This is of particular interest," said Trushaw. "It has high security with jamming devices that, as you can see, affect our surveillance. We've detected a lot of traffic in the area, but we've scant information about it."

"Let's put the facts on the table," said Kat, half rising from her seat. "Your main aim is to destroy, or at least weaken, the organisation. You want me to find out information, especially about any use of genetic material. Killing Baden-Hauf, for you, is incidental to that."

"Baden-Hauf would be a great source of information. We don't want him dead," Trushaw responded.

"I didn't come here to capture him. I came to kill him. He murdered my partner! I vowed revenge, and I will have it." Kat shook, the tip of her tail flicking.

Coren placed a hand on her shoulder. "Calm down, Kat. Let's take this one step at a time."

Trushaw agreed. "You can have your revenge, Kat, but surely you want to destroy the whole network? We need information first, and he's our best lead for getting it."

"So Baden-Hauf is your key to going further?" Kat glared at The Agency's leader.

Coren watched Kat, not afraid she'd back down. They had come too far and there was too much at stake. Baden-Hauf had to be their focus. "You want information from him, which means we have to capture him." He looked from Kat to the Director. "You also want us to find out what they're hiding in that building. And this will help stop the killing of sapient species on this and other worlds?"

"That's about it. A tall order, but if we can break them here, discover their leaders and networks, in fact any information at all, we may be able to cause a big dent in their organisation." Trushaw's smile finally reached her eyes.

"So, I need to get into Mokala Game Park and find out what's happening?" reiterated Kat.

"We'll be with you, Kat," said Coren. He looked at Kreltes. "How do you propose to get us into the park?"

The thin man coloured. "I said there might be a way to infiltrate the park, but only for one of you."

Kat stood tall. "That will be me. I'm not risking Coren or Hana in there. Besides, I need them to create a diversion to help me get out. Any ideas, Coren?"

Coren didn't like the idea of Kat going in alone, but if only one of them could go, it made sense for it to be her. He didn't bother arguing. Instead, he grinned. "I have just the thing."

Chapter 16

Kat ignored the background hiss of air as she breathed slowly, deeply, bringing herself to hunter awareness, preparing for the final stage of deployment. She had been dropped from a small stealth craft at high altitude, hundreds of kilometres from the park, the latest protosuit taking her on the final stage. The suit was a sleek unit, slightly larger than her body, its transparent shield deflecting the air as she descended. A row of calibrations flicked across her retina, calculating descent, distance, airspeed and location. The suit would begin to self-destruct at 500 metres, eroding into constituent parts with nothing to find or detect, the residual effect easing Kat to the ground.

The Mokala's detectors would register even her insignificant mass, but Kreltes believed she would be identified as a large scavenger bird that frequented the park. She hoped he was right, but should investigators be sent out, nothing would remain of her entry.

She was on her own. No weapons, no technology other than the micro-chip in her head, nothing to alert the electronic defences of the target. Despite Coren's repeated assurances they wanted to come with her, it was too risky to drop more than one of them inside the park, and only she had inbuilt defences such as her camouflage ability, speed, and claws. Her team would be on the other side of the perimeter fence as near to the compound as was safe, providing backup and ready to help. They could observe, and discharge weapons into the park, but they couldn't enter. Even messaging had to be restricted to nano-second bursts to avoid detection.

Kat would depend on her natural abilities together with her

wits, stealth, and skills as a hunter. To minimise the chance of being seen she had altered her fur to a sandy orange. Her compostable camouflage pack carried dried meat from local species plus a degradable water bottle. If she was detected, Kat would just be one of the park's big cats.

Her mission was simple, to gather information. At a minimum she planned to extract whatever she could from the highest-ranking hunter or employee she could capture, any incident being covered by the natural dangers of the park and not the incursion of an intelligence operative. The Director had made it abundantly clear that no one who saw her could remain alive if they were to use any information she procured. She would dispose of her captive in the manner of an Earth cheetah.

She had surprised herself how easily she had accepted being a predator of humans and what was surely murder, but in a war with game hunters threatening the very existence of sapient species there was little alternative. She had a job to do; the stakes were too high to allow for her cultural qualms.

The protosuit shuddered, lights warning Kat of the final descent. The early morning light outlined a series of rocky outcrops near where she would land. The point between light and dark was the easiest time to avoid detection. Dawn was the best hunting period and Kat needed time to find her lair and prey.

She prepared for the final drop, the hiss of the wind fading away. Pieces of suit disintegrated into sooty crumbs as she slowed and curled into a crouch for the final fall. An animal darted away, laughing hysterically. *Probably a hyena; not a danger on its own.* Trushaw had instructed her on the range of species to be found in the park.

Ready in hunting form, Kat arched her back, all four paws underneath her body, with her hands close to her face for protection. Her low body-to-weight ratio would help her to land on her feet, slowing her velocity while falling. She dropped the final few metres before landing at a run, surveying the surroundings as she did so. Satisfied she hadn't been detected, she slunk up the slope towards a craggy spike of rock skirted by thorny bushes.

The sun began heating the air, a shimmer distorting the scrub and skeletal trees that sparsely occupied the extensive flat ground. Spirals of dust whirled across the arid landscape, whether disturbed by animals or drawn by the rising breeze she couldn't tell. Vultures rose on the updrafts. She watched them for a while in case the birds showed any interest in her, but they continued circling on outstretched wings. Fascinated by the massive birds, unlike anything she'd ever seen on Crofta, she had to finally tear her gaze away, thankful their presence should help disguise her arrival.

She scented the air for any other evidence of life, drawing the range of alien odours into her lungs. Trushaw had provided samples for her to recognise as part of her pre-drop training. The rank stink of hyena came over the background iron tang of rock; different insect smells mingled with a distant odour of decay; a hint of small animals, birds, and a slight floral note drifted from a hardy flowering plant.

And old cat. Cheetah, similar to Tar and herself. The familiar waft almost had her sprinting towards it. For a moment she had forgotten her mate was dead, no longer able to race over grasses and rocks with her. She'd willingly trade the plains of Crofta for the harshness of Mokala Park if she had Tar by her side.

Kat controlled her emotions and opened the retinal scan, bringing up the park layout. As she turned her head, portions of the park zoomed closer. Soon she was facing the buildings over ten kilometres away where she believed her targets would come from. She settled down to wait. Prepared to endure the heat of the day and more while eking out her rations, she would wait, for she was a hunter. Patience was in her psyche.

A distant plume of thick dust caught her attention. A small two-man hover came towards her, sleek and fast, an anomaly in this rugged landscape.

Kat sank lower, ears flat, fur assuming the rusty red of the rock surrounding her. Despite her racing heart, she felt calm. The temperature was already high, above blood heat, her smell similar to local big cats. If they had seen her land, she had little chance of escaping detection. If not, the only way to find her would be to stumble across her.

The vehicle settled to the ground. Two men stepped out, one with a bulky detector, the other with an ion rifle.

"Around here?" The voice was staccato and flat.

The man with the detector spun in a circle, looking at the screen. "Nothing unusual. Keep on the lookout, though. The sign could have been a hyena."

"Hyena. I hate them nasty brutes. I'd like to fry one of them." He took aim at the rock where Kat hid.

Kat crouched lower, stifling a growl.

"Don't, you fool. They don't want anyone taking random shots. It's their preserve. At the very least they'll dock your pay."

He dropped the nozzle of the rifle. "Shit! Can't you hurry up? It's pissing hot out here. If it weren't for the pay, I'd quit."

"Just being thorough, like you should be. You know there's a big hunt on tomorrow. We can't afford any slipups. It's more than our lives are worth for anything to go wrong. These hunters are as important as they get."

He pointed the detector higher. "The trace showed something in the air, too. Reckon we should check it?"

"Look over there." He slung the large gun towards the sky. "Is your eyesight bad? Them's vultures. Almost as bad as hyenas but hard to hit from here."

"Vultures? Not worth a shot. But you're probably right. They follow the hyenas. Or is it the other way round? I can never remember. Both scavengers, anyway. Not worth it, any of them. So, must've been a vulture, there's nothing else showing up. No metal, nothing abnormal."

"Abnormal? What about what they're experimenting with to release into the park? Talk about abnormal. Reckon I'll look for another job when they do that."

"Yeah, I know what you're saying. Even with the ion gun I wouldn't feel safe." He switched off the detector. "Let's get outta here."

Kat watched the hover rise and head back the way it had come, her mind awhirl. She could have attacked them even with one of them waving an ion gun around. But they were only guards and it didn't sound as if they knew what was going on. But tomorrow there was to be a big hunt. *What did they mean by abnormal?* No matter, she would be ready.

She waited the rest of the day until the sun approached the horizon, unmoving other than to keep to the scant shade of the rocks and to sip at her water. The slight cooling as the sun left the land prompted her to move. *Time to scout a good site for an ambush.* She rose, crept through the thorny bushes and out into the eroded landscape.

Kat found a high, narrow ridge covered by the ubiquitous thorn bushes as the sun fell with a startling suddenness, bringing a drop in temperature. Old animal trails had created passages under the vegetation so she slithered through, slinking on her belly, able to see through the skeletal branches to the vague track the hover had used. She settled to wait out the night, rationing her supplies, half dozing, primal senses on alert. Small creatures moved nearby, but nothing of any threat. Once, she lifted her head at the cough of a big cat, but it was far away.

She patiently settled again.

A crackle of dry grass made her tense. Wan yellow moonlight, not the red she was used to, revealed what her nose told her—a large male cat, pale and ghost-like, slipped along the track below her. She hunched lower, breathing shallowly, watching. Its gait was familiar, not an ancient lion or leopard; cheetah perhaps. As much as she would have liked to greet him, she let him go. Not only was she unsure how he would react, she couldn't let herself get distracted.

He disappeared down a narrow gully.

Another waft of scent came minutes later, so familiar that Kat's eyes widened and she moved involuntarily. It was so near to a frenine's that it didn't make sense. She began to wriggle from her hiding place, but halted abruptly when she heard a rumble. Dawn wasn't far away. The hunters had started early, their vehicle's engine harsh and alien.

Kat froze. *How did they expect to hunt with all that noise?*

An acrid odour of men and weapons enveloped her before she saw them. Subdued laughter erupted as the r-drive all-terrain vehicle came into view, the driver up front concentrating on the track and a man beside him monitoring an onboard detector. Two men sat in the elevated back seat, one carelessly holding an ion rifle. The vehicle was open to the elements, an aspect Kat could employ. She recognised the driver from the day before and flattened herself down as they halted the vehicle.

"This is near where we picked up a hyena," he said, scanning the area. Kat froze her traitorous tail as her instincts kicked in.

"Hyena? I paid big bucks for a proper carnivore, Baden-Hauf," snapped the man, his florid face reddening as he turned to the man next to him, waving the gun.

Kat's chest vibrated in a silent purr. *Baden-Hauf. As Trushaw predicted.*

Her target smiled, bringing no relief to his harsh face. "Now Mr Troznec, it's early yet. The hyena is a good sign. They follow the big game you're after. Right, Diron?"

The man with the detector looked up. "Yes, sir. And we'll find one with this." He patted the machine. "If anything larger than a fly moves, we'll know."

"You'll get your trophy, Mr Troznec, be assured. Not only do we have traditional African species in the park, there are a couple of exotics as well, all ready for the hunt. It'll be hard, as it should be, but you'll get what you paid for if we have to stay out here all day and night."

Kat, as still as the rocks surrounding her, watched them pass, the whine of the engine and their chatter noisy enough to drive away any prey. The detector was obviously key to their hunt, to finding any unfortunate animal in the vicinity, then running it down with the power and versatility of the vehicle. She worried her different scent signature might reveal her, even though the detector was probably tuned to focus on particular species. *Or maybe they used embedded chips if the animals had ever been in captivity.*

Regardless, the tracker would make her challenge harder. She'd have to take care to stay out of its sweep, or else she might end up being their prey instead of the other way round. It hadn't detected her high on the rocks, so it either wasn't very sensitive or it wasn't programmed for genoids. That made sense. Kat was surprised they hadn't climbed the boulders to check the ridge, glad the hyena hadn't roamed higher.

She mused as she climbed through the thorn bushes to reach a vantage point. Taking out four people would require finesse and it would require her ultimate hunting skills to keep at least one of them alive, preferably Baden-Hauf. Lord Baden-Hauf of the Intergalactic Council. Lord Baden-Hauf, slaughterer of Tar. A growl rumbled through her body.

She followed the vehicle from a distance, tracking the dust trail and the hunters' loud voices, which rose higher as the heat of the day increased. It was an arduous trek simply due to the detector.

Without technology it would have been simple, but anything out of the ordinary would raise a warning on the machine. She couldn't take that chance.

When hunting with the pride, there would be periods of quiet where they would bunker down for a while, observe their prey, and make plans before acting. Hunting as a loner was much more difficult and made her appreciate the rare times when a single male was ostracised from the pride and had to survive on his own—the sudden thought hit her, that that was her future. A pang twisted her gut.

Kat, she admonished, *keep it together. Time to worry about that later.* She continued moving forward in the torrid conditions, belly to the ground, shoulder blades the only moving part above the sparsely grassed ground. A fly buzzed around her face but she merely slitted her eyes, refusing to allow any distraction.

The sun reached a scorching midday. She paused behind a tuft of stringy grass and raised her head until she could see her quarry. The vehicle had halted under a cluster of camel thorn trees where there was little cover for an approach. The driver and his offsider erected an envirotent for the comfort of the important men. They were professional enough to position the detector with a wide field of view; if she were to take advantage of the situation, they would be warned.

She huffed and backtracked until sufficient thorn bushes covered her position while giving a modicum of shade. The pursuit throughout the day had been fruitless, with no opportunity to attack without high risk. She had to rethink. The best site she had found was where she had first encountered the hunters, back at the rocky ridge. *Surely, they had to return along the track at some stage. If they had had a long day, it was likely their defences would be down and they were unlikely to expect an attack.*

Yes, she decided, *it's my best chance.* She settled down until the grumble of the vehicle brought her alert. It moved away at speed and disappeared over the horizon. Something had pricked their interest.

Kat headed back to her ambush site for a long wait, briefly wondering how Coren and Hana were coping without knowing what went on. Trushaw couldn't aid them by using her imaging technology since the slight risk of it being detected could put Kat's operation in jeopardy. She forced herself to relax and prepare for the coming confrontation.

A sudden crack of an ion rifle and a cut-short yowl echoed across the park.

A kill. She snarled, angry that she might have prevented the hunters if she had stayed. But she couldn't have acted earlier and saved whatever victim had been shot without giving away her presence and losing the benefit of surprise. She had to get information, and then kill. Her frustration fuelled a simmering rage.

The sun was sinking towards the horizon when she heard the r-drive returning. After sipping her water, she stretched in preparation, then climbed to her pre-determined vantage point where the track passed directly beneath the jumble of rocks.

The sound grew. Her tail twitched. The vehicle came into view, the men sitting in the same positions as before with the hunter still cradling his rifle. Baden-Hauf was there, her target. Her blood heated with the need to kill him, but she had promised Trushaw to try and capture him first. His information was more important to The Agency than her revenge.

Kat stiffened at the sight of a limp, furred body stretched over the rear cargo rack. Her tail thrashed. She pushed aside the memories it triggered. *Now was no time to think of Tar.*

The r-drive bumped as it went beneath her.

She pounced. Straight at the hunter with the rifle.

She knocked Baden-Hauf hard with her flank as she slashed at Troznec's jugular. Before the blood even spurted, she stretched over with clawed arms and gripped the heads of the two men in front, already turning in alarm. She yanked hard, slamming their heads together before biting down on Diron's skull, jaws crunching through bone.

The vehicle spun off the track and crashed through the acacia, the driver screaming. Thorns pricked Kat's skin as they careened over rocks and washouts. She threw herself across the driver, seeking his throat, kicking at someone grabbing her legs. She tore at the warm flesh of the driver's neck. His screaming stopped. She pulled away from whoever had hold of her ankle.

The vehicle tipped on its side, engine racing, throwing her into a boulder. She twisted, scrabbling against the surface to desperately find the remaining man, the final threat. Her enemy.

Her mind fuzzed and her limbs felt as if she were swimming

through glue. Try as she might, she couldn't spring onto the top of the wreck, her legs ignoring her commands.

Baden-Hauf lay sprawled on the ground nearby, eyes wide and face a bloody mess. He pushed himself away on his backside, hand groping for a weapon on his belt.

Kat tried to spring at him, yet again her limbs refused to move. Her head swam and her veins tingled. She remembered feeling a sharp prick. She'd been poisoned. *Had it been the thorns, or had whoever grabbed her ankle injected a sedative?*

It made no difference. Losing control of her body, she convulsed on the ground.

Baden-Hauf loomed over her, puffing. "You must be Kat, the frenine Gorind warned me about. You were supposed to be dead by now!"

Her eyes roved, the only part of her that could move. She looked for something to distract him, but instead saw the limp carcase of the big male cat.

Tar's dead eyes stared at her.

She spiralled into oblivion.

Chapter 17

Coren watched the vid screen in the backup vehicle manned by Velhker and Kreltes at its hidden location, not far from the massive perimeter fence enclosing the park. The stealth craft, kilometres up, appeared as a mere blinking dot on the screen. When the release order came, he imagined Kat dropping into the frigid air, an even smaller dot driving to earth at a perilous pace, a fragile living being with no right to exist in such an alien environment.

They all watched for an indication that Kat was on the way into the park and had made the journey safely. A small blip gave them some comfort until it was swallowed up by the target's electronic jamming blanket.

"That's all we can do. She's on her own now." Velhker drove back to their base, everyone silent in their own thoughts.

Once they arrived, Coren set about creating what he needed for the diversion to get Kat out. In a storeroom that Velhker had directed him to, he rummaged through cupboards, discarding objects but taking care to replace them where he'd found them. He knew exactly what he wanted, but so far had seen nothing even close. "Ferking new technology. Give me old-fashioned parts you can join together yourself, not all this clever self-adjusting rubbish. Too specific for purpose. Little use in improvisation."

He slammed the doors shut and went across to the shelves on the opposite wall. Odds and ends of composites, metals, and glass compounds lay haphazardly in dusty piles. "This is more like it."

He grabbed a collection of pieces and sat on the floor, legs crossed in front of him. Only a single light shone in the centre of the room. He adjusted his position so it illuminated his work. He twisted and pulled the pieces, cutting off bits where they stood out, jamming others in with his knife, screwing and riveting where necessary.

When he had built enough units to his satisfaction, he unfastened the small bag he'd secreted in a hidden pocket of his pack and extracted a number of cylindrical containers. At least he'd been able to smuggle these away from Crofta. Being unstable, they were illegal to transport without a permit. He unscrewed the lid of one and gently shook a few pink grains onto a spare flat piece of metal. Using tiny tweezers, he dropped the grains into his new devices, counting them individually.

"That should do it. If these don't create a big enough diversion, nothing will. A quick tweak and they'll be primed. Another tweak and they'll blow whatever I want to smithereens." Satisfied his devices were ready, he stashed them in his pack. He left the storeroom with a spring in his step.

A while later, Coren paced the conference room, cold drink in his hand. He couldn't stop wondering what Kat was doing, if she was alright. He knew it would be hours, if not a day or so, before she issued the signal for them to create a diversion for her to get out, but not knowing what was happening was driving him crazy. He stopped his pacing next to Velhker, who was scanning through old vids. "I have to go back to the park and check on her."

Velhker looked up and frowned. "You can't. We need to keep well away for now. You might alert their security."

Coren crushed the disposable cup in his hand, spilling the cold fluid over his fingers. "I'll stay high, on the rocky outcrop a few klicks back from the perimeter. I can use those powerful optics you've got. I can't just sit here and do nothing."

Kreltes butted in. "We can't spare one of us to drive you out there. There're other operatives we need to monitor, other ongoing projects."

Coren tossed the crushed cup into the recycling chute. "I don't need a babysitter. Give me a vehicle. I can go on my own."

Kreltes snorted. "You think you can drive one of those? They don't have such sophisticated technology on Crofta. You've got to be—"

"I can! Let me prove it to you. Surely you can spare a few minutes to see I can drive it. I can handle any vehicle, on the ground or in the air." Coren puffed up.

Rising to his feet, Velhker waved Kreltes down. "Prove it and you can borrow one. But don't say we didn't tell you when you fail."

Coren stomped out of the room, determined to show his ability to these Earthers.

Velhker led the way to the same vehicle from where they had watched Kat's drop. He motioned for Coren to sit in the front passenger seat and headed to an open, flat area behind the space apron. In the middle of the deserted space he pulled to a gentle halt and stopped the motor. "Your turn. If it's not as smooth as I did, you stay with us. These things are too valuable to risk."

Coren swapped places with him and adjusted the seat to his liking. Confident he could perform well, he fingered the controls. Not only had he driven these vehicles in virtual reality in the many war games he played, he had studied the controls every time they rode in one. He pressed the starter, remembering to squash his knee against the safety button on the door.

Velhker raised one eyebrow but remained silent as the motor purred to life.

The vehicle shot forward. Coren gasped as the controls proved more sensitive than he had imagined. Even the slightest nudge from his fingertips caused a response. He backed off and slowed down. Using his weight on the seat, he manoeuvred in a large figure of eight, then followed his exact tracks in reverse. The vision was superior to anything he had ever used and he loved the sensitivity of the controls. Forgetting Velhker sat beside him, he put the vehicle through its paces, getting faster and turning sharper as his confidence levels grew. After deliberately skidding and righting the vehicle with a reverse thrust, he laughed with joy.

"Enough!" Velhker held up his hands. "You can drive it. Drop me back at base and do what you have to, but don't get seen. Keep tuned to Kat's retinal chip frequency in case she sends a message, and be back before dark. I'll call you earlier if needed."

Coren dropped Velhker off and revelled in driving across the svelte before tackling the steep climb up the rear of the rocky outcrop he had selected. He smiled, enjoying driving such a state-of-the-art vehicle. He'd shown them. A boy from a backward planet way out in the galaxy could drive, and drive well. He'd always had a knack for vehicles, the *ScarthepD2* a perfect example. Now their allies knew it too.

When he reached the highest point where he could leave the vehicle without detection, he climbed the last few metres, keeping out of sight. Having made himself as comfortable as he could lying on the stony ground, propped on his elbows, he used his optics to scan into the park.

Nothing moved.

He checked his comms to see if anything had come through from Kat.

Again, nothing.

Was that good or bad? He sighed, and settled in for a long wait. He wouldn't leave Kat out there on her own, even if there was nothing he could do from here. If nothing else, he was closer to her comms for when she got in contact.

Then he thought of Hana. He should have told her what he was doing, but hadn't wanted an argument. He suspected she was jealous because of his interest in the sexy frenine, and Kat's privileged life. Hopefully Velhker would have let her know. Guilt riddled him. Even if Velhker had told Hana, she'd still be annoyed he'd gone on his own. *Should he go back? Not yet. He'd wait another hour and see if Kat contacted them. If she didn't, he'd return to base.*

Still no news had come from Kat after a couple of hours. Coren hadn't seen anything move other than a small herd of striped beasts, zebra perhaps, a bit like the zeena of Crofta but larger, and black-and-white. They'd seemed settled, nibbling at the sparse vegetation as they made their way into the shade of a few spindly trees, flicking their tails against insects.

Imagining Hana's fury if he didn't return soon, he slid back down from his vantage point, pins and needles in his arms from leaning on them too long. Once out of sight behind the crest he stretched and made his way to the vehicle, careful not to slip on the loose surface.

When he returned to base, all was quiet. If Kat had made contact, he'd have known over his comms. He headed to the control centre to look for Hana and found her in one of the small rooms off to the side, looking over Trushaw's shoulder at something on a screen. She turned as he entered and greeted him with a hug. *Phew, she didn't know he'd been gone.*

Hana turned back to the Director as Coren left the room. Trushaw was scanning a list of names again, the same she'd been searching through for the last hour. "I can't see a connection. There must be one."

Hana waved at the keyboard. "I keep offering to help. Why don't you let me try?"

"That's kind, but I can't imagine you can do any better than me."

Hana moved closer. "Please. The Agency let me look at live data on the system, so I'm not a security risk. And I may have access to information on that planet that you might not have."

Trushaw's eyebrows raised. "Really? I think that's unlikely."

"I have family in high places. Tell me again who you're looking for." Hana accepted the seat that the Director reluctantly vacated.

"She's officially a legal representative of their company, but we suspect she's a secret investigator." Trushaw went on to describe why they wanted to find this particular operative, for a project not related to Kat's mission.

Now it was Hana's turn to raise her eyebrows. "Let me see." She entered a series of codes into the terminal, opened a file, and instigated a search for variations of the name the Director was after.

Trushaw looked on in amazement. "I didn't know that data existed. How did you get access to it?"

Pleased she had surprised the older woman, Hana shrugged. "I told you, I have family connections."

"Surely they don't let you have free access to sensitive data. That'd be worth more than their jobs, maybe even their lives."

Hana kept looking at the screen. "They don't know. I hacked their home systems ages ago and installed spyware to keep me informed of their new access codes." She looked over her shoulder at the Director. "You're not going to give me away, are you? I'm doing this for you."

Trushaw shook her head. "Whatever works. I'm the last one to criticise you for breaking into datasets. I'll work with any information I can get."

The two of them followed the trail of links, engrossed in the chase. Hana enjoyed working with the Director, speculating on where to search next, discussing the possibilities of what the operative might be up to.

The extent of The Agency and what they delved into shocked Hana.

This certainly wasn't a slipshod operation. The way Trushaw, Velhker, Kreltes and their people went about their business inspired her. Sure, they had access to the very best of technology, but they were unfazed by it all, competently handling all aspects of every mission from what she had seen. Even though they'd mentioned they had other projects, it hadn't really sunk in for her that they were running multiple projects at the same time, some maybe even more important than seeking the illegal hunters. *They must have intergalactic backing of some kind, so why all the secrecy? Why weren't they working within the law? Unless, of course, the legal authorities were behind some of the problems they were trying to solve.* The ramifications spiralled through her mind.

Only after her neck became stiff did Hana remember they were waiting for contact from Kat. *How could she have forgotten? Poor Kat, alone out there in the park with murderers.* She left the Director and went in search of Coren in case he'd heard any news.

Chapter 18

Kat's eyes flicked open. The smell of antiseptic filled her nostrils. She struggled to her feet, wobbled, and crashed into a transparent wall. She dropped back to a cold floor, head throbbing with pain.

What had happened? Memories flooded back of blood and smells of the kill. Tar's dead eyes, staring at her, grew large in her mind. She shuddered.

But he had died on Crofta. She was certain. How could he have been alive on Earth?

Then she remembered the big cat patrolling below her hiding spot. His scent hadn't been identical, but very close. She pushed the thoughts away, crouched down and tested her body for injury. No bones were broken, but bruises spread around her midriff, her wrists and ankles, and her throat. She must have been tied onto the vehicle, like the body of whoever the big cat was. No doubt the bouncing of the r-drive had added to her injuries. She struggled to recreate the sequence of events, remembering the queasiness and dizziness. Somehow, she'd been drugged and captured.

She dragged her mind back to her current situation. The ambient smells located her in the Mokala game park, probably in the compound. Whatever was planned for her couldn't be good. She had killed Baden-Hauf's staff and an important client, not forgetting his son on K-Astar3. No doubt he would take his revenge. *So why wasn't she dead? There was only one reason she could think of. Baden-Hauf must suspect she'd had help to get inside the park. Would he torture her to find out what she knew?*

Her friends! She tried to activate the nano-receptor in her head to send a message, but either the signal was jammed or she hadn't communicated the keyword correctly to Velhker. She berated herself for using a keyword in the frenine native language—it was probably impossible to translate into common speech. She was on her own.

That would be her strategy. She'd have to convince Baden-Hauf she had acted alone out of revenge. But then she would have to explain how she had entered the park, bypassing security. Her muddled brain couldn't work out a plausible story. All she knew was that she'd deny her friends' and The Agency's existence if she possibly could. *She had overcome Gorind and his thugs, she could do the same again.*

She staggered to her feet, glad that this time she didn't wobble. Her head cleared as she inspected her surroundings. She was trapped in one of a series of circular armoured-glass cages occupying the centre of a dimly lit long room. Most of the cages were occupied by the still bodies of different species, presumably drugged or dead. But the nearest cage drew her attention, containing the pale brown body of an unmoving animal, a big cat.

Kat breathed deeply to drag any essence of the body to her but the antiseptic smell overpowered her senses, making it difficult to determine whether the animal was the big cat she had seen. Her eyes told her the body was devoid of life, which made her wonder why it was caged.

Her heart ached. He looked exactly like Tar in hunting form, the same strong muscles, the same lithe shape, fur the same colour of her pride back home. She tried to forget the painful memories by stretching, but the images lingered beyond the physical pain from her injuries. Sharp jabs stabbed through two tiny med patches on her stomach. She tentatively patted them, feeling the wounds beneath the dressings. They didn't feel like wounds from the thorn trees or from her capture.

She hissed. *What had they done to her?* They could discover her identity from her wrist chip, they didn't need skin samples. *But what did it matter, with Tar gone, and her captive? She should never have sought revenge. Mesat had been right—she should have let the authorities deal with Tar's murder. Now she had jeopardised the lives of her new friends, too.*

Kat tottered the two strides to the corner of the cage and sniffed at the water dispenser. With no sign of a way to escape she drank her fill, not caring if it were drugged, curled up on the floor, and sank into a torpor to enable her body to heal.

The lab door sighed open, breaking through Kat's consciousness. She sprang to her feet at the sound of several people approaching.

"You're awake, Kat, good. Or should I say Katerina Ellana Schlorati?" Lord Baden-Hauf's well-modulated voice matched his coiffed blond hair, his looks only spoilt by a recent deep gash down one cheek, too soon for any skin regeneration to have taken effect. He looked pleased with himself.

Kat snarled, pressing up against the glass, holding herself in check in order to not waste energy.

"Sorry about the cage." The big man lifted his shoulders and smiled, lightly fingering his wounded face. "How's the head?"

Kat glared past him to a tall thin woman with a heavily lined face dressed in a white laboratory uniform and an older man tending to overweight with a plump face and small eyes. He was dressed similarly to Baden-Hauf in a tan suit with a darker open-necked shirt and kerchief. *Almost a uniform*, she thought. "Let me out! You can't keep a frenine captive!"

"Calm down. I can do what I like. Who's going to care, anyway? You're a fugitive."

Baden-Hauf waved over his companions and introduced them. "You'll get to know Dr Guirden rather well. She's overseeing our work and is responsible for our ground-breaking innovations."

His eyes flicked along the line of cages containing the bodies of furred animals, then back to his male companion. "Mr Bakker is one of our financial supporters, keen to see a top assassin in the flesh. The tales of your exploits are already gathering attention."

Kat fixed Bakker with a steady gaze, recognising the calm demeanour of a fellow hunter. She resisted the urge to lash out, knowing that would make them really believe she was an animal. "I'm not an assassin! Frenines are pacifists. I only seek revenge for the murder of my lifemate."

The financier smiled with his lips only. "I think Dr Guirden's research should include this one, too, rather than eliminate her. She would enhance the demand for our operation."

"I agree, Bakker," said Baden-Hauf as he turned to walk out of the room. He threw a grin over his shoulder. "I'll provide a haunch of fresh meat to get you acclimatised, Kat, while we attend to other duties. Don't go away, will you?"

A thud of something hitting the floor made her swing around. The smell from a slab of freshly slaughtered animal rose from the cage's feeding chute. Feigning indifference to her enemies, Kat sat down to feed, not caring what it was. She'd need all she could eat if she were to recover her strength and escape.

The hum of an auto trolley accompanied the entry of the white-coated Dr Guirden through the lab door, a viewer and several loose instruments on its grey surface.

The colourless eyes of the scientist levelled at Kat. "I find it fascinating to see you in the flesh. All too often I have to work with dead specimens. They don't show the intricacies of skeleto-musculature structure, how the animal moves in nature, and how they react to stimuli. I need all these to ensure laboratory-raised animals act appropriately."

Kat stared into her dispassionate eyes, keeping her expression neutral. She had decided her best approach was to remain calm and rational. If she hadn't escaped in five days, Coren and Hana would set off their diversion without her signal. All she had to do was stay alive and keep her wits about her until then.

For now, she would try and talk sense into this doctor. "I assume you know the background of frenines?"

"Of course."

"You'll know then that we're a sapient race of genoids regarded by galactic convention as equal to humans."

The doctor drew a breath before waving a hand. "Go on."

"Why do you allow our people to be hunted? For sport? Why do you perform the outlawed practice of regenerating species?" Kat controlled her rage with effort, her breasts pushing against the barrier as she waited for a response. "While you're thinking how to answer, I'd appreciate some clothing."

The doctor stepped back and rubbed at her chin. "That shouldn't be a problem."

She spoke into her communicator before looking up, a slight smile adding character to her face. "As to why we regenerate, and recreate species, I would have thought it obvious. If we didn't, real animals would be slaughtered. If you're worried about species going extinct, then don't be. As long as we have laboratories we can produce to order, especially as we have that male frenine over there. Excellent specimen, from Crofta, like you I believe. We have his DNA in our store now and can produce copies as needed."

Kat could no longer suppress the growl that erupted from deep in her chest. That was Tar. She was certain.

"Don't worry. The animals that are hunted aren't real, merely regenerations or new genotypes. Our biggest problem is ensuring they react well enough to give our backers a worthwhile experience."

Kat snarled and pointed at her belly. "I suppose I've been added to your store? Did you take samples of my DNA? And what about you? Can I order a copy of you to track and kill, or should I go for the original?"

Dr Guirden ignored the last comment. "We didn't have any young female frenine DNA before'—she flapped her hand—"but a copy won't be you. It won't be real."

"Real? These creations of yours live and breathe and think. What's not real about that? Are you living in a fantasy world?" Kat stomped the confines of the cage, her anger escaping in flailing arms and swishing tail. She halted and pushed her hands against the barrier opposite Dr Guirden. "Don't you know what's happening? Your people are travelling to planets like mine and slaughtering us. Your copied animals are not keeping the big thrill seekers at home."

Dr Guirden looked down at her viewer and pressed it. "I don't know anything about that. The lab is my world. I'm only interested in science, not the business side of this venture. Without the hunters, I wouldn't have made the amazing discoveries I have. You should be thanking me, not railing at me. Without my inventions, rare species would have no future at all. If clones have to be killed in order for my funding to continue, it's for the greater good."

No wonder the big cat she had smelled in the park had been so close to Tar's scent. Fury simmered within her, a lifetime of believing that genetic engineering was wrong adding to her indignation at the doctor's smug certainty in what she was doing. She hissed. "Cloning is against all galactic treaties. It reduces biodiversity and leads to susceptibility to diseases and worse. How can you think what you do is good?"

Dr Guirden's eyes lit up. "But that's where my discoveries are different. My research has moved on from using base DNA. I use real eggs for testing. These animals aren't pure clones. I treat embryos so they're all slightly different, like in nature. That's why I removed your ovaries."

Kat shoved her face closer, snarling. "You removed my ovaries? My ovaries! How could you?" Not only had she lost Tar, but now she had lost any chance of having cubs with another mate. *These criminals had killed off her hopes and dreams, and now severely affected the future of frenines by eliminating her bloodline, after all her efforts with fertility treatments.*

The lab door slid open, disrupting her thoughts.

The doctor turned to take a pale-coloured body suit from an assistant and slid it down an access chute. "Try this on. I'll be back later."

Kat trembled as she dressed in the basic overalls, clawing a hole to accommodate her tail, fuming over what the woman had told her. *To remove her ovaries! What gave her the right? But they could have killed her first, so it didn't sound as if her life were in jeopardy, at least not from the doctor, not yet. What other body parts would she want? Would Kat end up being dissected, one piece at a time, for this woman's research?*

Before the door slid closed behind Dr Guirden, Baden-Hauf entered the room and sauntered over to Kat's cage. "Do you like her?"

She hissed at him. "She's evil!"

He stood with his hands clasped behind his back. "Evil? No. She's very focussed, I'll give you that, but how is that different to any scientist? I see you're dressed. Pity. Why hide such a gorgeous body? And it makes it harder to record your movement, you know."

Kat stopped her pacing and watched him, sensing a trace of unease in his arrogant manner. He must know he was operating outside the law.

Baden-Hauf turned and walked to the wall, where he pressed a button on a control panel. A dome of light descended over the cage. Background noise ceased as he walked back through the light wall. He smiled at her. "This is a sound shell. It keeps things private. Nothing is recorded inside or out."

Kat sharpened her guard, every hair tingling. "So?"

He pushed his face against the glass, looking into her eyes. "My son, Rast. You'd think I'd want you dead, wouldn't you?" his eyes hardened. "But I wasn't close to him and time has muted my desire for revenge. In my world, business takes precedence. We got off to a bad start, here at Mokala, unfortunately for my companions." He held up a hand to stop her response. "You're not being blamed for their deaths. We should have known better, even Troznec. Big game hunters know the risks and are required to legally acknowledge those before they hunt."

Kat pivoted to keep her eyes on him as he strolled around the cage.

He grinned. "You've given us a huge boost in our standings. The risk takers have been shown that hunting big game with us is a deadly adventure. Things have been getting too tame, hence the expansion of operations by the more unscrupulous to off-planet, to worlds such as Crofta."

Kat flinched. "Like you, you mean. You murdered Tar!"

Baden-Hauf held up both hands defensively. "It was necessary to give Dr Guirden the opportunity to harvest DNA from a Crofta frenine. Such pure bloodlines. A magnificent specimen."

Kat struggled to prevent the tears streaming down her face. *A specimen? Was that all Tar was to him? But she wouldn't give this murderer the satisfaction of seeing her pain.* "Why did you bring him back here? Couldn't you have taken what you needed back on Crofta, and let us at least bury him with respect? Or did you need to hide the body to protect yourself? With all your power, you could have done that on Crofta."

Baden-Hauf shook his head. "I don't have the freedom there you might presume. Besides, my chief scientist is here on Earth. But I'm deeply sorry for your loss."

"Sorry? Sorry? For murdering not only my lifemate, but affecting the chances for frenines to preserve our bloodlines and increase our numbers? Is that all you can say?"

"I can't undo what's been done, Kat. And now you've seen our organisation, I can't release you either. Instead, I see this as an opportunity to get to know you better. If I can forgive you for killing my son, you can surely forgive me."

Kat's mood swung between rage and misery, the need for vengeance and a loss of hope. Her inner body clock told her it was the middle of the night when the lab door hissed open.

This time her visitor was Bakker, the financier of the operation. His face flushed pink as if he had run there, his overweight body no doubt unused to exercise. He wasted no time on greetings. "Your attack on Troznec will serve to limit the illegal element which is a problem that reputable associations such as ours have to cope with."

"What associations are that?" asked Kat.

Bakker looked over his shoulder at the empty room. "I shouldn't say this, but a number of influential people and organisations control our business—including Lord Baden-Hauf. His power stretches further than you can imagine."

Kat didn't need reminding. She hadn't believed he had little influence on Crofta after both he and his son spent so much time in that area of space. But Bakker seemed willing to talk. She should get all the information out of him she could while he was here. "Where is the base of your operations?"

He rubbed a hand over his left arm, ignoring her question. "If the powers that be had their way, they'd use you for the duplication program, then charge exorbitant fees for one big hunt of a real frenine. Either way, the future's not looking good for you."

Kat pointed to the control panel. "If it'll make you feel better, Baden-Hauf used that to turn on a sound barrier. Do you know how to use it?"

"I can work it out." Bakker moved to the control panel and pressed the button, causing the dome of light to descend, before returning to the cage. "Now, to continue. I'm opposed to the direction some people are leading our business. They have too much control and have to be stopped. Your arrival has put certain things into motion."

Kat flattened her ears as she leant forward. "Like what?"

Bakker looked towards the door again. "I'm proposing to get you out of here, to your backup people and off-planet."

"Really?" Kat stepped back. "What backup people?"

"Come, Kat, I'm not stupid."

She thought for a moment. "You'd assist me to make your business operations legal? Not kill sapient species and operate within game parks with natural animals only? I find that hard to believe. It sounds like a trick."

Her instincts told her that him rubbing his arm was an unconscious sign of lying. "How do I know you're not releasing me to be hunted outside the park? That would be even better for your business, surely, and you're in this for the credits, not the hunt, from the look of you."

"Good question. Your brains prove you shouldn't be here. I can understand why you wouldn't trust me. But what have you got to lose? Anything I've done here is in keeping with normal procedure. There are monitors all over the place. I bribed the security guard to let me in and not have my presence recorded."

"What about my ovaries? How do we get those out? And any DNA samples." She indicated the patches over her wounds.

"Your loss is regrettable, I agree, but I couldn't stop that without raising suspicion. But I don't have the authority to enter Dr Guirden's lab. I can't retrieve any of her samples. What's it to be? Will you allow me to help you?"

Kat glared at Bakker's open face, trying to see what he was hiding. It seemed too easy to accept his story, sounding too much out of character for someone involved with HuX. The stakes were massive. *But, as he had said, what had she got to lose?* "Alright. But I have conditions."

"What?" he fidgeted, his hands in his pockets.

"I want my ovaries and my DNA back."

He grimaced. "I've said that's not possible."

Kat growled. "It has to be. Use your credits to find a way. Bribe another guard. I'm not leaving without all of me." Although not prepared to give in without a fight, she would only abandon the samples if this were a genuine opportunity to escape. This might be her only chance.

She glanced over at Tar's lifeless form. Her guts squirmed. "I want Tar's body too, plus anything taken from him." She pointed at the nearby cage.

Bakker looked over at the body. "That's your mate?"

"Yes," she snarled. "I want every bit of him or I'll take my chances on my own."

His face ran through a range of emotions. "You make it hard to help you."

Chapter 19

Kat pondered Bakker's offer, struggling to reconcile him as an ally. From reading his body language he seemed genuine, but someone else might be manipulating him. However, with her future already in jeopardy, there was little risk. She decided to go along with his proposal. Anything was better than being caged. Out in the open would give her a chance against her captors. She wasn't fool enough to accept Bakker at face value, and certainly wouldn't be divulging anything, especially about her support people, but she might get more information from him before they parted. If she could get away from Mokala Park she could find help and return to Trushaw at Ysterplaat.

Bakker promised to be a goldmine of information about the hunter network. *Could she risk taking him with her?* She hadn't obtained much intelligence from her time in the park and, being caged, she had little hope of more. Her drop into Mokala had been a gamble. *Maybe the gamble was paying off after all. Or was it too easy?*

Kat paced the confines of her glass prison. The failure of the retinal chip's electronics against the park's security added to her uncertainty. Bakker had left a while ago with instructions to be patient. She hoped Coren and Hana would be as well.

Time passed. No sound penetrated the laboratory except a vague hum; it was a sterile place, far from the grasslands of Crofta. A bad place to die. *Had Bakker changed his mind or was he toying with her? Perhaps his plans had fallen through or he'd been caught doing something he shouldn't.* She couldn't rely on this uncertain ally to save her. She must find another way.

More time passed. A chunk of meat with an unfamiliar, gamey

odour dropped out of the food chute with a thud. "More cold meat," she snarled. "They don't have a clue what frenines like. Or maybe they don't care." While she ate, she focused on possible ways to escape. *Was the feed chute a possibility? But with a one-way flap and automatic locking it offered little. What if she broke the water bowl to flood the room? Could it short the power to her cage? Would the ensuing pandemonium give her a chance to get free?*

The sound of the lab door closing startled her. She chided herself for being distracted and not paying attention to her surrounds.

Bakker sidled up, a furtive smile on his face, eyes flickering. "I've made sure the sensors are disabled."

Kat remained still yet alert. "I can't go without my ovaries. Plus Tar's body and all his DNA."

Bakker blinked, sweat beading on his forehead and upper lip. "Sorry, I can't do anything about the dead animal—I mean, your partner. He's too big to move. As to your bits, I have no idea where they are. We can't waste time looking. Do you want to get out or not?"

Kat hesitated. "Where does the doctor spend most of her time?"

"She has a lab with a cool store, even more secure than here. You're not thinking of trying to get in there, are you?"

Kat bit her lip. "Is it close?"

"Several doors down, near the acclimatisation pens, but we need to get out of here, fast." He released the cage door and held it open, rubbing an arm across his forehead. "Hurry!"

Kat remained still. "Do you have the plans of this place?"

"Plans? We haven't time for this."

Kat growled.

Bakker frowned and waved her out. "I have the building layout on my console."

Kat waited one more moment, then leapt silently from the cage.

Bakker backed nervously away.

She stifled a purr at her release and the financier's nervousness. "Don't worry, I won't hurt you, providing you don't betray me. Let's go."

The moment the lab door slid open Kat was struck by the lack of sounds, having assumed the quiet had been due to the glass walls of her cage. Although she'd known it was night, she had assumed there would at least be a hum of auto-trolleys or the murmur of conversations behind closed doors from security guards or late workers. No machinery whirred, no instruments sounded in other labs. Low lighting outlined a white corridor ahead of them, with doors leading off at regular intervals.

Kat was curious, but Bakker kept a hurried pace, flicking glances at the sensor panels as he passed. He halted at a curved panel. "This leads outside. We'll have to be extra careful here. I think all of the sensors are disabled, but I can't be sure how long that'll last." He pressed at his hand-held console. The panel slid open to a harsh glare of lights.

Kat hissed. "I can't go without what they stole from Tar and me. Our DNA is too important." She slipped back behind the wall, prepared to attack if necessary, her claws extended.

Bakker carefully stepped into the light. "We don't have time. Follow me."

"No! I can't leave. Not yet." She turned to move back inside.

A hand grabbed her upper arm and yanked. "It's too late. Do you want to get us caught?"

Even though alarm bells rang in her mind, Kat vacillated, not wanting to hurt Bakker by pulling against him. She still needed him to get her out. She snarled, resolving to return once reunited with the team, but ripped her arm from his grasp. "I'm coming, just don't touch me again or you'll regret it."

Bakker grimaced. "Stay in the shadows. As I said, I'm not sure whether all the devices are disabled, so keep up."

Kat squinted away from the light, her body low and alert, tracking the darker spaces, every part of her body resisting leaving. She quashed the desire and followed him outside.

Her guide stopped at a hemispherical building and touched his console. The side rose to reveal a low opening. "In here."

Low lighting flickered on as they moved into a vast open space to a gust of chemicals and oil. An array of vehicles from hovers to heavy duty r-drives were lined up in neat rows. Bakker touched his console and one of the vehicles lit up. "This hover's allocated to me."

He moved towards it as Kat scanned the space. A light glowed on her retinal display, a flashing message showing her friends had been trying to contact her. She paused to mentally message her waiting friends, grateful for The Agency's technology.

"Are you coming?" he asked.

"In a moment," said Kat, feeling a surge of relief as a confirmation pinged back.

"You'll need to conceal yourself. It should appear I'm going off base as normal, as I often do nightly hover runs. The longer we can delay knowledge of your escape the better."

Kat grunted as she stepped into the vehicle, her belly wounds pulled taut, and her unused muscles stiff. She hunched down below the panelling and curled up as small as a cub, her eyes focussed through a tiny window in the nose of the vehicle. "I'm ready."

The hover whined as it lifted and moved out of the building. The outer perimeter loomed from the dark. A section of the high grey wall dropped when Bakker drove up to it. He manoeuvred through and increased speed, heading away from the park and into the dark wilderness along a winding road cut through jagged rock and skeletal trees, the hover's lights creating an eerie atmosphere. Bakker hunched forward as if urging the vehicle on, although it automatically followed the path via its electronic guidance system.

Kat kept on the alert, still crouched in the nose of the vehicle, hoping her message had been fully understood.

"Shit!" screeched Bakker.

A black shape had appeared from the shadows.

The hover's brakes slammed Bakker back into his seat and Kat against the hard panelling. With a crunch, the nose of the hover hit a vehicle in front of them.

Bakker reached for his gun.

Kat clamped a hand on his arm, claws digging in. "Leave it. I know who they are." She extracted his laser from its holster. "There's been a change in plans."

"Hey! Give me back my gun!" Bakker lunged towards her.

"Not yet. My instincts are saying you're not to be trusted. You'll have to prove yourself first."

Bakker sighed and released the top. "Wasn't getting you out enough?"

"Thanks for that, but my fur is standing on end. I'll be happier when we're safely away from here." Familiar shapes emerged from the shadows, approaching their hover. Kat waved at her friends.

"We'd almost given up on you," called Coren.

Hana leant over and hugged Kat before peering cautiously into the hover. "Who's this?"

Kat introduced Bakker. "He helped me escape. He claims to be on our side."

The plump man rose reluctantly from his seat and joined them on the roadside. "These are your friends, I take it? How did they know to be here?"

"Like I said, a change of plans," Kat said, her voice a throaty purr. She turned to them. "Bakker's one of Mokala's financiers."

She signalled to him with her hands. "Get back in, quickly. Coren, you drive Bakker's hover. I hope you've brought the devices you were going to use for the distraction. We've unfinished business."

"You can't mean to go back into the park?" Bakker's face paled in the hover's lights. "I've only just got you out of the compound. They're sure to know something's happened by now."

"Fine." Kat held out her hand. "Give me your holster and your console."

"Kat, the only way you could get back in is if security thinks it's me returning, through the codes. If you're recognised it'll be your suicide." He fidgeted on the spot. "You do know that helping you is causing me significant financial cost, not to mention my standing with IHO. Why did I let my heart rule my head?"

"The codes, Bakker."

"Fine. These are the codes to the gate and the inner door." Bakker typed in a sequence of numbers before he tentatively held the console and the holster out to her.

"Wait a moment." Hana flicked her gun at Bakker. "I'm sure there's more. A state-of-the-art facility like Mokala wouldn't be that simple. It must use DNA at the very least. Bakker?"

Even in the moonlight Kat could see his face redden.

"I can't give you my fingers."

"No, but a micro-sliver of skin should do. Coren, do you have a vibro-knife?"

"There's one in the medical kit in my pack."

As he dashed back to the vehicle, Hana called out, "And something to seal it in, Coren."

When Coren returned, Bakker retreated, his hands in the air. "Don't cut me!"

"It won't hurt, it's only a few cells deep. Hold out your hand."

Bakker tentatively held out his right hand, keeping his left firmly behind his back.

"Let me do it," said Hana as Coren reached forward. "I'm more used to such things. I suggest you hold very still, Mr Bakker."

"Damn," he yelped as Hana carefully operated the vibro-knife.

"There, didn't hurt, did it?" Hana held out the slice of skin on the tip of the knife. "Kat, if you wrap it in the sealant it'll be fine for when you need it."

"Thanks Hana. Can you keep Bakker in your vehicle while we go back? I have a feeling we need to watch him."

"Where would he go? Can't we trust him to stay? He's hardly likely to run off into the park. I want to come with you," said Hana.

"We can't risk it. We need what's in his head. This'll give you a chance to start recording information. If anything goes wrong, get him to our base for further debriefing. What I have to do has to be done quickly, before there's an alarm."

"I'll let our friends know what you're doing," said Hana, her face showing concern. "We've set up a rendezvous point."

"Good. Hopefully we won't be too long," said Kat, inserting the laser into Bakker's holster, before strapping it on and dropping into the passenger seat of his hover.

"Do you know what you're doing, Kat?"' asked Coren, taking the controls.

"I have to do this. Swing around and let's go."

Hana's voice hardened as she nudged Bakker with the gun. "Get in the back. Far side." She pointed the gun at the hover's rear seat.

"Careful. It might go off," the sweating man warned as he slipped into the seat. "We are friends, after all."

"Not with me; I trust Kat's instincts. Sit still and start talking. I want to know all you can tell me about Hunters Extreme." She sat at an angle on the front seat, making sure Bakker could see the gun and her determination. Hana's eyes fastened on his reddened face while she communicated via her comms-link to the Ysterplaat base.

After a moment Velhker's voice sounded in her earpiece. *See what you can get out of Bakker, Hana. We'll record what he says and analyse his body's responses.*

Bakker scratched at his arm for a moment. "I don't remember Kat mentioning you. Hana, is it? Aren't you a little young to be helping her? She's a fully mature frenine, whereas you—"

"Look, Bakker, I know you helped Kat out of that place so I'm grateful, but you're still an unknown. What's in it for you? It seems to me that you're selling out your organisation by helping us. If you're really a financier, credits are your priority, and you'll get none by supporting us."

Bakker squirmed on the seat. "I've already told Kat why I helped her escape. I've not been happy with the way IHO is heading. I don't approve of the illegal aspects of HuX's business, and couldn't stand aside and let her, a rare frenine female, be chopped up and used as DNA material. This is about credits, but I don't operate outside the law. My reputation is important."

Hana studied him a moment. "You're still taking a huge risk. From what I've learnt, IHO isn't known for its kindness, particularly its concern for rare species."

Bakker shrugged. "I've been trying to steer it a certain way, add my influence from the background. But the other financiers want bigger returns, quicker. They've pushed the organisation over the line of legality."

She watched him for a long while, still disquieted at his apparently simple explanation. *No*, she communicated to Velhker, *he's hiding something. Something's not right about him.*

Keep it up. This is useful, he replied.

Her intuition had never let her down, and it rang alarm bells in her head. "What do you want to do now, when the others get back?"

"Why, help you." He spread his arms wide. "Your aims and mine are the same. We should join forces, remove the rough elements of the IHO and co-exist. After all, we have the same goals in mind."

"We're not in this for credits. Nor to hunt and kill animals. Is that what you mean?"

Bakker leant forward until Hana raised the gun. He relaxed back with an air of superiority. "No, you foolish child, that's not what it's about. We hold special reserves for those who want to hunt, to satisfy their natural urges. In so doing, we ensure there is regulated culling of overpopulated game species. Sapient species are never targeted. We're in the business of doing the right thing for all concerned, now and into the future."

Hana coughed a disbelieving laugh, biting back a retort about him calling her a child. "Your idea of sapient and mine must be different. How is a clone not still sapient? And why you, Bakker? What's your influence in such a large organisation other than credits?"

The smile never reached his eyes. "I'm a small cog in a huge wheel. But credits talk with these people, and they need it for their research. If I were to withdraw funding, they'd be set back by years. So, they listen to me. Hence, I use my influence for the betterment of all concerned."

That almost sounded like blackmail, yet credits certainly talked within Hana's family. She had soon realised they put their financial interests ahead of love, especially of her. Even so, she found it hard to believe that was Bakker's only power. *If he didn't like the way IHO operated, why did he support them at all? That nagging voice in her head wouldn't let her accept him at face value. What couldn't she see?*

Leave it for now, came Velker's voice in her ear. *He seems to be telling the truth, at least how he sees it. We'll continue interrogation at base.*

Hana relaxed while keeping her gun on Bakker, pleased someone else had taken responsibility for what to do with the man.

Kat leant forward and spoke over Coren's shoulder. "Keep the lights on and act normal. We'll have to appear to be Bakker if we want to get in."

"Fine," said Coren, eyes on the road as he accelerated the hover towards Mokala Park's main gates.

"What are we doing, Kat?" asked Coren. "I thought you wouldn't want to go back."

"They have Tar!"

"What? How can that be?"

Kat gulped. "They transported him from Crofta for research. I'm not leaving him here. They've extracted his DNA, and mine, as well as that of other sapient species. They're making copies of genoids to go hunting. I can't let—."

"We're coming to the gate," interrupted Coren.

"Drive up to it. I hope it'll still open to the hover as Bakker said." Kat pulled Coren down out of sight with her and punched in the code on Bakker's console.

Security lights flickered on to light the road as the vehicle nosed up to a grey wall. A section of the barrier slowly slid out of sight. Coren drove the hover into the compound, stopping near the doors Kat pointed out, where she had left from a short while before.

"This'll do. Although it seems quiet, we'll need to leave the vehicle here for a speedy exit. Hopefully we can be in and out before we're noticed. I know where I'm going." She jumped out, keeping low.

Coren followed, lugging his pack as usual.

After a quick scan of the surroundings, Kat entered the code Bakker had given her into the wall console next to the door. A panel opened with a blinking light. She carefully pressed the sliver of skin against it and sighed in relief that the door slid open. Thank goodness it only detected living DNA and not fingerprints like the old-fashioned sensors. The skin hadn't had time to degrade.

They raced down the corridor to the room with the cages, Kat focussing on the console. "Here," she whispered. Again, she tapped in the security codes to open the door. It slid open to the vast room holding the glass cages. So far Bakker had delivered. *Maybe she had been overcautious about him.*

She slowed as she approached the cage holding Tar's limp body. Tears threatened to erupt. She sniffed and placed her hand on the protective glass, talking to him in her head as if he were still alive.

Coren exhaled behind her. "We'll never be able to carry him. He's huge."

The reality of the situation struck Kat hard. "I'm not leaving him to be chopped up and copied again. Can you… Can you cremate his body?"

Coren extracted a cylindrical device from his pack. "Sure, Kat. And I'll make it so that everything in this room is in pieces, but we'd better be the hell away from here when it blows."

"What if people try to disable it?" Kat couldn't bear to picture Dr Guirden slicing into Tar again.

"Don't worry. It's booby-trapped. If anyone touches it, they'll be blown up too."

Kat hesitated. She had known it would have been near impossible to take Tar's body with her, but had still held out some hope. She said a silent "goodbye" to her mate before stepping back.

"Do it. Then let's find the samples. And," she continued,

remembering what Bakker had mentioned, "we need to find the orientation pens to see what they hold."

"Are you mad, Kat? We've gotta get moving. Things have been too smooth so far."

"Set it for twenty minutes, then we can go."

Coren attached the device to the wall of the cage, not bothering to hide it, and activated the countdown. "Let's get outta here."

Kat turned without another look, not daring to farewell Tar in case she broke down, focussing on following Bakker's directions to find Dr Guirden's lab. "Down this corridor."

She counted, "One, two, three. Next door. This must be the doctor's room where she keeps the genetic samples." The glow from an array of monitor lights lit the room, revealing banks of hand-sized compartments set on white benches. Shadows moved within a transparent room behind them.

"Hurry, Kat. There's something living in there. I thought it seemed too easy," whispered Coren.

Kat grabbed a console from the bench and magnified the view. A drop-down menu appeared, displaying a list of names. "DNA. Frenine, along this row."

She scanned the list until she found "Male frenine, prime—Crofta'. She sprinted for the shelf, ripped open the door, and confirmed the label on the capsule. Her heart leapt. *It had to be Tar's! The date was right and there couldn't have been another male frenine killed without her knowing about it.*

Another capsule had her name on a label. She grabbed it too, placed them into a lifeseal pac she'd taken from a shelf, and tucked the whole thing into her waist pouch. The pac would ensure the live tissue wouldn't deteriorate, no matter the environment, for months, if not years.

She stared along the line of shelves, aghast at the extent of the DNA storage facility. "We can't take it all. It'll have to be destroyed."

"There's more along here," said Coren. "Other species?"

Kat joined him and read the console. "Yes, some I can't recognise. But…dineeth. Would you believe it? Dineeth." *Did the mystic know?*

She pushed the thought aside for another time. "Can we destroy all this, too?"

Coren grinned. "I made heaps for the diversion to get you out."

Kat nodded in approval.

He set three of the explosive containers along the benches. "How long do you think we need?"

"Five minutes should be fine."

Coren did as asked with smooth efficiency. They picked up their bags and headed out the door.

"This door," she muttered, "marked "Breeding"." She flung it open to see long rows of cages lining both walls, many pairs of eyes watching them.

"Ferking hell!" Coren yelped, "Look at all those animals. All locked in."

"Yes," Kat growled, "all kinds, grown to be hunted and slaughtered. We can't leave them. They've got to be freed. Hopefully they'll have a chance of escape, or at least survival, if we release them into the park."

"Fine. I've got a couple of devices left. If we blow a hole in that wall and destroy the locking mechanism, they should be able to get out. Best I can do."

"Great, let's do it, then get out of here." They wasted no time, Kat clamping on the remaining devices and Coren setting the timers.

"Let's go," urged Kat. They rushed back into the corridor.

"Hold it!" ordered a hard voice.

The crack of an ion gun rang in Kat's ears.

Chapter 20

Kat twisted as she dived to the floor, seeing Dr Guirden trying to sight an ion rifle. She inwardly cursed at getting too absorbed in what she had discovered and not detecting the woman.

The thump of Coren on the other side of the corridor shoved her self-anger aside as she scrabbled for her gun, crabbing across the floor as ion beams crisped the crete. Her hand grasped an empty holster; the weapon must have fallen out as she flung herself down.

"Leave the gun!" screamed the doctor. "I've widened the beam so I'll get you no matter what."

Kat hissed and crouched against the wall, her mind awhirl.

"Fine. You win. Here's my laser," called Coren.

"What the—?" Kat couldn't believe her ears. *Why was he giving up?*

Coren stood, hands raised, the weapon clattering to the floor.

The doctor's eyes flicked between them, the ion rifle awkward in her hands as she gestured with it. "Get up, Kat! Over with him." The woman's face was white, her body rigid with tension.

Kat rose, arms held away from her sides, angling herself to keep the DNA lifeseal pac in her waist pouch hidden by her body, and shifted towards Coren.

"Who are you?" Coren asked the doctor.

"I'll ask the questions. More to the point, who are you? How did you get the frenine out?"

Coren waved an arm to engage the doctor's attention. "I'm here to rescue my friend."

"Friend? You're a friend to this animal?" She swung the rifle towards Kat.

Kat remembered the charges set to explode and crouched slightly. *So that was what Coren was doing. They needed to move, and soon.*

"Where're you taking us?" Kat snarled.

Dr Guirden blinked, weapon dropping slightly. "Back to the cages, where you belong. Come on. Move past." She flattened herself against the side of the corridor. "Try anything and you're dead."

Kat turned to Coren. "Do as she says."

"Ow!" He bent and clutched at his foot. "My ankle! Must've twisted it when I fell."

Dr Guirden stabbed at him with the tip of the rifle. "None of that. Move."

Kat put a hand under Coren's armpit and squeezed, their heads nearly touching. "Two minutes."

Coren nodded as he struggled to his feet.

Sweat beaded the doctor's forehead. "Move!"

They limped their way down the corridor, hunched over, towards the cages where the bomb on Tar's prison ticked down the time, Coren dragging his leg.

Whoomph! Whoomph! Whoomph!

A pressure wave from the lab knocked them to the floor. They covered their heads with their arms, curling into balls. Panelling rippled with a screech, adding to the cacophony of the explosions. The doctor crashed over them, the rifle and debris flying past.

An alarm pealed.

Several moments passed before Kat tentatively lifted her head. "Are you hurt?"

"I don't think so," answered Coren, peering around. "We'd better get out of here."

He bent over the doctor. "She's out cold, but alive."

Kat couldn't bring herself to kill in cold blood, even though the doctor was her enemy. "Do you reckon we can take her back to Ysterplaat? She'd be a store of information."

Coren raised an eyebrow. "I bet she's heavier than she looks, but we can try."

They heaved a limp arm over each of their shoulders and dragged the doctor towards the exit, stumbling over chunks of panelling and glass. Coren puffed as they passed the smashed doors to the DNA storage room and the orientation pens. "My devices did a good job.

I hope the captives have escaped."

Kat grunted, the only acknowledgement she could muster. When they reached the exit door, she pressed the console to open it.

Nothing happened.

She cursed. "There must be a security lockdown. You'll have to get the rifle and blast our way out."

"It's down the far end of the corridor, Kat, back near the cages," said Coren. "You're quicker than me."

Knowing he was right, Kat slipped from under the doctor's arm and sprinted down the corridor, snatched up one of their lasers still lying against the wall, and clambered over wreckage to find the ion rifle. Lengths of gnarled piping hanging from the ceiling and exploded from one of the walls made it hard to see where the weapon had ended up. The alarm continued to scream, egging her on at the same time as panicking her. She stopped and mentally composed herself. *Calm down. Use your wits. Tar's been dead since Crofta. He won't feel anything when his cage blows.*

Finally, Kat noticed the tip of the ion rifle half buried against a buckled door. She gripped its barrel and pulled. It jerked out of the rubbish with a shriek of metal. She flinched and mumbled, "I hope it still works."

A cough startled her.

Still crouching, she looked up. Straight into the nozzle of a laser. A dark-uniformed guard stood over her as the door behind him shuddered open. Kat dropped the ion rifle, sprang into the air, and launched at him as his finger tightened on the trigger. A sizzle hissed under her legs. She came down hard, clawed hand ripping at the man's face. She kicked out, driving the guard back into his companions, who were clustered in the doorway.

Kat snatched up the ion rifle and sprinted down the corridor, leaping over debris. Lasers hissed behind her. She raced towards Coren. "Out of the way!" She fired at the door locking plate ahead while still running, punching a hole in the material. "Open it!"

As Coren tore the door wide, the sizzle of a laser burnt Kat's side. She heaved the doctor through the opening with one hand, trying to ignore the sting under her ribs. "Find something to jam the door! We have to get to the hover."

"Use the gun, Kat! Melt the door to the wall. I'll get her to the hover," Coren puffed as he dragged the doctor's limp body on his own. "Ferking hell! We should have left it closer." He tugged the woman by her arms, step by step along the building's wall.

Kat sprayed the bottom of the door with the ion rifle until it stopped working. A bubbling strip of metal oozed to the ground. Hoping she'd done enough to at least delay their pursuers, she dropped the useless weapon and hobbled after Coren.

Boom!

Kat's ears rang from the explosion. She reached Coren and gasped, "Give me an arm." They pulled Dr Guirden to the hover, heedless of her torn clothes and dripping blood.

Kat could no longer stop her tears flowing. Tar was truly gone now.

oren dropped Dr Guirden's arm as they reached the passenger side of the hover. "Leave her," growled Coren, "We're out of time."

"We've got to bring her!" yelled Kat. "Help me!"

A series of thuds came from behind them in the direction of the buildings, the pursuing guards bashing their way out. Coren helped heave the scientist into the hover, then scrambled in, followed by a breathless Kat.

"Hit Bakker's console. Hope it still works." He settled into the driver seat as Kat punched in the code.

The barrier retracted. "Great! It's still working. That's surprising." Kat leant forward, as if to urge the hover forward. The barrier stopped halfway into the wall, then started to close again. "Damn, we'll be trapped!"

"No way!" Coren slammed the controls into place. The vehicle shot forward and jammed into the diminishing gap, halting the barrier. His fingers danced over the controls, stabbing at buttons. With a squeal of its toughened body, the hover tore free and accelerated up the road.

he journey through the night across the African landscape seemed endless. Staccato light flashed as beams from the hover's headlights bounced off trees and rocks. Dr Guirden's groans elicited no sympathy from Kat as they sped on their way, her mind preoccupied with the memories of Tar, mingled with the satisfaction that they had struck a blow against HuX. The vehicle slowed, pulling up next to the hover where Hana's face showed through the glass.

"Kat," said Coren, "do you want to go with Hana and Bakker? If you lead, I'll keep driving this and try to get rid of any tail. Hana knows where we're meeting Trushaw's team."

Kat hesitated. "What about Guirden? At least Bakker is on our side."

Coren grimaced at the unconscious form of the doctor. "She's out cold, and I don't trust Bakker. Do you?"

Kat's instincts still niggled, raising the hairs on her neck. "No, not fully. But what if the doctor comes round?"

"Don't worry about that. Once we've gone a short way and I feel safer, I'll stop and tie her up. I've plenty of things in my pack."

Kat shook her head. "No, I'll stay with you. We haven't time to stop and we'll waste what little lead we have. We'll have to trust Bakker a bit longer. Let's go." She messaged Hana to head to the rendezvous.

As Hana's vehicle sped ahead of them, Kat placed a clawed foot on the recumbent body jammed at the base of the back seat. "We don't want Dr Guirden hearing anything when she comes around, and I want to learn a lot from her. There's far more at stake here than I realised. I'll tell you more later, but for now, let's get somewhere safe."

They drove on through the night, skeletal trees and jagged rock formations leaping out as the hover lights flashed over them. The drive in the alien landscape proved unnerving, especially with Coren using dodging tactics to confuse any pursuers. Damaged parts dropped off the vehicle ahead, leaving an easy trail to follow. She admired Coren's skill in keeping close behind Hana and avoiding the debris. Occasionally, they caught glimpses of spotlights or heard the whine of pursuing hovers, but none came close.

Coren swiftly turned around an outcrop of boulders and changed direction, away from where Hana headed.

Kat gripped the rail in front of her. "What are you doing?"

"Laying a false trail. At least if we get caught, Hana and Bakker can get to The Agency's team safely. Bakker's knowledge is important." Coren puffed with exertion from maintaining control of the vehicle over the rough terrain.

Kat silently agreed that bringing down HuX was worth more

than their lives, especially with Tar gone. But she still had her revenge to seek. "Do you think their security can track us by heat or aerial visuals?"

Coren grimaced. "Maybe your captive will save us from that. I assume she's valuable to them. And Bakker. They wouldn't want to lose a rich patron, and they probably don't know yet he was responsible for releasing you."

The body beneath Kat's foot rolled with the movement of the vehicle but the doctor didn't stir. Kat wondered whether the explosion had injured her more than it appeared. She hoped not. *What if there were more stores of DNA in other labs, more animals, even on other planets? Would Bakker know of them?* Kat's mind whirled with all the machinations the future might now hold.

When Coren was convinced he had lost any pursuers, he headed back to where Hana had gone, the hover spluttering and losing power. They caught her up where the road wound through an ancient system of eroded hills. A rough layby appeared on the left.

Ahead of them, Hana swung in and stopped the vehicle. As it sank to the ground a section of the rock face lit up. They pulled up next to it, their engine dying before Coren could power the hover down. "That was close. This old thing has had it."

Kat kicked open what remained of the door with a shriek of metal. Flickering light outlined two figures ahead as if they were part of an antique film projection.

"Hold it!" ordered a voice Kat recognised as Kreltes, the scientist from Ysterplaat's control centre. "Who do you have with you?"

Glad Kreltes was acting as pre-arranged in case they had been taken hostage, Kat called out the 'we're fine' password and roused the doctor with slaps to her face. When Guirden moaned awake, Kat lifted her foot from the captive's back. "Get up, and don't try anything."

The woman pulled herself from the vehicle and eased herself into a standing position, rubbing her head. "What did you do to me?"

Coren twisted one of her arms behind her back. She screeched in pain.

"You were caught in an explosion," said Kat, not caring if Coren hurt the doctor. "Fortunately, one which destroyed the DNA storage and most of your lab. You're lucky to be alive. Now be quiet."

She looked over to see Hana holding Bakker loosely by an arm next to her vehicle. Kreltes and Velhker strode towards Kat, masks covering their faces, lasers at the ready.

"We're lucky to be here," she said, tilting her head towards Dr Guirden. "She was set to put us both in cages until Coren's devices blew up."

Velhker waved his laser at the doctor but spoke to Coren. "Have you been followed?"

Coren shook his head. "There were two or more hovers after us, but I lost them in the veldt."

"Good. Who is this?"

Kat pointed to the doctor. "She's in charge of genetics in the game park and reproduces native species for hunting. I expect you know from the comms link about Bakker, with Hana. He's one of their financiers, but he helped me escape. He claims he doesn't approve of their methods, but we've no proof. He could be lying."

"I agree. He didn't give anything away to Hana," said Velhker. "I'll incapacitate them both until we're back to base."

She stepped away from the doctor as Velhker grabbed Guirden's arms.

"Hey!" yelled Bakker as he was trussed by Kreltes. "Don't I deserve some leeway for getting you out of the park?" He froze and crumpled to the ground as Velhker's stun beam turned his limbs rubbery. Guirden fell in a similar heap before both were moved into the lit area by Velhker and Kreltes.

As she followed the two men, Kat realised the back of a heavy-duty vehicle had been hidden by a concealment projection to blend in with the surrounding rocks. She'd never seen anything like it, even better than her natural camouflage ability. Coren had joined Hana and embraced her. Hana returned the hug, whispering something not even Kat could hear.

Kreltes opened the hatch of the large, imposing vehicle that looked able to sustain a barrage of artillery, its whole body covered in scales like an Earth armadillo, with no obvious means of locomotion. "Let's go. The hovers will be picked up soon. This r-drive 42 utilizes the old rail network and will get us to Ysterplaat in short order. I'll keep the captives restrained in the back."

Kat climbed into the vehicle, briefly meeting the doctor's glazed eyes above her gagged mouth and muffled ears. She purred in satisfaction as she settled. The r-drive whined and they shot off at an impressive speed. The vehicle quickly linked onto the old metal rail that showed as a long line disappearing into the dusky dawn.

Kat closed her eyes and attempted to catch up on some sleep, but myriad questions roiled in her mind. She was no nearer to satisfying her need for revenge against Tar's murderer. Instead, she had discovered an organisation bigger than she'd feared, with vast resources and contacts all over the galaxy. *With someone as powerful as Lord Baden-Hauf involved, how deep in the Galactic Council did the rot go?*

She wasn't scared of dying, only of failing to stop the hunters, and now she was embroiled in Ardan's organisation. *If The Agency was so powerful, why did they need her and her friends?* She had no intention of handing her and Tar's DNA over to them. She still didn't know if retrieving it was of value, only that she couldn't risk leaving it behind. She had to keep it safe until she returned home. Maybe she could bury it as a memorial to Tar.

Did Mystic Nivlac know more about the hunter organisation than he'd let on? Had he known about the dineeth DNA they had? Maybe he was part of Ardan's network. The more questions she raised, the more she knew she had to stay with this to the end, glad at least she had Coren and Hana by her side.

Aslight bump alerted Kat when they left the rail and headed down a primitive metalled road that led into the white solar-panelled buildings of Ysterplaat, already converting the harsh sun into power.

Coren placed a hand on Kat's leg and smiled. "Had a good cat nap?"

Kat squinted and gently pushed Coren's hand away. "Not really. Too much going through my head, and my side still hurts. It's been a harrowing few days. I could sleep for a week."

Kreltes had applied a field dressing before they left, but the anaesthetic had worn off a while ago. The r-drive dived into a tunnel that disappeared under a low hill on the outskirts of the city. Kat peered out of the side window. "It looks like we're here."

"Not long now," said Velhker from the front seat. "Trushaw should be waiting for us. She'll be very keen to interview IHO's personnel. You've done a good job."

Velhker held her eye for a moment before turning back as Kreltes drove into a brightly lit space which Kat recognised from the last time they had been there. The Director's diminutive figure waited by a long grey wall leading to the offices. She smiled grimly as the vehicle drew up.

They trooped down the tunnel, Bakker and Dr Guirden held firmly by Velhker and Kreltes.

Bakker tried to pull his arm free. "Hey, you," he addressed Trushaw. "You're in charge, aren't you? Well, I'm on your side!" he added as they were led into the large, grey-painted room with guards around the walls. "I released the frenine!"

Dr Guirden looked hard at him but didn't say a word.

"Sit," ordered Trushaw, gesturing at the seats set around a table. "We'll get you some food, then we'll talk."

Velhker punched orders into the food dispenser, handed around the rehydrated rations, then left without a word.

Kat observed the captives. While Bakker eyed Trushaw, nervously rubbing at an arm, Dr Guirden stared around with hard eyes. It all looked as it should be: a grey-suited guard on the door, Trushaw and Kreltes watching the IHO personnel, her friends eating. Yet her instinct told her something wasn't right. The hairs on the nape of Kat's neck bristled. Things seemed too easy: Bakker on their side, the DNA base destroyed, and Ardan's people able to question Dr Guirden. Between her and Bakker, The Agency should get enough information to shut down HuX's operation.

So why wasn't she satisfied? She caught Hana's eye. Surreptitiously, the woman jerked her head towards the door. Kat stood up. "I need to get clean," she said. "Coming, Hana?"

Coren ignored them, still chewing.

Trushaw looked up. "We'll wait to debrief when you're back."

Bakker's eyes tracked them to the door.

Hana took a breath to speak but remained silent as Kat's hand touched her forearm. They entered the female facilities and Hana leant across to Kat's ear. "I've got a bad feeling about this, and it's to do with Bakker."

"I agree," said Kat. "I think we need to keep a close eye on him, even though he acts like a friend. The opportunity to bring him here was too good to pass up, but I better make sure Trushaw takes more precautions with those two. Then we'll have to wait and—"

Whoomph!
A loud rumble shook the floor, knocking them down.
"Holy Hell!" yelled Hana. "What was that?"
Kat scrabbled to her feet and dashed back to the meeting room.

Chapter 21

Kat burst through a cloud of putrid black smoke into the rubble of the room, Hana close behind her. No sign of anyone remained among the barely recognisable heaps of table, chairs and vid equipment. Sirens wailed. Kat gasped in horror and clawed at her ears. "Oh shit! I knew it. I knew it."

"Where's Coren? Coren?" Hana shouted, throwing rubble aside. After tearing aside a large sheet of board, she screeched.

Kat screwed up her eyes trying to make sense of what she saw. A figure, dressed in green, sat in the only chair still upright in the destruction.

Trushaw. Headless.

Kat listened, dimly aware of Hana's urgency. A sound penetrated her consciousness. A rumble from outside gradually overcame the buzzing in her ears. She remembered the space apron outside the complex and recognised the sound of a spaceship taking off. She took a step towards the door before shaking her head and turning to help Hana search for survivors.

A rush of grey-suited figures poured into the room, overwhelming Kat and Hana, pushing them onto the smouldering floor despite their protests.

"No! No!" yelled Velhker, emerging from behind the shattered food dispenser in the corner of the room. "Not them! The others. They've gotten away. Some of you go after them! The rest, stay here and help."

Kat scrambled to her feet, hearing someone retch. It wasn't Hana, tearing at rubble with her bare hands, choking dust and fumes clouding the air. Kat clambered to the other side of the room to look for survivors.

Kneeling beside the chair, Velhker wiped his mouth with his hands, his head turned away from the Director's remains. "They killed her. That's what they were here for. The murdering bastards."

Kat couldn't let him grieve now. "Help us, Velhker. Coren's here somewhere. Kreltes, too."

Velhker stood and wiped his hands on his jacket before heaving at the scattered sheets of wall panelling.

"Here!" Hana scrabbled at tangled wires and rubble.

Kat rushed over and helped, revealing a leg in green trousers. "It's not Coren, Hana. He was nearer the door, wasn't he?" She beckoned to Velhker. "This must be Kreltes."

Velhker's round face drooped and he rubbed at his eyes. "Damn them. They targeted us, murdered Trushaw."

Kat joined Hana to push through the rubble. She heard a groan. "Here!" They pulled a large sheet of panelling up. Something under Kat's hand moved as she tugged.

A muffled voice swore. "You've got claws, Kat."

"Coren?" Hana reached under a tangle of broken ceiling tiles and pulled. Coren's head popped out.

"I'm not broken," said Coren, his eyes dazed.

Hana hugged him to her chest and heaved. Kat smiled and rubbed a clawed hand in his hair.

"Get him out," ordered Velhker. "The place still isn't safe and we need to see if there are other survivors."

The crash of falling panels and tumble of debris as rescuers and medical workers pushed frantically through the rubble rattled Kat's nerves.

Coren and Hana sat huddled together in the corridor, dusty and forlorn, small medi-pads adhered to Coren's superficial wounds. He'd been told by a stressed, white-coated med tech to wait there for further treatment.

Kat hovered nearby, anxious to help though mindful she might be more of a hindrance. She turned away as two sheeted bodies were carried past.

Hana joined her. "I had no idea, Kat," she murmured. "If you hadn't looked at me when you did, I could've been in there. It could've been me sitting there with Trushaw without a—" she gulped as tears tracked down her dusty face.

"I know." Kat placed an arm around Hana's shoulders, "We saved each other. I felt something, had a hunch, and you confirmed it. If only we could've got the others out too."

People hurried past, some carrying equipment and others moving rubble. Feeling guilty and useless, Kat slid down the wall next to Coren with Hana on his other side, to wait for the rush to die down. She had seen death before, plenty of it, but not *people. How many more would die before HuX were brought to account?* She didn't even notice when Coren was taken off to have his injuries properly examined. One moment he was there, the next time Kat looked, he was gone. Hana remained nearby.

A white-coated woman with green trousers looked down at them, her face grim. "We have time for you now, if you would like to come this way?"

They rose and followed her along a corridor, eventually entering a room containing a number of benches overlain with the slight smell of antiseptic. Several women dressed in light green waited for them.

"You need checking over before we do anything else," said Velhker.

"You too," said Kat.

"Haven't time. Short-staffed." Velhker barked a laugh, then sat shakily on a bench.

"Sorry sir, but she's right," said an older woman with a pleasant, lined face. "I'll have someone look to your needs." She signalled for Kat and Hana to follow her. "You'll need a thorough examination. We don't know if there are noxious chemicals in the air. "The woman led them through an inner door to a similar room containing several benches and seats plus a shower in one corner. "I'm Viese, head med tech. You'll need to shower before I check you over. I understand you weren't in the actual explosion?"

"No, we were out of the room," said Kat. "The others weren't so lucky."

"No," Viese agreed. "Those murderers knew who to target, I'm afraid. Anyway, please remove your clothing and wash. There's no telling what pathogens might have been in the explosives. After we check you over, you'll have new clothes."

"I'll be happy to get rid of these and be clean," said Kat as she pulled off her overalls. "I'm ripe, even for a frenine."

"You go first," said Hana. "I agree, you need it."

Kat waited until Viese was out of the room and passed her waist pouch to Hana. "Can you hang on to this for me? I don't want anyone else to have what's inside, not even for an instant."

When Hana agreed, Kat grimaced at herself in a mirror and walked under the shower. The feel of warm water running through her fur was bliss as she soaped off the grime of the past few days, taking care not to touch the laser burn on her side. She still wasn't sure what to do with her and Tar's DNA. Burying it seemed so final. At least the refreshing wash improved her spirits. She would have stayed in longer had Hana not banged on the screen. She opened the door.

"My turn." A naked, brown Hana stepped past into the shower, handing Kat her waist pouch, before Kat even had a chance to turn off the water. The frenine apologised for taking so long and looked for a towel.

Viese returned at that moment and held one out. "You look good for your time in captivity, although that patch on your side suggests you didn't enjoy it."

After she had dried, Viese ran a scanner over Kat's body. "I'll redress that wound in a moment. Laser burn, wasn't it?"

"Yes." Velhker or Kreltes must have messaged ahead of their arrival. "I've had some problems, but I feel alright, just very tired."

"Apart from the burn and the surgery, you've several other cuts and bruises. You also have nutrient deficiencies, but nothing a few days' rest with good food won't put right."

"If we have time," said Kat. "Can I dress now?"

"Over there," said Viese, indicating a pile of clothing in a corner. "I'll check your companion now."

Kat found black trousers, a jacket, and a dark, short-sleeved shirt. She was comfortably dressed with the DNA package safely clipped onto her belt by the time Hana had been checked out and found her new clothing. Everything fitted them well, even to the point of Kat's trousers having been adapted for her tail.

"You've both passed as healthy enough, so I'll take you to the meal room where you'll get something better than food dispenser product," said Viese. "Come with me."

The aroma of frying food brought a rush of saliva to Kat's mouth and her stomach grumbled in response.

Hana waved at Coren as she and Kat entered the meal room. "He's beaten us to it. Typical man, more concerned with food than hygiene."

"This's good," mumbled Coren, taking a mouthful of fried meat from the plate in front of him. "Try some."

Hana sat next to him.

Kat sat on the other side of the table and focussed on the large plate placed in front of her. The meat was almost raw though hot, with Crofta spices, eggs, and a few vegetables all cooked to her taste. Even so, it was all she could do to chew and swallow. Her stomach churned with the after-effects of her release and the ensuing drama.

Images of Tar's body being blown to smithereens flashed through her mind. Her legs trembled and her heart raced. Her face felt clammy and nausea rose in her throat. She had her ovaries and Tar's DNA, all the other DNA samples had been destroyed, and hopefully all those caged in the orientation pens had escaped, but it didn't seem enough. *How could anyone treat sapient species like that?* She shivered and tried another mouthful, knowing she needed the sustenance.

"You reckon that was planned, Kat?" asked Coren.

Coren's question dragged her back to the present. "Planned?"

She chewed and considered the situation. "Whether the killings here were, I'm not sure. Do you think they waited until we were out of the room before attacking? Maybe Guirden didn't want me killed, but Bakker? He played me and I fell for it. It must have been his intention all along to let us lead him here, to The Agency's base."

She was swamped by guilt at what had happened due to her naivety. Trushaw. That nice, clever woman. Her staff. She shook her head and put down her cutlery. She couldn't eat any more.

"Kat, we all fell for it, even Velhker," said Hana. "He listened in when I was questioning Bakker. He was happy enough to get him back here. No one is to blame, only the perpetrators."

"I saw him do it," said Coren, taking a gulp of hot coffee. "He flicked something from his hand, something flat, straight at Trushaw. Then the blast, and I knew nothing else. He fooled us all."

"Which hand did he use?" asked Kat.

"His left, I think." Coren scratched his head. "Yes, his left. Why?"

"Remember, Hana? He was always playing with his left arm. That's what triggered my instincts. He must've had the device there, even though he was searched by Velhker. Some part of his arm must be false and the device was hidden inside."

Hana groaned. "I should have known something wasn't right when he deflected all my questions while I was waiting for you. And you're right, he did keep fiddling with that arm. Bastard. I'd like to blow *him* up."

Kat glanced over to the table where Velhker sat with Viese. "We'll need to share what we suspect."

Velhker saw her looking and motioned them over. "Bring your food and we'll go over things."

"I don't blame any of you," began Velhker, eyes scanning across Kat, Hana and Coren. "We were all taken in, though how Bakker knew to go for Trushaw, I don't know. Maybe they've infiltrated The Agency's network, like we have with HuX's. That's to find out another day. Meanwhile, Director Trushaw is a great loss, the linchpin of our operation. I know most of it, and of course there're records too, but this is a significant setback. She was a good woman, and a great leader."

Kat looked down the table to where Viese sat with three grey-uniformed people and raised her eyebrows at Velhker.

"You've met Viese, whose duties double as head med tech and supervisor, then there's Braun, essentially my equivalent but hastily rushed into operations."

The podgy, square-faced man smiled tightly.

"And Rasult, to take the place of my friend, Kreltes." The large man, whose eyes remained on Velhker, inclined his head.

"I must say again that Trushaw's murder is a great blow to our mission to destroy HuX, not to mention the other projects she had under her control which I can't talk about." Velhker pushed his half-empty plate away from him. "But we can't stand still. The spaceship stolen by Bakker appears to be heading to a rendezvous with a ship in Earth orbit and it's suspected they'll be on their way to Crofta."

"Crofta!" exclaimed Kat. "Why? I thought HuX was based here or on K-Astar3. You don't think they're going after the frenine prides, do you?"

"I think the asteroid is an important meeting place, for obvious reasons, but there's a good chance you're right. We've had our suspicions about Crofta for some time," continued Velhker. "That's one of the reasons Ardan is located there. Also, why we've kept a low profile trying to track the comings and goings of people of interest."

"And why you involved people like us," said Coren through a mouthful of bread.

Velhker nodded.

"Why did Bakker go through the process of rescuing Kat and then killing Trushaw?" asked Coren. "Surely there were better ways of targeting your organisation, getting you lot off their backs?"

Kat agreed. "Bakker can't have known my friends would be waiting for me. I might have had him drop me off anywhere."

Velhker shook his head. "I'm sure he'd have made certain he didn't leave you without a tracking device or some other way to stay in touch. That's partly why we checked all your clothes."

Kat hadn't thought of that. "Did you find anything?"

"No, but that doesn't mean there wasn't anything. Who knows what technology they have access to? That's why we destroyed it all."

Rasult spoke for the first time, his voice as deep as his size. "I'm newly come to this side of things but have been giving the whole attack some thought. I believe if we look at it from the criminals' perspective, we can see what they've gained. One, they now know where we are based on Earth and to some extent the size of our operation, although killing our leader may indicate they had more intelligence than we suspected. Of course, that could have been luck, though they would've seen that she was obviously the one in charge.

"Two, the field team we had against them. They now know all of you." He shrugged towards Coren.

"Thirdly, they can extrapolate our suspicions. They know you three are from Crofta and that the frenine Baden-Hauf killed was Kat's mate, with ancient ancestry which they'd prize. So I agree, that could be a prime reason why they might be headed there."

He grimaced. "They know we're getting closer, which is why they risked freeing Kat, hoping she'd lead them here."

Kat cringed. "So it is all my fault. If I hadn't agreed to Bakker's plan, Trushaw would still be alive. If only—"

"You mustn't think like that," interrupted Velhker. "We brought them here, not you. By targeting our head, they may anticipate gaining time to do whatever they need to on Crofta, and possibly close up operations on K-Astar3. If so, they'll disappear again and we'll be back where we started."

"What about their game parks here?" asked Hana. "That'll have to be a big loss."

"No," laughed Rasult harshly, "the operations of this and other game parks are, in the main, completely legitimate. The legalities are watertight and there'd be little to gain in attempting to dismantle them. And they do preserve endangered species. Now you've destroyed the DNA storage, there's no evidence they were doing anything outside galactic agreements."

"When we destroyed the compound and labs, we helped a lot of caged animals escape," said Kat, her voice quivering. "They should have spread into the park. They'll be evidence of what she's been doing."

"Right. But our primary concern now is to get at the criminal element of the organisation, thus target people like Bakker and Guirden," stated Velhker.

"No time to rest then," said Kat, ruefully rubbing her side.

"Your ship is ready to de-planet when you are," said Braun. "We'll make sure our operatives in the region are fully briefed for your arrival."

"That's settled then," said Kat, "we're going hunting again."

Chapter 22

"Ferking hell, the one thing I hate!" yelped Coren as the *ScarthepD2* rose from the horizontal to the vertical with a shudder. As much as he loved space travel, the disorientation that came with being thrust onto his back never failed to disturb him. If he ever became an engineer, he'd invent something that took the shock out of space jumps.

"Relax," said Kat, as she looked over at him and Hana on the flight deck. "Are you both ready?"

"Sure, let's go," Hana said, looking relaxed. "Shall I inform Control, Kat?"

As Kat acknowledged Hana, Coren smoothly manipulated the controls, slipping into the mindset for take-off. Excitement gripped him, better than any vid game. He screwed up his eyes and drew in the last whiffs of the African air, vowing to return to Earth sometime when this mission was over.

The force of the engines thrusting him deep into his seat drove away the memories of Dr Guirden's lab and the horrific deaths of Trushaw and Kreltes. Ysterplaat and the African continent were soon far below, merely coloured specks on a globe, as they orientated next to the Earth's meteor-pocked moon to prepare for their first jump. He glanced at the rich greens and blues of Earth filling the screens on his left before Hana's voice broke into his reverie.

"Co-ordinates entered, Coren. We can initiate jump sequence."

Coren tore his eyes away from the mesmerising planet and concentrated on the controls. "Jumping in 3, 2, 1—"

The vision through the flight deck ports blurred. He looked away, having no wish to put more pressure on his stomach from rapid space transit. The only sound caused by jumping was the creaking of their craft. Even the best ships still suffered under the incredible pressures of the action and the *ScarthepD2* was well built. He looked over to his companions. Kat had already shut her eyes and curled up her legs, a posture he recognised meant she was deep in thought—she wasn't going to be much of a conversationalist for the trip—whereas Hana was alert, watching the instruments.

Coren's stomach churned. "Do we have anything decent in the galley? All this spacing makes me hungry."

"I wondered when you'd ask. You could go and look. I have to check the co-ordinates for the next jump."

"But I'm the pilot, Hana."

"We're on auto now," replied Hana, not looking at him.

Coren remained where he sat, too tired and comfortable to move. If he stood up, his stomach was likely to complain at the movement. "We've plenty of time for you to do that. You know your way around a kitchen better than me."

Hana turned and stared at him. "About time you learnt then, isn't it? I don't see you asking Kat to get the food."

Coren rose with a grunt and headed to the galley.

He came back with two meat burgers, even though he knew Hana preferred vegetarian, and a lightly cooked portion of meat for Kat. He roused the frenine with a word, rather than risk shaking her arm; he'd been caught out with that before and nearly had his eyes scratched out. They ate in silence before their second jump, the first having taken them from Sol's orbit to Alpha Centauri.

Having finished only half her burger, Hana collected the plates. "I guess I'll have to do the galley run next time if I'm to get what I want."

"I'll do the next galley trip," said Kat.

"You can do the one after that. We'll take turns, like it should be." Hana glared at Coren.

He reddened and wiped crumbs from his face. "She'll probably bring me a salad sandwich," he whispered to Kat.

Kat looked at the two of them. "I don't know why you're sniping at each other, but this spaceship is too small for arguments. How about whoever goes to the galley asks what everyone else wants first?"

Coren coughed and looked away.

Hana grimaced. "Sorry, Kat. I guess we're still stressed out. We're being petty when there are much bigger issues at stake."

Kat placed a hand on each of their shoulders. "We've been in the wars, had to fight, and support each other. We've been tracking and competing with top level criminal minds. We've been attacked, shot at, and blown up. But we've survived, despite our relative youth and limited experience. I think we can be proud of ourselves."

Hana tilted her head. "And it's not over yet, though we're happy to be here with you. Despite having rich and well-connected relatives, they thought the best thing for me was to be brought up in an orphanage. This is certainly better than that or living in the slums of Sensuna. It's incredible to have access to so much technology— I'm learning so much."

Coren gave a wry smile. "I doubt you can understand, Kat, being brought up in luxury by a supportive pride."

Kat clicked her claws in and out. "Like Hana, I'm an only child, and I am, or rather was, part of a pride that cares for everyone in it." She swallowed at the thought of her exile, but that was a problem for the future. "Tar was an orphan, so the females in my pride adopted him. We grew up together, but he wasn't like a brother; we always knew we had a responsibility to continue the frenine species. That's why he and I—" She choked back her cracked voice.

Coren patted her shoulder. "It's alright, Kat. We understand."

Hana looked over at her console. "We're about to initiate the next jump. Places everyone."

Crash! Bang!

Instead of the normal quiet that followed a jump, the spacecraft reverberated and shuddered.

Kat grabbed the edge of her seat, despite being strapped in. "What's happening?"

"The force-field's on, Hana, isn't it?" screeched Coren.

"Yes, but something's got through!"

"I know that. Check!"

"The system's functioning normally," Hana's voice rushed. "It can't be the ship."

"No," Kat said, focusing on the port's vid screen enhancer, "it's a rock, a large one too. And look out, another's about to hit!"

"Prepare to jump, Coren!" ordered Hana. "It's not safe here! Where are they coming from?"

Crash! Bang!

"Ferking hell!" Coren yelled. "The co-ordinates for the next jump, are they in the navigation pod?"

"Yes Coren, we can go!" Hana added.

"I've found what's causing it," shouted Kat, looking at the enlarged external view on the vid screen. "A stealth fighter, hidden in the asteroid belt. Not one of ours. They really must want to stop us."

"How—" began Hana.

"Done!" shouted Coren, jamming down on the navigation pod's jump button as another crash shook the spaceship.

The quiet during the jump was calming.

"How did that happen?" continued Kat. "We're shielded, plus we shouldn't be able to be tracked, especially when emerging from hyperspace. What don't we know?"

"The enemy would have the specs of this ship and they'd have a fair idea where we'd emerge from a jump," said Coren. "They must have planned for the asteroids to destroy us and shifted them here. A laser wouldn't get through our force shield."

"If they did it once, will they do it again?" asked Hana, gazing through the narrow port into the pitch black of hyperspace.

"Yes," replied Kat, "we have to assume they will. How can we prepare for them? What can we do to stop them?"

Coren smiled. "Be sneakier. If we reverse our jump, do we end up in the same locale? I mean, is there much chance it'd vary?"

Hana considered the question for a moment. "No. From what I've read, it'd be much the same, unless you deliberately try to avoid the same space. Jump technology is designed to move a certain mass a certain distance. It involves some complicated mathematics, but if the specs of a ship are known, then I guess the jump distance is known."

"So," continued Coren, his forehead wrinkled in thought. "If we're met by the same ship when we emerge from this jump, we know they have our details. If we immediately reverse our direction, go back to the starting point, we can assume they'll work out what we've done and do the same."

"Yes, Coren," said Hana, "the point being…?"

"Well, we know where they were, don't we?"

"Yes, it's recorded in the navigation pod. It's not the same ship as Bakker and Guirden left in, though."

"Even so, they're definitely the enemy. As we know where they're going to emerge from their jump—"

"Yes!" exclaimed Kat. "We arrange a similar surprise for them, a pile of those rocks they were lobbing at us. Two things in the same space, at the same time, and kaboom!"

"It might work, if we're quick," said Hana. "We'll have to have the co-ordinates ready to activate on emergence and rely on their confusion to give us time to return to our previous position, just clear of the rocks they hit us with, and move enough asteroids into place with our ship's tractor beam. Probably the best chance we've got to get rid of them. What do you think?"

"Let's do it," confirmed Kat.

Hana jumped to punch in the co-ordinates. "You need to hit the button once we've rebooted from the jump, Coren, and we can go again, in reverse."

"Right," called Coren. "Emergence in 10 seconds."

The countdown seemed interminable, each of them scanning the narrow port in front of their seats, seeking a view of their attacker. The pitch black dissolved into streaks of light that rapidly resolved into the stars of the galaxy around them.

Kat peered into the void. "Anyone see anything?"

"There!" pointed Coren, "Just emerged. And, dammit, rocks already on their way."

"Hold it! Hold it. A few seconds more," warned Hana. "Now!"

Coren slammed a hand on the jump button. The rapidly looming rocks disappeared as the blackness of the jump overtook them. "Shit, this isn't much good for my insides," he complained.

"Alright," said Hana, her fingers flashing over the screen in front of her. "The tractor controls are simple enough, Kat. I'm adjusting them so that when we return to normal space we can latch onto several asteroids near where the enemy was. If you're quick enough, they won't know what hit them."

Kat concentrated on the tractor beam controls, trying to not think of what might go wrong. No matter what, she didn't want to end up as debris floating in space forever.

Coren's voice broke the tension. "Emergence in 10 seconds."

This time they were ready. The tractor beam's pale glow lanced out the moment they arrived in normal space, latching onto a small cluster of asteroids and beginning the arduous process of moving them to the precise co-ordinates.

"It's too slow," shouted Coren, "we'll never have them in position before that spacecraft is back."

"Quiet, Coren, let me concentrate," ordered Kat. "Hana, how's it going?"

"They're moving. It's a lot of mass to overcome, but they're moving. No sign of the enemy yet," said Hana, watching the navigation screen.

"Nearly there," said Kat, "nearly there."

"Still no sign," said Hana. "We're rebooted ready for the next jump."

"In place," added Kat. "Be ready to jump when, and if, the enemy arrives. The energy outburst will be formidable if we've got this right."

"Nothing," murmured Coren. "Looks like they didn't fall for it."

"No, wait, something's happening," yelped Hana. "I think something's emerging nearby!"

A dazzling light blasted their area of space.

"Go, Coren!" yelled Kat.

Coren slammed his hand on the jump button as the glare lit up the darkness of the cabin. It snapped off as the blackness of the jump took over.

Kat remained tense as they emerged from the jump, waiting long moments before releasing a sigh. Nothing followed them this time. They all glanced at each other.

"It worked, didn't it?" whispered Coren.

They waited, tense, a few more moments. Still nothing followed them. They settled into the last leg of the journey, a tiny speck in the vastness of space.

The twinkling lights of K-Astar3 contrasted against the myriad of stars that surrounded them as they slowly approached the terraformed asteroid. After the final jump, the trip had been uneventful, Coren enjoying the experience of piloting such a sophisticated spaceship.

A number of secure sub-ether messages had been waiting for them when they had emerged from their last jump, giving them the most up-to-date intelligence on the whereabouts of their quarry. They also now knew that Ardan would be waiting for them at the asteroid. They landed at The Hub in accordance with his instructions instead of at their departure port of Primal Field; he had assured them there would be no trouble.

"No one to meet us this time?" noted Kat, as she observed the absence of hoverbots on the quiet landing apron.

"Probably just as well," said Hana. "Last time things got a bit hot."

"You can say that again," added Coren.

They entered the checkpoint and quickly passed through security into the central hub with the white walls curving in front of them.

"Back again," murmured Kat, scanning the scattering of people for anyone she recognised.

"Ardan seems to have smoothed our way again," whispered Hana. "I wonder where that rough-looking lot from last time is?"

Kat scanned the room. "I don't recognise anyone or see any more threats. What did Ardan say for us to do now, Hana?"

"Book into the Star View and wait."

"For how long?" asked Coren. "We've had bad experiences with that place."

"I'm not sure," Hana replied, "but I can't imagine it'll be long."

"I hope not, after what we've been through," growled Kat. "I'm keen to get back to Crofta as soon as possible."

"I'll get a flitter," said Coren, as they reached the slot marked with a shooting star logo. The small remote dropped into his hand and they left the building.

They climbed into the vehicle and headed for the Star View. After easing into the garage space alongside the long, squat building, Hana checked the entry screen. "It seems we've been allocated separate rooms this time. One for you, Kat, and one for me and Coren."

"Organised by Ardan, I hope? We don't want a repeat of what happened with the space rocks," commented Coren.

"I'll double check," answered Kat. She held a small device to the display. "Definitely him. That's his signature code. We can go in."

Coren grunted and led the way along a narrow corridor.

He touched the wall below a glowing number and waited as the door hissed open. Kat carried on to her own room, the door closing behind her with a solid thunk.

Chapter 23

Kat looked around the room designed for one, exhibiting the same wear as the larger room they had been in. The grey walls had splashes of orange trying valiantly to lift the tiredness of the room, while the only bed was wedged between two small side tables. The bathroom was poorly hidden by a light screen against one wall. As Kat eased her pack to the floor, she noticed an incongruous white scroll sitting on one of the tables.

She walked over and gingerly picked it up with the corner of her shirt, every hair on end with suspicion. "Who uses paper these days?"

As if in answer to her question, the paper unfurled in her fingertips, opening up to a clean white sheet. She flipped it over, inspecting it closely, but could find nothing to indicate who it came from or what it meant. She put it back on the table and went into the bathroom, turning on the mister to have a much-needed clean while pondering the strangeness of the paper.

As Kat re-entered the room, the background odours of the room had another level. She sucked in a lungful of air through her nose, seeking to analyse its constituent parts. The source came from the paper. Recognition struck her. It was aimed specifically at her.

"Clever," she murmured with a smile. She had detected two out-of-place scents—the first she remembered with distaste, the sewage outflow in the slums of the waystation; the second a strong smell of humus. She knew what that meant.

She padded down the hall to Coren and Hana's room and scratched on their door. "Coren?" She waited, then scratched more urgently.

Coren's tousled head peered through the door. "Kat. Can't we get some sleep?"

"Yes, but I need the flitter." She held out a hand.

"What for?" he asked as he passed over the remote.

"I need to go out. Sorry I disturbed you. Don't worry, I'll see you soon." She turned on her heel before he could ask more questions.

Kat climbed into the vehicle and drove quietly out towards the slums of the waystation. She buzzed with curiosity as she followed a slow path deeper into the ramshackle region of the asteroid, her senses alert for anything untoward, but all seemed peaceful. Her intuition told her it was safe, but she had a laser on her hip, courtesy of The Agency, more as a precaution than real need, and kept a close eye out for any possible wrong turning. Surprisingly, the closer she went to the sewage outfall the easier it was to navigate. It seemed the waystation did maintain this region, despite its location.

The smell grew stronger, almost thick in the air. She stopped and stepped out of the flitter. Creeping forward, she kept to the side of the ruined buildings, ears and eyes open, hand on her laser. With her nostrils closed in order not to be distracted, breathing through her mouth, she entered a wide area encompassed by eroded sides of the slums. Pipes snaked from the waystation into large rectangular holes. The odour was so overpowering, even with her nostrils shut, she wondered why such a meeting place would be chosen.

"Where are you?" she mouthed as her eyes watered and nose ran.

As if on cue, a familiar figure beckoned from an opposite corner of the clearing, then disappeared.

Kat dashed over as Mystic Nivlac slipped into a small opening in a building halfway up a narrow alley. She waited for her eyes to adjust to the almost complete darkness then followed, calling a greeting into the gloom. "Why here? Why now?"

"I had to be sure that only you would come," he whispered. "I want to aid the next stage of your quest."

Kat walked towards his voice, discovering they were in a box-like room with a low ceiling and no other exits. She breathed in the pleasant smells of humus as she sank to the floor. "You have the oddest ways of getting in contact, and the weirdest meeting places."

His eyes lit beneath the hood of his hat. "I'll endeavour to answer the many questions filling your head, but first let me congratulate you on surviving what must have been a truly harrowing time."

He leant forward and pushed at a small pot on a flameless fire. "Tea?"

Kat accepted and let her senses absorb her surrounds while the dineeth busied himself preparing two small cups, letting the silence drag out between them. The space around them had the same look and feel of the mystic's home on Crofta. She hesitated. Was he going to drug her again?

He must have read her thoughts and chuckled. "It's only peppermint, my favourite. Refreshing, and will help to counteract the outside odours."

She sipped with pleasure, the hot liquid reviving her flagging spirits and filling her with longing for everything to slow down, her quest to be over, and life to return to normal. Except it wouldn't be normal, not without Tar, and the pride having ostracised her. She gulped her next mouthful to prevent any tears, choking on a burning throat.

"I had forgotten how impatient you are," Mystic Nivlac said through a waft of steam from his cup. "Let me tell you what I know, and why we are meeting like this."

He stroked his muzzle with a furred hand. "The prime objective of your mission is accomplished, though you probably believe you haven't achieved as much as you've lost."

She leant forward, eyebrows raised, and clicked open her claws. "That second part is right! Tar's murderer, Lord Baden-Hauf, is still alive and nowhere to be found. My sponsor's organisation has been infiltrated. Two of their key players are dead. And I've discovered more about what's going on than I could ever have feared in my worst nightmare. These people have a lot to answer for! How can you possibly think my objective has been met? Whose side are you on?"

"Wait. Hear me out. I accept all that you say. Believe me, I am on your side, and that of all sapient genoids. Your achievements on Earth were remarkable, despite the loss of a truly great champion for our cause."

Kat took a deep breath. "You know about Trushaw? Are you part of The Agency?"

The dineeth shook his furry head. "Not exactly, though Ardan and I have worked together in the past. I assumed he'd told you of my involvement in this project. The very fact I'm here indicates that."

Kat's tail flicked in frustration. *Why did the mystic have to keep so many secrets?* She wasn't surprised, but anger at not being trusted simmered in her gut. "Tell me something good that's come out of what I went through."

Nivlac sipped his tea before placing the cup on the floor. "The positives include the increasing competency of your group, the fear you've sent through HuX, and the information we can get from Bakker and Dr Guirden."

"But Bakker and Guirden have escaped. And Guirden was the one harvesting DNA and manipulating clones for hunting! Then Bakker murdered Trushaw and Kreltes, not to mention wrecking their Ysterplaat headquarters. Are you sure it was worth it?"

"Really?" the mystic jerked back. "I thought they'd helped you to escape, not that they were the murderers."

Kat's tail lashed the air. "It was all a trick to get me to lead them to The Agency's base. They bolted the moment they'd exploded their device. We've no idea where they are now. I thought that was what you wanted to tell me. I've been travelling the galaxy and am nowhere nearer to my revenge for Tar's murder. Baden-Hauf taunted me at Mokala, only to disappear again. I was so close!"

Nivlac looked genuinely hurt and drew back, as if worried she might lash out. "This is terrible news." He topped up their cups with a shaking hand. "No, I wanted to share with you what I had learnt about Baden-Hauf. But that will have to wait. Update me on what you found in the game park laboratory. Was there biological material?"

"I assumed you knew that too. I found Tar's body, and a cloned version of him roaming in the park. Both shocked me, hard. And his DNA was there, in storage. They took mine, too."

She didn't mention the removal of her ovaries. Some things were too personal. "They had racks and racks of samples from species all over the galaxy, many I didn't recognise."

He leant forward again. "And dineeth samples?"

"Yes."

"And you destroyed them all?" Mystic Nivlac tensed on the edge of his seat.

"Yes!"

He relaxed and sat back. "That was the most important job of all. Well done, Kat. Destroying the DNA samples so no one can use them for nefarious purposes was a primary part of your mission."

"Not for me it wasn't! But I'm glad I did it. It had to be done. You don't know the worst of what was going on there. The experiments! That doctor was playing with the genetics of a range of species, adding foreign DNA into other animals, making better prey for the hunters. That's got to be stopped!"

Nivlac remained calm, his only reaction a lifting of one shaggy eyebrow.

Kat jumped up, furious at herself for not seeing the obvious before. "You knew! Are you saying that was the purpose of my mission all along, to destroy that DNA and any aberrations that the lab had developed? I'm sick of being everyone's pawn, having to kill against my wishes, endangering my friends, and being treated like a fool."

The mystic looked away, fiddling with the burner and teapot, folding up the pouch of peppermint leaves.

Kat regained her seat with trouble, knowing that if she remained standing, she'd leave without finding out what the mystic had to share. She suppressed a growl deep in her chest and steadied her recalcitrant tail. "Tell me what you know. Don't hold anything back this time."

He leant back. "Harvesting DNA for cloning is an illegal practice, as is regenerating species for the purposes of hunting, let alone their practice of gene manipulation, creating monsters. It was vital that this material be destroyed and the practice stopped."

"I understand all that, but why not tell me that was what you wanted?" Kat couldn't restrain her body any longer. She sprang up and paced the tiny room, thinking back to the time she had lost in the mystic's cave. *What had he done with her mind?* "Did you imprint that on me when I was drugged? How are you any better than them?"

Nivlac waited for her to settle, then resumed as if there had been no difficult pause. "Would you still have gone? All you wanted was revenge for your mate's murder. I had to make the suggestion subliminal. If you were caught, no one could discover your purpose. I told you I would let you know what you owed me for helping you achieve your revenge. That was it. You've met your side of the bargain, now I'll do mine. Let me tell you more." He went on to explain his thoughts on where HuX could be operating on Crofta.

Kat forced herself to quieten as she considered the mystic's words. "You might be right. I'll think on it."

With great effort, she swallowed her grievance at being manipulated. After all, the end result was what she wanted, too. There was no point dwelling on the past. All she desired now was to kill Lord Baden-Hauf.

She held out her cup for a refill, then sipped the cooling brew as she digested what she had learnt.

And she admitted: "You're not just an eccentric old dog who lives in a hole in a cliff, are you?"

Chapter 24

Kat slid the flitter into the garage space, her head spinning with so much information. She scanned the surroundings as she exited the vehicle, looking for anything untoward. The whole galaxy had taken on a different complexion with her new knowledge, though everything seemed to be as she'd left it, nothing indicating danger.

More to the point, and what caused her the most angst, was how much her pride, in particular the elder, Mesat, might know about the mystic's role. *Was that why she'd suggested Kat seek him out? So why had she been exiled when she'd followed his instructions?*

She walked down the corridor and touched her room plate, her mind whirling with a million thoughts like the stars in the arms of a galaxy. Despite lying on her bed and using all her relaxation techniques, sleep eluded her.

When a knock came at her door, she jumped up, glad to have a distraction, but knowing she couldn't yet share the information with her friends, not until she was certain it was correct. She activated the security screen to see Hana standing outside, and triggered the door lock. "Come in."

Hana's eyes regarded her suspiciously under her fringe of black hair. "I heard you went out earlier."

"Yes, I needed to clear my head. Is Coren up?" Kat tidied her bed and donned her clothes.

Hana stood there, not answering, her arms folded under her breasts.

Guilt riddled Kat, but she dare not upset Hana or Coren. "Please, trust me, alright?"

"If you say so, Kat," Hana sighed. "Yes, Coren's up and eating in the room that passes for a diner in this place."

"So, no word from Ardan?"

"No, nothing."

"Come on then, I'm hungry," said Kat, putting an arm across Hana's shoulders.

They walked to the end of the hall and entered an off-white room holding four cube tables and bench seats. A dispenser hatch offered a minimal menu. *Same tired décor*, thought Kat.

"Welcome to Hotel Paradise," said Coren with a wave of a spoon. "After you've selected from the extensive range of food, join me at the packing crate tables."

"Thanks for the offer, Coren." Kat smiled and opted for a meat-egg combination optimistically called Free-range Mix.

"I suppose Hana has told you that there's no word yet," said Coren as Kat and Hana sat with their meals.

She mumbled an acknowledgement through her food. After swallowing, she added, "I think we should go back to The Hub after this and check."

Coren stared at her. "Are you going to tell us where you went?"

Kat pushed the remote over to him. "Just a drive to clear my head."

They finished their meal, the silence among them palpable, then headed outside. When they reached the flitter, a winking light on the console greeted them.

"Looks like we've got something," said Coren, as he touched the *message received* icon.

The words shimmered into a holo:

Welcome.

Be ready to take off.

Meet in room A2, The Hub.

Ardan.

"About time. Let's get out of this dump," Coren added.

Kat agreed and settled in for the short drive to The Hub.

A2 was located through a panel in the wall to one side of the exit sign in The Hub. A frosted door hissed open to reveal a grey-clad figure sitting at an incongruous timber veneer desk, a row of uncomfortable chairs before it. He looked up, brushing a hand across his thinning hair before standing. He forced a smile as he gestured towards the seats. "Come in. It's good to see you safe."

He introduced himself to Coren and Hana as he slid open a hatch. "Let me offer you refreshments. There's quite a range." He moved several trays to the edge of his desk and waited while Coren took a selection of snacks. The women only took drinks.

"You've been through a lot," Ardan continued, "exposing the extent of corruption and pursing major players in this insidious network. Well done, all three of you."

He frowned at them. "Needless to say, I'm devastated to lose Director Trushaw. She was a great leader and a close friend." He paused while he watched their expressions. "But good has come from it as we have exposed HuX and those who head it. Even now my intelligence has confirmed that Crofta is the destination of Bakker and Guirden."

They sat forward, keen to know more.

"If I can ask you all for one more effort in this fight against HuX, we may be able to bring the dreadful practice of hunting sapient species to some closure."

"'Why should we continue to put our lives at risk?" asked Hana. "It's Baden-Hauf that Kat is after. Can't The Agency deal with Bakker and Guirden now?"

Ardan's eyebrows almost met. "As you know, The Agency's prime focus is to prevent the exploitation of sapient species on all worlds, linking in with each planet's animal welfare operations. After what you've seen, don't you want that too?"

"Of course," agreed Hana. "But what can we do that you can't?"

"Our financial resources and assets are significant. However, we need to utilise outside personnel such as you three as we have few permanent staff. You'll be well recompensed."

Coren drummed his fingers on the desk. "Where does your funding come from?"

Ardan leant back and raised his eyebrows. "From many sources. Wealthy patrons, large corporations, some government departments, anyone basically who cares about our purpose. It's not for me to reveal exactly who, but believe me, our resources, not just financial, are extensive."

He smiled at the earnest expressions on Hana's and Coren's faces. "When we arrive on Crofta, I'll have Relina give you access to our databases should you wish to follow up anything. That's how much I trust you."

Kat sat still, silently musing, while Ardan continued to speak to Coren and Hana. She half listened to them planning the trip to Crofta, meeting with Relina and his other operatives and determining their first moves to capture Bakker and Dr Guirden, but once again, nothing was said about her target, Lord Baden-Hauf. However, it seemed her destination lay in accord with what Ardan wanted, so she'd go along with the plans without comment at this stage.

They orbited Crofta, Kat watching the orange-brown planet with a mixture of joy and trepidation, the red moon bringing back painful memories. She wanted to run on the grasslands, feel the wind in her fur, scent the zeena and feast on a fresh kill, but knew she would have no such luxury yet. She still had a job to do. A tear leaked from her eye. She swiped it away.

An arm snaked over her shoulder. "We all want to finish this, Kat."

"Leave it, Coren." She pushed his arm away.

Coren returned his attention to the controls in front of him.

"We've got clearance to Sensuna. Time to strap in," said Hana as she initiated the entry sequence.

"One more," murmured Kat, "then I'm staying put. If I survive."

They landed and passed smoothly through customs, then settled to eat in the spaceport diner, still alert in case they were being observed.

"What next?" asked Kat, already regretting not paying full attention to Ardan's briefing.

"We've got access to the technology in Ardan's offices," answered Hana. "That should help us identify when the murderers arrived."

Although Kat suspected she knew the final destination of the criminals, she didn't know when they would arrive or whether they would have support personnel. She needed to follow the path laid out for them by Ardan.

Coren looked sadly at Kat. "We know this is hard for you, Kat. Don't forget we're on your side." He went on to share the plan with her and ended by saying they had accommodation arranged nearby.

At least she didn't have to confront the pride yet. As much as she wanted to be reunited with them, she'd need a good argument for them to lift her exile. She couldn't think about that until her revenge was satisfied. When they arrived at the hotel, Kat stretched out on her bed. Yet another hotel, in another place, although the furnishings were far superior to the Star View's. That night she tossed and turned, dreaming of bodies ripped apart only to become whole again.

The morning brought her more uncertainty on how to proceed. Without any answers, she refreshed herself as best she could and then met Coren on the ground floor of the hotel.

Coren appeared to be assessing everyone as they exited the grav lift.

"Morning, Kat. You been out yet?" he asked.

"No, not yet. Just checking around. Where's Hana?"

"She went off early, to meet up with Relina at Ardan's office. Keen to get at the technology, I reckon." He smiled. "Eaten?"

"No, I'm not hungry. Let's see what Ardan's got for us."

"The offices are in Founder Square."

"That's right, I've been there before," confirmed Kat, remembering her first encounter with Ardan and the deal they had agreed on, what felt like so long ago.

It didn't take them long to walk to the offices located in one of a number of similar-sized buildings made from brown crete matching the local stone. A number of people strode through the wide entrances even at this early hour. Flitters buzzed through the square like a co-ordinated dance. Kat watched carefully but saw few non-humans. A dineeth, dressed in loose, non-descript clothing, scurried past the offices as they entered. She thought she saw several frenines near a café across the way, but nothing remarkable. *Natives prefer to avoid the city.*

They headed towards two transparent-walled grav lifts situated in the centre of the building and entered one which took them gently upwards in response to Coren's request for Level 7. Kat kept her hand on the laser in her equipment belt, apprehensive to see whether their destination was the same as where she had previously met Ardan. They glided to a halt and were greeted by a stern-looking man dressed in the common grey uniform worn by most inhabitants of the building. He held a small console to their faces before stepping back and asking them to follow.

A corridor carpeted with a spongy green material led to a solid door, a lock in the middle of its surface. The door swung open in response to their guide's hand wave and they entered a room lit by holo screens and ambient lighting. Electronics hummed.

"About time. Relina and I have done a lot while you were sleeping. It makes a change for me to be first up, Coren," said Hana, smiling at her companion.

Relina looked up from a holo screen and waved.

"Relina really knows her way around data tech. Better than me, even."

Kat smiled at Hana's boast and moved forward to listen to Relina.

"You'll remember Ardan saying he believed Bakker and Guirden were heading to Crofta. I was puzzled at first'—she paused and glanced at a nearby technician—"how he knew. My first task this morning was to track the spaceship to K-Astar3, which proved easy enough, but after that the trail went cold."

Hana took over. "Monitoring comings and goings from the waystation revealed a number of ships, from small freighters and passenger ships to several large cargo transiters, as likely targets, any one of which could have carried our friends."

Relina resumed. "We've gradually whittled it down to two which landed in Sensuna yesterday and another landing in a secondary spaceport in the plains, near Fieldsway, I think you call it?"

"Feldenswey," Kat corrected. "They could have gone there to avoid registering with the authorities, which makes sense; that would give them easy access to their hunting grounds and whatever illegal infrastructure they need."

"We don't know that for sure, Kat," said Relina. "There's more to do to narrow it down, then we have to decide how to proceed."

Kat bit her lip to prevent herself from telling them what she knew. Far better to let them follow the trail in case Mystic Nivlac's suspicions were wrong.

Chapter 25

Kat hovered behind Relina's chair, pondering what to do next. Hana sat at another monitor, tapping at the keyboard, scanning lists of names. Another tech did the same on the other side of the room.

Coren shuffled from foot to foot. "Is there anything Kat and I can do to help?"

Relina looked up with a grin. "A strong coffee and a house triple-decker roll from the eatery on the ground floor would go down well. I haven't had breakfast yet."

"Me neither," added Hana, "but make mine a fizz with a veg burg."

Coren shrugged and headed back to the door. "Anyone else? This'll be on Ardan's cred, you know."

Chaz, the other tech, added his order, but Kat didn't feel like eating and shook her head. "Where's Ardan? Is he in his office?"

Relina didn't bother looking up. "No, he's off-planet. He should be back later today. I could check for the exact time if it's important."

"No, that's alright." Kat had hoped to talk to him privately. Instead, she rested a hand on Relina's shoulder. "Can you show me any maps of the area where you think HuX's location might be? It would be good to get my bearings. It's a while since I've been into the city outskirts."

She moved over to Hana's side. "You probably know the area well, as the orphanage is out towards Feldenswey, isn't it?"

Hana never took her eyes off the screen. "Yes, but we never really knew the area. We were restricted to the buildings and grounds, and once we got away, we didn't stick around to explore."

Relina wheeled her chair back. "Chaz, can you open maps of Sensuna and surrounds for Kat in the conference room please?"

The tech obligingly stood and indicated for Kat to follow him.

Although looking at the maps would be useful, Kat had really hoped to talk privately to Relina in Ardan's absence. She still couldn't decide whether to tell Coren and Hana about her meeting with Mystic Nivlac. It would have helped to discuss it with the older woman.

The maps were easy to navigate and she quickly zoomed in on Feldenswey. Barren areas separated dull crete buildings with no windows. Little traffic moved on the live streaming, mainly automatic cargo transporters and the occasional hover or flitter. She focused in on the secondary spaceport on the plains, her instinct telling her this would be where Guirden and Bakker would have landed. The spaceport was much smaller than The Hub on K-Astar3. All she could make out were several craft docked with no obvious activity, though with the sealed tunnels to the central building for control and quarantine she wouldn't expect there to be much happening outside.

No vehicles were parked near what was presumably the entrance, and the gates to the central building were closed with no security in evidence; all the surveillance was probably remote. She shifted focus to the orphanage where Coren and Hana had met, feeling disquiet as she studied the rows of long buildings that looked like kennels, tiny windows and doors only opening onto an enclosed yard. A larger building surrounded them in a square.

She increased the magnification until people came into focus. Despite the blurriness of their features, she could tell there were many different species—human, frenine and dineeth, and other species she wasn't sure of—children of all colours, shapes and sizes. They filtered in a steady stream from the dormitories to one side of the rectangle and disappeared into the building. *Would that be classrooms? A dining hall?* She couldn't be sure, and she didn't want to upset Hana by asking her before she had confirmation of what was going on.

She shuddered and rose from her chair to walk up to the projection. A vehicle sped towards the front gate. An arm extended out the window and made contact with a sensor on a post. The gates slid open for the vehicle to go through, and then the process was repeated at another gate. *Why did an orphanage need double gates? It wasn't a prison.*

Or maybe it was.

She froze rigid when a person emerged from the vehicle. She knew that shape. The way he walked. His arrogant strut and bulging belly. *But he's dead! How can he be here?* Alarms rang in her mind.

But there was no doubt. It was Gorind.

She dashed out of the room and raced outside.

Hana pushed back in her chair and swung around as Coren returned with the food order. As well as her drink and veg burger, he handed her a sticky pastry. He'd always known what she liked.

Relina also stopped working but the tech ate at his desk. Hana, Coren and Relina sat eating together around the central table.

Coren suddenly lifted his head, eyebrows raised, to ask: "Where's Kat?"

"She's in the small conference room," Hana mumbled through sticky lips.

"She's not. I passed there going out and coming back. That's too long for her to be using the relief station. The lights were on, and the projection shows our old orphanage. Isn't that a bit odd?"

Hana puzzled for a moment. "Maybe she's gone out to Feldenswey. But why wouldn't she tell us she was going? Her communicator is still here so we've no hope of contacting her."

Coren guzzled a mouthful of his drink. "She's a secretive one. Maybe she's gone to see her pride. I can't believe they've exiled her for doing what was needed. You'd think they'd be proud of what she's doing."

Hana shook her head. "The frenine homelands are on the other side of the grass plains, among the rocky tors. You know that."

Coren shrugged. "I was only guessing. She doesn't have to be going where the projection shows. She's always going off on her own, like she did on K-Astar3. Did we ever find out what she was up to then?"

Hana frowned. "No, and I didn't believe her saying she needed a drive to clear her head. She definitely looked like she'd been on a mission when she came back. Has she said anything to you, Relina?"

"No." Relina tapped her knee with her fingers. "Let's think about this from a different angle. We suspect Guirden and Bakker landed at Feldenswey, but they'd surely be gone from there now so it shouldn't be because of them. We assumed they were going to the IHO headquarters, but what if they're here for something else?"

"Like what?" Hana paused to think. "Oh no! I've had a terrible thought."

"What?" Coren grabbed at her arm, squeezing tight.

Hana didn't pull away. "They must need to replace the DNA that was destroyed at their lab where Kat was held. They're not hunters, so where else could they get samples?"

Relina cocked her head. "You mean, where else would they find a range of sapient genoids in one area?"

Hana jumped up. "Yes. We know exactly where that could be, don't we, Coren?"

Coren looked blank for a moment and then jumped to the same conclusion. "Ferking hell! The orphanage! If that's where Kat's going, we'd better get there too. As much as I hate the idea of going anywhere near that place again, we can't let her go there by herself."

Relina looked quizzical. "Why the orphanage? Isn't that where you grew up?"

Hana took a deep breath. "Yes, and the matron there is a monster. But the orphanage is home to all manner of species, human and genoid. What if Kat worked out or somehow knew that's where the samples came from? She'd be livid, but would want to protect us from that, I bet."

Coren rose slowly. "Sounds likely. We need to catch her."

Relina waved them on. "You'd better go. I'm no field agent, so I'll stay and look after comms while trying to find out more. There's an Agency vehicle in the basement you can use. It'll be quicker than hiring a flitter."

She tossed a remote to Coren. "Keep me informed as much as you can. But be careful. Don't use your personal communicators near the orphanage unless it's an emergency. There's too much riding on everything to allow our conversations to be intercepted. I'll fill Ardan in as soon as he returns on-planet."

Kat parked her hire flitter behind a copse of thorn trees and crept to the other side of the dense foliage to study the terrain. The orphanage boundary, a high-tensile mesh fencing razored along the top, looked more like an Earth prison from the historical vids she'd watched. She almost expected guards with old-fashioned rifles to be patrolling the border with shaggy dogs at their heels. *But that was ridiculous. Why did an orphanage need high security?* An alarmed boundary and hi-viz lighting would be enough to alert staff if a child wandered too far.

The place didn't look the same as when she'd visited on the school excursion. *Could it have changed so much or had her bad experience affected her memories? Regardless, this was where she needed to be now.*

Only a few lit windows showed any living beings resided there. No one walked the crete paths or tended the short-clipped grass, not like when she'd been watching the live feed. Everyone must be busy inside. But no sounds of music or playing children reached her sensitive ears. In fact, she couldn't see any playground equipment outside. Thinking back to the map projections at Ardan's offices, she couldn't even remember any sports fields or other signs of outdoor activities other than what looked like an army training ground with obstacle course equipment.

It all seemed peculiar, nothing like a well-run orphanage should be. She had always thought the hardships hinted at by Coren and Hana had been exaggerated due to them missing their families. The reality of this place shed new light on what she had gleaned from them. A shiver ran through her fur despite the warmth of the day.

Movement off to her left caught her eye. The same person she had seen on the surveillance strode around the outside of the fence. There was no denying that bulky body. Gorind. He hadn't died in the fire when Coren had rescued her. Deep down, she'd always suspected that had been too good to be true. Every muscle tensed as she held herself at full alert. A well-equipped, uniformed Gorind headed her way, scanning the open spaces with optics and methodically stopping to investigate clumps of vegetation like the one she hid in. *What was he up to?* All her frustrations boiled up, overriding her natural caution, and she had a score to settle with him. She had to take the offensive before he spotted her.

Sneaking back around the copse, she removed her clothes and transformed to full hunting feline, the better to be silent and quick. Each time Gorind looked away, she slunk from cover to cover, endeavouring to get behind him while gradually closing the distance. When she was as close as she could get, she crouched low, breathed deeply to pump her lungs full of oxygen, then sprinted up behind him.

With a mighty leap, she launched herself onto his shoulders, snagging her claws in his camouflage jacket, raking the back of his legs with her hind feet. They crashed to the ground together, his weight and her momentum rolling him on top of her.

Gorind grunted and struggled to reach his gun.

Kat flicked it out of the pouch into a bush with one foreleg, trying to get her hind legs up to gouge his belly. She recoiled as she hit hidden body armour. Strong hands locked around her throat, pushing her jaws away from his florid face. She slashed at an arm with her front paw, the satisfying rip of flesh and his gasp driving her on. Using her tail as leverage, she rolled over on top of him but couldn't hold her position.

He rolled her on her back, forcing a knee between her legs. "I thought you'd return, pussy," he croaked, his foetid breath gusting over her.

Clamping her mouth and nostrils closed, Kat didn't answer. Instead, she remembered his grubby advances when she'd been at school, him torturing her when he held her captive, and how he had turned up at every point through the nightmare since Tar's murder. Anger drove her. She wanted to kill, to murder her tormentor. She had no intention of letting Gorind get the better of her this time.

Coren accelerated away from the car park, impressed with The Agency's top-of-the-range flitter. "This isn't the same vehicle Relina was driving when Kat and I followed her home."

Hana fiddled with the controls on her side of the dash. "Maybe it's held in reserve for special occasions. It's got remote viewing, self-maintaining fuel generation, individual thermostatic seating, even a bar!"

Coren peered ahead. "Is there anything we can use to see where Kat is? Maybe Ardan had the vehicle fitted with the same gear as in the office."

Hana tapped at a panel, then shook her head. "I don't think so. That's odd, but maybe it's more for carrying guests, such as their financiers."

Despite Coren speeding along the roadway, swerving around turnings as if on a racetrack, the vehicle holding its passengers comfortably. He barely had to think where he wanted to go, or change speed, and the controls adjusted. "Do you think this flitter is one of those new intuitive lux-drives? I've only seen them on vids."

Hana nudged him with her elbow. "Stop thinking about the vehicle and focus on where we're going. We'd better have a plan for when we get to the kids' home, if that is where Kat has gone."

Suppressing his excitement, Coren returned his attention to the task at hand. "We could go in via the old tunnel we kids found. Remember, it ends in the storeroom behind the kitchens."

"Unless it's been discovered since we were there." Hana shook her head. "I don't fancy going through that again anyway."

Coren grunted. "I've still got a few of my gadgets. We could blow up the front gates. That would be satisfying."

Hana stared hard at him. "So much for being discreet. Let's whistle and yell as we go."

"No need to be like that," he replied, speeding into another sharp turn. "I don't want to go near the place either. We don't even know if Kat went there. If she did, she wouldn't get in without permission. If by any chance she is in there, they'll know something's up anyway."

Hana slumped back into her seat. "Don't take this the wrong way, but I don't think you'd fit down the tunnel these days. I doubt I could either. We'd better think of another way in."

"Better be quick, then. At this rate it won't take us long to get there." Coren accelerated along a straight. "Good job there're no speed limits out this way."

Soon Coren pulled over at the turnoff to the orphanage. "Now what? I haven't seen another vehicle, let alone one Kat might have driven."

Hana peered through the front windscreen. "There's dust ahead. Let's see who it is."

Without being too obvious, Coren drove on, slowly gaining on the vehicle in front. Too large to be a flitter, there were no distinguishing marks identifying the hover's owner. He kept well back as it approached the double gates to the orphanage.

An arm reached out of the side window and touched the console before a head appeared, no doubt identifying himself.

"That's Bakker!" Hana squeaked. "Don't let him see us! Turn around!"

"Is there anyone else with him?" asked Coren as he pulled up.

Hana peered through the windscreen. "Yes! Two others. Get us out of here!"

Hana's frantic cry prompted Coren to action. He reversed up the approach road, trying to look as if he had made a wrong turn, before swinging The Agency's vehicle around and heading back to the turnoff. He pulled off the road again. "Now what?"

Hana groaned. "We'll have to use the tunnel if we can still locate where it comes out. I don't want to, but we've got to find out what Bakker and the others are doing here."

Coren placed a gentle hand on her leg. "Don't try and find them on your own. All you need to do is let me in through the back gate where the rubbish goes out."

"What if the security locks have been changed? They might have biosecurity now, or something fancier than the system we knew." Hana's quiet voice trembled and sweat broke out on her forehead.

Coren sat back. "Can you think of another way?"

The pause before she replied seemed to take forever. "No. I'll do it."

Without waiting for her to change her mind, Coren set off back down the access road until he reached a rough track that followed the fence line to the rear of the property.

"What's that?" Hana pointed forward, craning her neck to see as Coren sped over the bumpy track.

"Where?" As Coren slowed down to look, he made out the forms of two people fighting.

"Stop! It's Kat, and some big bastard." Hana already had one hand on the door release.

Coren screeched to a halt near where the two still fought, grabbed his pack with one hand and followed Hana to the melee.

Just as he went to dive at the man's legs, Kat yanked one of the man's arms from her throat and wriggled from underneath, gasping for air. The man tried to grab back at her but she knocked him onto his belly and straddled him. Her clawed hands held his head to the ground, shoving it into the dirt. Her tail lashed in fury and a deep snarl rumbled from her throat.

"Kat! Stop! You'll kill him!" Coren yelled.

Kat paused, turning glazed eyes towards him.

Coren took the opportunity, handing a quick-tie cargo fastener to Hana and grabbing the man's legs. He pulled them close together so Hana could lash them and stop him kicking.

"I wish I'd killed you," Kat growled, grabbing a flailing arm and twisting it up behind his back. Coren grabbed his other arm. Between them, they got the man's wrists together and Hana attached another cargo fastener to keep him secure.

Coren rolled the man over to see his face. "You! We thought you were dead."

Gorind writhed, squirming and kicking with legs together, trying to sit up and smash them with his head. "You'll pay for this, you filth," his voice rasped from his scarred throat. "You're as bad as the pussy. You can all rot in the same jail."

Coren grabbed Gorind's wrists and rolled him back onto his belly, then knelt on his shoulders. "I don't think so, Gorind. Time for the truth to come out."

Kat's chest heaved as she rubbed at her throat. Standing tall, she extended her claws. "We'll strip off your body armour and see how tender your throat is. Whether your blood is as red as a frenine's."

"Kat, are you alright?" Hana placed a restraining hand on Kat's shoulder. "Did he hurt you?"

Kat snarled before visibly relaxing. "No more than he's done in the past. Thanks for the help. How did you know to come here?" She smoothed her fur and licked blood from her arm, still unconcernedly naked.

Coren averted his eyes. Even in full feline form, Kat's nakedness threatened to make him forget why they were there. "We'll tell you later, but we saw Bakker and a couple of others going through the front gate."

Hana shuffled her feet. "Kat, are you alright to look after Gorind while we find out what's going on? You look as if you need a rest."

Kat extracted a small gun from Gorind's side holster and pointed it at his head. "If one of us is going in, we should all go in. I can shoot his legs to disable him. I'm not going to risk him getting away."

Coren blanched at Kat's cold-blooded tone. "I've got rope. We can tie him to a tree. That should stop him."

Chapter 26

Hana fingered the security remote that Coren had found on Gorind's belt. They gagged and trussed him to the trunk of a needle tree like a fat pig ready for a spit-roast. If he tried to move, the long thorns would only pierce his flesh, not sever the cord. Kat had sullenly agreed to not maim him, despite her earlier rage.

Hana left the others while she checked out the orphanage's garbage gate to see if the security had been changed since they lived there. As she couldn't see any exterior locks or controls, she tried Gorind's remote.

Nothing happened.

With a heavy heart she crept back to where the others waited, close by but out of sight. "It's no good, we won't get in that way."

Coren rested a hand on her shoulder. "We can't risk being seen near any of the other gates, not with Bakker here. It'll have to be the tunnel. Are you up to it?"

Hana shrugged. "I don't have a choice, do I?"

Kat stepped forward. "Why don't I go? I can squeeze through the tiniest spaces in this form with no clothes to snag."

Hope rose in Hana's chest, then plummeted into her stomach. "The exit from the tunnel is hidden where it comes into the storerooms so it'd make it harder for you than me. And you won't easily find your way to the back gate, especially if things have changed." She took a deep breath and began stripping down to her underwear. "It's alright, it's best I do it."

Coren led the way to the start of the tunnel, slashing strangling vines and dead wood out of the way. "No one's used this in an age. Maybe the current kids don't know about it, or perhaps the tunnel's collapsed on itself."

"Thanks, Coren," said Hana, peering into the dark, obscured hole. "That really helps my nerves. Let's get on with it. And I won't use my communicator unless I really have to. Wait for me near the back gate," she added as she clipped her communicator belt around her bare waist and then removed her boots.

Hana crawled on all fours through the last of the undergrowth and into the tunnel entrance, dried dung and other detritus crumbling under her elbows. She pushed aside thoughts of any creatures that might live there. Her body blocked the light as she wiggled forward into the darkness. The tunnel had never been very wide, but Hana was sure she hadn't grown that much in the years since Coren had first shown it to her. He had used it often, but she had only been through once before. It wasn't an experience she was ever likely to forget.

Soil dribbled down her neck as she brushed against the ceiling. Roots snagged in her hair like fingers raking her scalp. Stones pressed into her knees and thighs as she was now forced to squirm along on her belly. *Why was she doing this? She was an organiser, not an elite fighter.* The tunnel descended to where the soil became damp and cool, almost a relief as sweat streaked her face. She couldn't free a hand to wipe the prickle away. Her nose itched. She clawed forward.

Something snagged her, holding her fast. *Don't panic!* Without being able to use her hands to feel around, Hana inched backwards using her toes. A rock scraped her stomach. It had caught on her belt. *Stupid! She should have removed that, too.*

Maybe she should have accepted Kat's offer and let her snake her way through. But what she'd said was right: Kat would have had trouble locating the back gate without being detected. Hana had worked in the kitchens often enough, even in her limited time at the orphanage, to know the maze of walkways.

She resumed forward progress, careful to hunch her hips over the protruding stone. Her back scraped the ceiling, grazing her spine, but she kept on. Hands, elbows, hips, knees. Hands, elbows, hips, knees. She daren't stop. Keeping her eyes shut to block any falling earth, she pushed on, focusing on her breathing as Coren had suggested.

Her fingers hit something hard. *No! It couldn't be blocked.* She couldn't bear to go back all that way even if she could turn around, and moving backwards would take an eternity. *What if the air ran out and she was stuck here forever?*

With the tunnel slightly wider where she was, she quelled her rising panic, squeezed her knees under herself and crawled forward to push against the barrier. It moved a tiny fraction. Encouraged, she bunched up to gain more leverage and shoved again. The box, or whatever it was blocking the hole, screeched as it moved across the crete floor of the storeroom. Hana froze, poised to wriggle back if anyone came. She listened, her eyes adjusting to the dim light. Hearing nothing and seeing no sign of movement, she caught her breath and shoved again. This time she could push her head through. She shouldered the box out of the way, choking back a cough from the raised dust.

No one was in the storeroom, so Hana scrambled out of the tunnel as quietly as she could and rose to her feet before pushing the box back to hide the entrance. After a quick brush down she listened at the door before trying the handle. It refused to turn. Locked.

Hana's pulse raced in panic before she remembered Gorind's security remote. Hopefully it was a master key. She waved it at the door handle. She tensed, despite the satisfying click. *It had sounded so loud!* After turning the handle and opening the door a sliver, she peered through the crack. All quiet. She slipped through and snicked the door shut behind her.

There was no time for stealth. If a kid or a member of staff saw her, she'd just have to run. Striding out as silently as she could, Hana moved through the corridors past other storerooms. She hesitated by the kitchen door, the clang of pots and pans of pots and pans taking her back in time. She shivered and hurried past, grabbing a convenient bag of garbage from one of the bins to provide an excuse.

The way to the rear yard proved clear. When she reached the back gate, on her now sore feet, she dumped the bag and took out Gorind's security remote. A laugh almost erupted from her as she saw why the remote hadn't worked from the other side. Old-fashioned iron bolts fastened a latch onto the heavy gate, a padlock securing it. She grabbed it in frustration before noticing the slight movement in the latch. A patter of rust fell as she wriggled it, giving her hope that the iron bolts were weak.

The rattle of the gate made her wait for a moment. With no one nearby, she wriggled the latch back and forth, rust falling in a steady rain until one of the bolts snapped. The leverage then made breaking the other bolt an easy task. The latch fell to one side. Relieved, she looked forward to getting her outer clothes and boots back.

Footsteps approached.

Hana didn't wait to hear someone call out. She yanked the gate open and squeezed through, pulling it shut behind her, cursing that she'd left the bag of rubbish.

With relief, she saw Coren waiting with her gear, anxiety lifting from his face. She signalled him to be quiet with one hand, while indicating they needed to move away with the other. They crouched by the fence, holding their breath, as they heard someone curse about rubbish being left lying around. The clatter of a bin sounded.

Hana willed the person not to see the broken latch. She rolled her eyes at Coren when the sound of footsteps led away from the gate. "I'll quickly get dressed and then we'd better hurry before anyone else comes."

Kat, still on an adrenaline high from her fight with Gorind, followed Coren and Hana through the gate. Although she had expected the stark buildings and prison-like fences from the sat images, she had still anticipated the inside to feel more like her boarding school.

Nothing could be further from the truth. She might have hated being away from home, and as anywhere, there had been bullies, pretend friends, and stuck-up social climbers, but at least there had been noise. Even during class time, there would be the sound of training vids, or kids calling out answers, or debating, or giggling.

Here, a slight clatter of metal came from the direction Kat presumed from Hana to be the kitchens. Other than that, there was nothing; no sound at all. She didn't need Hana's finger to her lips to tell her to remain silent. That presented no challenge to a frenine. She swivelled her ears to catch any hint of where Bakker might be.

Coren and Hana communicated with hand signals, signs she didn't know. She suspected this was the kids' language from when they'd been in the orphanage. They'd have needed a way to communicate without being found out. The whole concept spooked her. *How had they stood it? No wonder they ran away at the first opportunity.*

A distant female voice, deep and throaty, caught her attention. She placed a hand on Hana's shoulder and indicated the direction it came from.

Hana led them in single file down the path.

Kat stepped with care, following the footsteps of the others. She'd had no idea Coren and Hana could be so quiet. Their faces had become blank, too, not a look she had ever seen on them before. The path followed the edge of the buildings out to an open square. The hover Bakker had been driving stood silent on the other side. Beyond that lay a dirt area that Kat had thought to be an army training camp from the air.

A line of children, of mixed ages, sizes, and species, lined up along the edge of the dirt, standing to attention with the deadpan expressions of her friends. Four human adults sat on cushioned chairs under the shade of a viewing stand raised above the dust. The deep female voice came from the person on the end. Another was obviously Bakker. Kat couldn't make out the identities of the other two, hidden as they were in shadow, but they all appeared to be following the woman's gesticulations.

Hana leant to whisper in Kat's ear. "That's Matron."

And Dr. Guirden. Kat was sure of it now, seeing the woman's face in profile. *But who was the fourth person?*

The man in question waved a hand in the air.

Kat caught a few words "…get on with…"

She flinched. She knew that voice. With great effort, claws pulsing in and out, she stopped herself from charging at him.

Tar's murderer. Lord Baden-Hauf.

Coren must have seen her stiffen. He signalled for her to wait. They had agreed a plan when outside the fence, but hadn't expected to confront their enemies in open country.

The three of them stood like statues as kids commenced performing on the ropes and climbing bars, fighting hand to hand or with weapons in choreographed displays, racing over hurdles and clambering through obstacles.

Coren signalled for Kat and Hana to move back into cover.

When they reached the security of the buildings, Coren leant against a wall and wiped sweat from his forehead. "What the ferking hell are they up to? We didn't have to do stuff like that."

"Looks like combat training to me," mused Kat.

"What would be the point of that?" Hana wore a frown deeper than any of them.

Kat fidgeted before taking a deep breath and straightening up. She couldn't hold back any longer. "I have a contact here on Crofta, a dineeth, a mystic. That's who I met while you were at the Star View." She tried to ignore the look of anger on her friends' faces. "Hear me out, please. I didn't want to say anything earlier because I needed to be sure his fears were right. He was concerned the orphanage has been raising children with special traits, such as strength, speed, and stamina. To use their DNA in the creation of game animals."

Her friends gaped, obviously wanting to shout out but not daring to make a sound.

She stilled under their gaze. "It seemed fanciful to me at the time, even though we know HuX use DNA for cloning. But then I remembered what we saw in the orientation pens. We didn't have time to look too closely, but what if their experimentation went further? What if—"

She caught herself touching her wounds. "Maybe they didn't only take swabs from these youngsters." From the little she'd learned from Dr Guirden, the scientist had been experimenting with reproduction far beyond cloning.

Hana gulped. "But how do they get the kids to agree? There could be copies of them on every planet, being hunted and killed. A lot of these kids are human, too."

"As if they've a choice against adults," Kat growled. "And I've told you that Dr Guirden manipulates the embryos so she needs the source material, eggs as well as DNA. She might only be using the genetic code for certain traits, but who knows how far her evilness goes?"

Hana pointed a finger at her. "This means, if we can get proof, they can be arrested by the authorities. What they're doing is illegal. Not to mention immoral." She turned to Coren. "Did you bring recording equipment with you?"

Coren grimaced. "Yes. Trushaw had some excellent stuff, for all the good it did her." He paused and shook his head. "We really need to vid what they're doing here, and find a way to catch them taking DNA samples or talking about their intent."

Hana suppressed a bark of a laugh. "Is that all? Easy, then."

Kat had other things on her mind. She could smell Baden-Hauf on the breeze. "You two do what you can, but I'm getting my revenge.

Even if I get jailed for it, or die, I'm not letting Tar's murderer leave here alive."

Kat crept along the inside of the boundary fence, glad she hadn't dressed after fighting Gorind, her fur blending with the background. Coren and Hana hadn't hesitated to support her in her desire to kill Baden-Hauf, merely adapted their plan to take it into account. She would forever be grateful to them for that, plus all they'd done to get them this far.

Coren moved along the fence in the other direction, ensuring they would be positioned on the far side of the training ground when Hana made herself known to Matron.

Once in position, Kat crouched into a comfortable pose, prepared to react in a split second. She studied the children of disparate species with growing horror as they performed for their small audience. Their exercises became harder and more dangerous, yet still none of them made the slightest sound. Only the clang of equipment or crash of weapons reached her ears. Every so often, one of the combatants would fail and be sent to the dormitories, fear etched on their faces. Only half of the original number remained. Occasionally, one of the four adults would clap. Even then, the children didn't react, or stop performing. Disgust roiled in Kat's stomach. She wished Hana would act soon, but she knew Coren would need more time to get in position without giving himself away.

"Matron!" Hana's call broke the air.

The large woman, with greying hair and wearing a shapeless, dull-blue dress, pushed herself to her feet at Hana's approach. "You! What are you doing back here? You should have kept running while you had the chance."

Hana kept walking, confidence in her stride. "I'm not back by choice. I'm back because of what you're doing here."

By now the other three adults had risen and stood watching.

Matron waddled towards Hana, a long switch in her hand. "I don't know how you got in," she scowled, "but don't think you'll get out as easily. Security will stop you."

Hana halted and held up her hand. "Don't come any closer. The authorities have been called. I just wanted to see what evil looks like up close."

Lord Baden-Hauf's laugh echoed. "What authorities? I am the authority on this planet. There's nothing you, child, can do to me."

Before Hana could respond, Coren appeared, pointing his gun at the group. "How come we're in here then, and your security guard is trussed up outside?"

Kat couldn't hold back any longer. She loped across the clearing, ignoring kids scrambling out of her way. Even with the confrontation between her friends and the HuX people, the children had kept up their performance. Now they scattered, most back to the dormitories, others to lie flat on the ground with their hands on their heads.

Baden-Hauf swivelled on one foot to face her. "What the hell?" he yelled. His hand reached to his side for a weapon. "Stay right where you are!" he ordered.

Kat launched herself at her enemy.

He ducked behind Guirden and Bakker before pushing them both at her. Such was Kat's impetus she couldn't avoid their flailing bodies. Their limbs tangled. Bakker grabbed at Kat's body, disrupting her efforts to get past and attack Tar's killer. She slashed down, a claw raking a long strip of skin from the man's face.

Bakker's scream pierced the air. Everyone except Baden-Hauf paused. He raced towards the nearby hover as Kat scrabbled for traction. By the time she sighted her prey he had nearly reached his vehicle, giving him enough time to turn and aim at her.

It took all of Kat's hunting skills to avoid his laser beams. This was a man obsessed with hunting, who had no doubt grown up around weapons and spent hours practising. She anticipated his shots and took evasive action even as she closed in on her quarry.

But her movements achieved what Baden-Hauf desired: time to reach his hover.

She snarled in frustration as he remotely opened the door and slid into the driver's seat. With a roar and a billow of dust, he sped away and headed for the front gates. They opened as he reached them.

Kat raced after him, all four paws eating up the distance. His vehicle sped away. Knowing she wouldn't outrun him on foot, but determined not to lose him, she headed for her hire flitter.

Coren waved his gun at Bakker and Guirden. "Don't think you can make a dash for it too. I won't hesitate to shoot. Get on the ground, face down, and don't try anything clever."

He signalled for Hana to tie them.

Matron stomped towards him. "You won't—"

A blast from his gun stopped her coming any closer, kicking up dust as high as her waist. Her face reddened as she blustered.

Hana checked the Earthers' clothes, stashing objects in Coren's pack as she found things in their pockets. She finished by thoroughly patting them down, before tying their hands with Coren's fasteners. "All clear," she said as she drew her laser and covered the matron.

Coren pointed to the woman. "And you. We won't make you lie down else we'll never get you up, but remember I have many old scores to settle."

He holstered his laser before walking over to Matron and reaching for her arms.

She swung a clubbed fist at his head and kicked him in the shins.

Coren yowled and staggered back.

"Look out!" yelled Hana as some of the children broke away from where the group had been performing and charged at them, swinging their fists and any weapons they could grab.

"Hold it!" yelped Coren, snatching out his gun, "We're from here. We're on your side!"

The children kept coming, seemingly determined to protect their Matron despite her cruelty.

Hana jumped in front of them, arms out wide, gun pointed into the air. "Remember me? I'm one of you. I won't hurt you. I'm here to help you. Please."

The plea worked, causing most of the charging children to slow down, puzzling through the new information. The older ones recognised Hana and must have remembered that she had been kind and helpful in her short stay. Their hesitation ran through the group, causing a slowdown in their approach.

Matron was fast to take advantage of the distraction despite her size and age. She hauled Dr Guirden up in front of her as a shield. "Shoot her if you want, but my son, Shastic, will be here any moment. He's Head of Security and won't take any nonsense from the likes of you.

Coren snarled. "Where is he, then? I can't see any security. The only guard we've seen was patrolling the exterior fence."

"That's him! He'll make you pay for this." Saliva dribbled down Matron's chin.

"Gorind?" Coren couldn't believe his ears. "Shastic Gorind is your son?" It was all he could do to stop laughing, but so much made sense now. "He won't be coming to save you. He's trussed to a tree."

"Rubbish. You couldn't beat him. Your bluff won't work with me." Matron had a huge arm around Dr Guirden's throat. "I'll kill her, and Bakker, and you'll take the blame. They're nothing to me. There's always someone who wants a taste of young flesh, and not just skin samples either. You'll be on X-Astar9 before you know it."

Hana swung around to focus on the large woman. "So it's true. You've been raising kids for monsters like these. Selecting the best and strongest for their cloning program. You're evil."

Coren stood over Bakker. The financier had his eyes screwed shut as if hoping to make the situation disappear.

Hana watched as Coren began arguing with the head of the orphanage, bringing up old slights and misbehaviours. Seeing that she was distracted, Hana moved closer and, with a swift hit to the woman's head with her gun, knocked her down. The matron slumped forward to the ground, unconscious, Dr Guirden breaking her fall with a squeal.

Hana pushed both knees to Matron's back and lashed her wrists together behind her with ties from Coren's pack.

"Ferking hell, I can't believe Gorind is her son. Who'd father anyone on her? It must've been in the dark." Coren grinned at Hana as she rolled the Matron off Dr Guirden. "I'd hoped you'd do that."

Hana breathed hard. "I wasn't sure I could hit her hard enough, but I thought of what she had done to me when I was here."

Coren pointed with his gun. "What do we do with them?"

Hana looked around. All the kids had disappeared. No staff had come to see what was happening, no doubt frightened to interfere in Matron's business. "Can we take Bakker and Guirden over to the fence and secure them so they can't move? Then we'd better drag Matron there too. After that I'll contact Relina and tell her what's happening. She needs to get help here as soon as possible."

Hana stood over Matron until Coren returned from restraining the two Earthers. He nudged Matron with his boot. "We can't move her while she's like this, she's a dead weight."

He extracted a vial from the medical kit in his pack and waved it under her nose. "This'll bring her round."

The woman sneezed and came to, wriggling like a lizard caught in a sack. "Release me now! It'll go easier for you if you do."

Coren shook her by the shoulders until she lay still. "That's for talking back, like you used to do to me. Stand up! Shut up!"

Between them, they hauled Matron to her feet and dragged her, fighting all the way, to the fence where Coren secured her to a post. "How long do you think Ardan's people will take to get here?"

"Not long, I hope. We'll have to wait until they come," Hana said, raising her comm unit, before squatting on her heels in the meagre shade of a shrub.

Coren straightened. "Will you be alright if I leave you here so I can help Kat?"

Hana gulped. "Oh sure, a frenine in hunting mode needs far more help than me. After all, she has one person to track, and I have three, four if you count Gorind, to contend with."

Coren squirmed under her gaze. "But they're secured and help is coming. Even in hunting form Kat is vulnerable against Baden-Hauf's weapons."

"What about what happened last time, with Trushaw? Have you forgotten so soon?"

Coren flinched. "Shit, you're right. I'll give Bakker a thorough check over."

He used a vibro-knife to slash Bakker's outer clothes and stripped him to his underwear.

Hana checked the pockets and linings of his garments before discarding them out of reach. "Nothing here. Check his left arm."

Coren tapped Bakker's limbs with the handle of his knife. Sure enough, the left forearm wasn't flesh. "Kat was right. He has a fake limb."

Bakker snarled. "Yes, a bloody dineeth took my real arm. All I wanted was one of its pups as a pet for my son. But I guess it did me a favour. Trushaw got what was coming to her."

Hana could no longer control herself. She slapped Bakker hard across the face. "She was a better person than you'll ever be." With deft fingers, she found the pressure point which revealed a hidden compartment in Bakker's fake arm. It was empty.

Coren moved Hana's arms aside and, using the vibro-knife, cut out the chip that enabled Bakker to control his artificial limb. "There, that should do it."

Turning away and shrugging, Hana tried to quell her fear of being left alone. "Alright. Help Kat if you can, but don't get shot!"

Chapter 27

Kat's hire flitter wouldn't normally have kept up with Baden-Hauf's hover, but she suspected he wanted her to follow him. His dust trail soon confirmed her intuition—he was heading for the plains beyond her home, where he had murdered Tar.

In case she was wrong, she pushed the flitter to its limits, not caring about the rocks that hit the windshield or any damage she caused the low undercarriage by speeding over rough ground. Adrenalin pumped through her arms; her head dizzy with emotion.

This was it. The last chance. If she couldn't kill Tar's murderer this time, she'd be better off dead. Then reality hit her. If she did kill Lord Baden-Hauf, she'd be better off dead rather than face a lifetime on X-Astar9 or be forever on the run. *Not that it mattered. Life without Tar wasn't worth living. What did her future hold without him? She no longer even had the support of the pride.*

As she'd foreseen, the HuX hover was parked where the dirt track ended. She pulled alongside and peered around. No one remained in the vehicle, and nothing moved out on the grasslands.

Kat had no intention of being hunted like one of the big cats on Earth. Taking care with her appearance, she donned the clothes that she'd left in the flitter, though she decided against the heeled boots. If she had to run, they would hinder her.

Fishing deep inside her pack, she withdrew the choker that Mystic Nivlac had provided. I seemed so long ago. Her mind whizzed over the places she'd been and things she'd done since then—being captured by Gorind, meeting Ardan, jumping around the galaxy, being rescued by Coren, betrayed by Hana, then trusting Coren's flying and believing in Hana's information, then together discovering the game parks on Earth.

And…the violation of her body. Bakker's trickery. Trushaw's beheading. The other deaths. She shivered. All she'd ever wanted was to chase zeena across the plains with Tar, to sunbathe next to his body, to raise his cubs, litter after litter, and restore the population of frenines.

Lord Baden-Hauf had changed all that.

Tar was dead. All she had left was the lifeseal pac of their cells. She didn't know why she kept them, only that she couldn't bear to part with the last particle of the future they had dreamed of. She hadn't set out to bring down an intergalactic hunting operation, only for revenge. *But the cost had been high, too high for so many innocents trying, like her, to do the right thing. Time for her to pay the price.*

She fastened the choker around her neck, ensuring the hexagonal diamond, the one that Mystic Nivlac had told her to use only in a dire emergency, nestled against her jugular vein.

After checking her clothes sat comfortably and wouldn't hinder her, she sniffed for the scent of her enemy. She found his track with ease, the tread of his sturdy boots obvious. *Had he anticipated this? How could he have known she'd come? Or maybe he had intended to hunt after his visit, maybe even using one of the children?* Horror slithered down her spine like icy water.

She followed his trail, walking as a genoid, not a feline. If he intended to shoot her, let him see that she was a genoid, a sapient being like him, not a game animal. Let him look into her eyes and see the person within. Let him cut her down in cold blood.

Then she remembered that was what she'd done to his son. He wouldn't feel any remorse at slaughtering her. He'd probably mount her head on his wall as a trophy and use her skin as a rug on his polished floor. The notion slowed her steps. This was no normal man she tracked; he believed himself above the law, believed himself to *be* the law.

She halted and peered across the vast grasslands, the desire to strip off her clothes and run on all fours almost overwhelming her. Only the memory of the last time she was here, with Tar's body slung over the r-drive, brought her back to why she had come.

Small boulders dotted the plains like marbles on an expanse of buff carpet. She settled into a jog and copied Baden-Hauf's strides towards the first boulder. His scuffed footsteps showed he hadn't paused there long. She looked ahead to the next one and sniffed the air. No hint of his scent reached her on the slight breeze. She jogged on to the next boulder.

Rock by rock, she advanced across the dry, grassy plains. Her prey kept ahead, out of sight. *What was he playing at, the supposedly competent big game hunter? They'd almost come full circle. Didn't he know where he was going?*

Whether he'd been trying to tire her, or didn't know the plains as well as she, Kat knew where they would end up—where she and Tar almost—almost—consummated their love. That had to be where they were headed, despite the roundabout route.

Stopping in a small patch of shade, she thought again about what she must do. She hadn't brought a weapon. Her claws and teeth would be enough, fitting for the kill. Maybe she should go natural after all.

A movement ahead caught her eye. *There*! Something glinted.

Retreating behind the boulder, she removed her clothes and piled them behind her. She kept the choker on and checked again that the diamond lay in the correct place.

Another flash!

Kat had patience. She could watch a herd of zeena for hours without moving. Eventually Baden-Hauf would reveal himself.

She didn't have to wait long. She heard a clink and saw his back. He looked toward Sensuna, the way they'd driven in. Maybe he hadn't realised she was already there. Whether this was the case or not, she took her chance, transforming into feline form and sprinting on all fours towards her enemy.

He swivelled, grinning, and fired at her. A trap! *Fool, fool, fool! Of course he'd known she was there. He'd have all the modern tracking technology.*

She dodged, but too slow. The beam sizzled across her thigh.

He shot again, making her zigzag in her run, slowing her forward progress. Another blast clipped her arm. She carried on regardless of the pain, focused on only one thing.

To kill.

At the last moment, the man must have realised she wasn't going to stop. He levelled his weapon for a head shot.

She launched herself high into the air, covering the distance with legs curled up to her body, tail balancing her flight. His shot went beneath her. She hit him in the chest. They fell and rolled together, her trying to get a grip on his neck with her teeth, him fumbling for something on his belt.

A sharp pain ripped her side. She snarled and lashed with her front paws at whatever she could contact, her claws sliding off his protective gear. She growled in frustration.

Baden-Hauf rolled on top of her, using his bulk to pin her down. "I'll skin you alive! No quick death for you, not like my son. I'll make you suffer!" He lifted a reinforced fist, his eyes hard.

Kat struggled, but his greater weight proved too much for her to push off. She brought her hind legs up, trying to gouge his belly with her hind claws, but he smashed her head against the ground. Her mind numbed. He had weapons, armour, and strength. Despite being determined, her will to live had faltered the moment she'd seen the spot where she and Tar had last been together.

Pulling one paw from beneath her, she reached for her neck. Time to end this battle. The bastard had won. She would join Tar in death. Others would have the responsibility of bringing him and HuX down. She'd done all she could.

She thumped the diamond against her neck, seeking oblivion. A needle penetrated her soft skin, straight into the vein as intended. A burning sensation sizzled through her veins.

Instead of the expected drifting off into death, strength beyond her imagining flooded her body. She shoved the man off her chest and ripped away his weapons, flinging them far beyond the rocks.

Her change in tactic took him by surprise. After a moment of hesitation, he bunched his muscles and fought back in a frenzy.

He was no match for Kat in her heightened state, even with his armour. His eyes reflected his horror. His mouth opened in a high-pitched scream as he faced his death. In a whirl of limbs and claws, Kat shredded his chest through his toughened clothing, ripping open his belly and slashing his face. Even once he stopped resisting, Kat continued in a frenzy, flailing at him until his body lay in a tangle of blood and offal.

As suddenly as the energy had hit her, it disappeared.

She sagged in a heap, totally spent, covered in Baden-Hauf's body fluids and fragments of flesh. She had achieved her goal, gained revenge for Tar's murder. The satisfaction she had expected didn't eventuate. Instead, a hollow space filled her chest, of loss, and horror at what she had done. *How many lives had she taken?*

With a shudder, her body convulsed. She collapsed next to her victim.

Coren hastened to The Agency's flitter and sped away from the orphanage. He smacked his hand against the controls as if that would make the vehicle go any faster. "Oh Kat, you shouldn't have gone without us! We're your friends!"

Grateful he'd had the foresight to get Hana to attach a tracker to the HuX hover on her way to confront Matron, Coren followed its signal. Turning off the smooth road, he didn't care if this fancy flitter wasn't designed for rough terrain, he'd take it wherever Kat had gone. His heart pounded as he pushed the flitter for more speed, ignoring the sudden sideways lurches as it bumped over the rough track, hitting hummocks. "Come on, come on! I've got to reach her before she catches him!"

He'd never been far out onto the plains before. The open landscape reminded him of the game park on Earth, perfect for big felines. He could almost understand why Kat loved it out here, but not him. Give him the city, warehouses of technology and a set of tools any day. He ran through what he had in his pack that might be of use to stop Baden-Hauf. They wanted him alive to account for his crimes and enable them to destroy the rest of HuX.

He gasped as he spotted two vehicles ahead, a hover parked neatly, a flitter haphazardly pulled up at its side. Neither had occupants. He slid to a halt behind them and, leaping out of the vehicle, shouted for Kat. "Where are you?"

His cry went unanswered.

Frantic, Coren grabbed the optics from his pack and climbed onto the top of the HuX hover, the tallest of the three transports. He scanned the dry grasslands, blinking dust from his eyes.

Nothing.

Adjusting the focus, he searched further away, looking for the slightest movement, the tiniest change of colour, that might give away where Baden-Hauf or Kat were. He had no doubt they hunted each other, but who was ahead of whom?

A splash of orange and yellow caught his eye, a grecka, one of the giant scavenging lizards. Crofta didn't have vultures and hyena like Earth to clean up carrion. These lizards did the job instead. Coren's stomach churned. The grecka flickered its tongue, tasting the air, and waddled as if intent on its quarry. While it was at least as long as Coren was tall, the mottled orange and yellow of its scales blended into the sand and grass whenever it stopped moving.

It rose onto its hind legs for a moment, then started to run.

Tweaking the optics sharper, Coren scanned to where it might be headed. His stomach threatened to empty his breakfast. A body lay in a tangle of torn fabrics.

No way could Coren cover the distance on foot to reach whoever it was before the grecka got there. Diving into the HuX hover, he pressed the starter, relieved it hadn't been locked. He could have overridden the controls, but that would have wasted time, and this was almost like an r-drive, suitable for cross-country work.

Roaring across the plains, Coren made straight for the body. The approach of the hover gave the grecka pause, but it only slowed. The smell of food must have been too much to overcome its concern for his arrival.

He was out of the hover before it had fully stopped. With a shot from his laser, he forced the grecka to hesitate, then turn and slink off. His hands had been shaking too much for an accurate shot to harm it. He'd worry about that later.

Running to the prone form, Coren almost didn't notice another body lying beside it. "Kat! It's you!"

He sank to his knees beside her, thanking all the deities that he'd ever heard of that the torn, dead body was Baden-Hauf's.

Kat didn't move.

Coren lifted her shoulders and hugged her close, ignoring the gore splattered across her, relieved her soft fur was warm against his face. "Kat! Kat!"

Hana poked around the corridors beyond the door marked *Private*, trying door handles and opening cupboards. She'd never been foolish enough to breach Matron's domain when she was younger, no matter Coren's prompting. They'd had enough trouble with her as it was. Even now she walked as if on eggshells, not only because of Matron, but because of Bakker, Gorind and Baden-Hauf. *What if one of them got free? Did Bakker have any more surprises?*

She had tried not to show her horror at the headless Trushaw, but nightmares plagued her. She'd never seen a dead person before, let alone someone she knew. And Trushaw had been so nice, a successful and respected woman, working to overcome evil. Life wasn't fair.

And now Coren had run off and left Hana alone in a place she feared more than anywhere else, with those responsible for Trushaw's death. He was still the old Coren when they were alone, but whenever Kat was around, she felt invisible.

She steeled herself to move deeper into the off-limits wing of the orphanage. Relina had suggested Hana look for evidence of HuX while she waited for assistance. Ardan had returned from off-planet and was coming with his people.

"So Gorind is Matron's son. That's a surprise. They did have the same facial features, especially that large nose," she reflected, talking to herself to stave off her sense of isolation.

Hana couldn't believe what must have been going on all the time she had been living at the kids' home. *No wonder the other girls had been shy and sensitive. It would only have been a matter of time before Gorind approached her.*

Her footsteps echoed on the bare floor, keeping her alert. Despite knowing Matron and the HuX people were securely tied, she couldn't help feeling there should be more people around. *Where were the staff? Why hadn't Baden-Hauf had his usual bodyguards with him? Why wasn't Coren backing her up?*

She reached a solid wooden door, a rarity, at the end of the corridor. A carved sign said "MATRON—NO ENTRY".

Hana tried the old-fashioned brass door handle. It didn't turn. "Maybe it's false," she thought aloud, unafraid of being overheard. She swiped the door with Gorind's security remote. She jumped at a quiet click but touched the door with her fingertips, applying a slight pressure, wary in case of a trap. The door swung inwards without a noise, revealing a sparsely furnished room.

Hana entered and closed the door quietly behind her. A large desk dominated the far side, behind which stood an overstuffed chair covered in zeena hide, worn into the shape of a large backside. There was no doubt who usually sat there. The only item on the desk was a touch pad. She moved behind the desk and tapped at the blank pad, jumping back as panels slid from the wall opposite the desk, revealing screens. "No bio-security. She must be confident nobody could get in here."

Images flickered on multiple screens, images Hana immediately recognised—the dorms, the classrooms, the dining hall, even the showers and relief stations. Children of all ages and species cowered on their beds while others met in small groups, obviously agitated. There were still no staff in sight. "This must be live. I wonder if she had this when we were here."

Staring at one screen in particular, Hana shook her head. "Coren would never have got away with what he did if she had. This all looks far too modern and sophisticated."

The images changed every few seconds. Hana turned away, not bearing to watch. She tapped more commands into the control panel. A small viewing screen rose from the desk, but the device was locked. Without time to hack into the system, she'd have to look for other evidence. The only other piece of furniture was a shelving unit holding identical folders. She grabbed one at random and examined the contents. "These are id prints, photographs. Like they used in the old days. There must be one for every kid that's ever been here."

She flicked through more folders, looking for information such as where the children came from, or where they ended up. Nothing. Just pictures. She selected another folder on a different shelf. The same. And another. Hundreds and hundreds of them.

She must be there too. And Coren.

"But these can't all be kids that lived here. There're too many." She flipped over a few of the folders to see each had a code on the back. *Maybe Matron had categorised them for their potential to HuX.* She grabbed a few at random, thinking The Agency might find them useful, and tucked them inside her jacket.

A door that looked like a closet lay flush in the corner of the wall opposite the main door. Hana didn't even bother trying the handles, using the security remote instead. The door panel slid back into a recess, revealing a smooth wall. She studied the dim glow of the panel, which looked like a giant scanner, and placed her hand against it.

An alarm screeched. "UNAUTHORISED ACCESS" flashed on the wall.

Her immediate reaction was to flee, but who was going to come?

Matron and the others were tied up. She dithered, then wondered if the alarm was linked to an external security group. Gorind's thugs might be on their way.

But where could she go? Coren had taken the Agency flitter, damn him.

Her mind whirled. First, she had to get the alarm turned off. Matron would be able to do that. Somehow Hana had to force her to cancel it. She quivered at the idea of dragging the obese woman into her own office, doubting she could force Matron to do anything. *Maybe Dr Guirden would be a better bet? If this was HuX business, she might have security rights, and she'd be easier to drag.*

Or should she hide in the tunnel until help came?

While she dithered about what to do, the alarm stopped. The glowing door ceased flashing.

With relief, Hana inhaled deeply. Then she saw a number glowing on the door, a number counting down. *It was a grav lift!*

A soft swish came from the panel. *Someone was coming!*

She turned to leave the office then stopped, mesmerised. The vid wall had changed, focussing into several large screens. Gun-carrying figures, anonymous in black uniforms and battle helmets, filled the grav lift. On the adjoining screen, white-coated staff ran frantically around a laboratory, presumably below the complex.

Hana's stomach churned. That's where the rest of the staff were, so many of them. She had to get out of there and contact Relina again. As she bolted for the office door, she used her communicator, no need to keep quiet any longer.

Chapter 28

Hana moved along the corridor, trying not to keep looking over her shoulder. What she wouldn't give to have Coren with her. They usually worked so well as a team. Now he wasn't by her side when she needed him most. She slammed the solid wooden door of Matron's office behind her. *Coren's not here because of Kat. What about my needs? I could be killed and he wouldn't know. I'm left to do the hard things while he runs after her.*

She shook her head to clear her distracting thoughts as she searched urgently for some way to impede those coming after her. Spying a heavy metal cabinet from the adjacent room, she dragged it against the wooden door.

"Relina, I've blocked the door as best I can. I'll go out through the kitchens," she said into her communicator. "I'll catch up with Ardan there…if I make it, but I'll mute the comms again in case it alerts anyone."

Hana forgot about Coren as smoke rose from the centre of the wooden door. She pocketed her communicator and ran down the administration corridor, scattering chairs and any loose bits of furniture along the way. As she reached the door to the kitchens, the crackle of a laser beam hissed past her head.

She slammed the door behind her and pressed Gorind's remote. As soon as she heard the click of the lock, she weaved her way through the preparation benches and toward the storerooms, vaguely hoping her pursuers would be distracted by the rows of pots and pans hanging on stainless steel hooks above their heads, the shining surfaces gleaming and reflecting their passage, and the stacks of crockery and cutlery all in their place. *Some chance.*

As she spied the last storeroom where the tunnel emerged, the outside door to the kitchens blew open, hitting the wall.

"Don't shoot!" yelled Hana as she spun around, relieved to see Ardan's grey-uniformed officers, not the black-garbed enforcers crowding the doorway. "I'm Hana! The enemy's that way," she pointed, "and they're armed."

"Get back!" ordered a large man. "Out of the way!"

As Hana slipped into the storeroom, Ardan's team spread out across the kitchen, taking shelter behind the benches and pointing their weapons towards the door at the far end of the large space.

"I can't bear to watch," Hana murmured as she shuffled back into the dark and relative security of the storeroom. At least someone had come to her aid. Damn Coren again. But realistically, he couldn't have helped her against HuX's forces.

"Hana!" a voice crackled tinnily. "Are you safe?"

"Relina?"

A crash blew away her next words. Looking around, she heard the familiar hiss of lasers as Ardan's team fired at the black figures crowding the smashed kitchen doorway.

"Relina, they're fighting in here. I'm sheltering in a storeroom. Is Coren back?"

"No Coren yet, I'm sorry. However, that's not why I'm contacting you. Have you seen Dr Guirden?"

"What?" Hana hunched down instinctively at another loud bang.

"One of our men reported she escaped her bonds. I needed to warn you."

"No! How?" Hana cried against the rising noise and screams of pain.

"Try the—"

"What?" Hana yelled.

The communicator hissed in Hana's ear. "Try the laboratory if you can. See if she's there."

"I don't know where it is." Hana swallowed her panic. *Coren, why aren't you here?* She thought back to the scenes she had seen on the wall screens. "Yes I do! It's deep under the admin building, on the north east corner. That's where the guards came from. There must be another way to get in than through Matron's office. But what can I do? I'm not strong enough alone!"

A supporting beam smashed into the corner of the door.

"Hana? Are you alright?" Relina's voice crackled.

"Yeah," she gasped.

"Fine. I've got to go. Others are checking in. Stop Guirden, if you can."

Yeah, by myself, she thought, standing up, suddenly conscious of the noise and the professional fighters around her. Still, if she could find Guirden, she could let Ardan's men know where she was.

"More of them," yelled a voice nearby.

"Force them out. Into the yard. We've more forces coming."

A blast reverberated, shaking the walls. Dust poured from the ceiling, blanketing the air, making the fighting seem surreal, black and grey figures twisting and turning in a macabre dance. In a concerted push, the remaining enemy forces rushed in a mass towards the storerooms, the laser beams losing effectiveness in the dust-filled air. Different weapons opened up with a crack reminiscent of ancient Earth rifles.

Hana hissed with alarm and moved further back, towards the hidden tunnel, as a melee of figures fought towards her. The wall shook again. She crouched lower. A loud crash blasted her eardrums. A wash of light illuminated the scene from where the outer wall had been.

"Hold!" yelled a powerful voice. "You're surrounded! Drop your weapons."

Hana stifled an urge to cough, remaining still, not wanting to leave her position. Someone shouted orders to round up the surrendering enemy forces. Screams and moans from the injured pierced her body as if she were wounded as well.

"Hana?" called a familiar voice. "You can come out now."

"Ardan!" Hana rushed to the tall, strong figure, hugging him in relief.

He stepped back with his hands in the air.

"Sorry. I'm so relieved to see you and glad that it's over." Hana brushed the dust from her hair behind her neck to hide her embarrassment.

"That's fine, but it's far from over," said Ardan, as he led her past the shambles of the kitchen and the fallen bodies. "We still have to find Guirden and stop her from destroying any evidence of their activities."

Hana took a deep breath. "How did she get free? She's got a lot to answer for."

"Let me know straight away if you see her, but your main priority is the children. See what you can do," said Ardan. "You know this place better than my team. I'll concentrate on Dr Guirden."

"Some of the children are in the dorms. I saw them," Hana said, "but I don't know where the ones from the training ground ran to. I'll do what I can."

"Good. Get them somewhere safe outside, as far away from the buildings as you can."

Hana didn't wait to hear more. Doing her best to ignore the wounded and dead enforcers lying prone in the corridor, the stench of blood and gut contents, and the cacophony of pain and anger, she raced from room to room, calling children to follow her. A few joined her and helped her search.

A tall youth, his lank hair hanging over his eyes, refused to co-operate. "What have you done to the staff?"

Hana reached for his arm.

He snatched it away. "Get outta here! I'm not going anywhere with you."

Another lad, part dineeth from his furry ears and long nose, joined him. "Yeah, how do we know this isn't a test? Checking our loyalty? We don't know you."

Despairing, Hana pleaded with them. "It's dangerous for you to stay here. At least get out of the building. Get to safety on the other side of the yard."

"We've been told to stay in our dorms when there's trouble, no matter what," the tall one stated, his arms crossed and feet planted apart.

Shots rang through the corridor.

"This isn't a drill. Please!"

Hana left them to decide their fate, running out of time to find other children who would follow her. Some came easily, some had to be coaxed. She sent the older ones to gather those in the other buildings. One small child, huddled beneath a desk, was so frightened Hana scooped her up and ran with her tight to her chest.

She sent the group of bedraggled and frightened children out across the dirt yard, to the safety of the boundary trees, the occasional shot still echoing in the air, hoping Coren and Kat would be safe. Once they were all moving away, she headed back inside.

"Kat! Kat!"

Kat opened her eyes to see tears glistening like stars on Coren's broad face. "Coren! It's you! I'm not dead?"

"Are you hurt? What happened?" Coren held her to his chest.

Kat blinked and pushed at him, trying to sit up. "I can't remember. Only that Baden-Hauf was killing me!"

Coren released her but kept one arm around her shoulders. "Don't try to get up. Catch your breath."

Exhaustion suffused every muscle of Kat's limbs. She leant against Coren's strong body, gaining strength from his solidity. "I couldn't fight any more. I—"

She couldn't tell Coren she'd intended to take her life. She had obviously misunderstood Mystic Nivlac's meaning about only using the diamond in dire emergencies. The memory of her whirlwind actions came back to her, one piece at a time. She would never have dreamed a frenine could fight so viciously. "I killed him."

"Ferking hell, Kat! You didn't just kill him. You shredded him! Good for you. Speaking of which, we need to get out of here. A giant grecka wants to feed, clean up the offal." Coren sprang to his feet and held out a hand.

Kat grasped and tried to pull herself to her feet. Energy failed her. "I... I can't."

Without a word, Coren scooped her up in his arms and carried her away from the carnage.

Kat fell into a torpor until a door clicked shut behind her. She lay on the back seat of a luxury flitter, the soft moulding material hugging her safely, as Coren gently wiped her fur clean of splattered gore. "Whose flitter is this?"

"The Agency's. Pretty flash, eh?" Coren moved into the driver's seat, started the flitter and drove off smoothly.

Kat couldn't move. Whatever the drug had done to help her overcome her enemy, it had drained her of every fragment of energy. She couldn't tell where her body ended and the seat began, allowing herself to be swallowed up in comfort. "What happened at the orphanage? Is everyone safe?"

Coren reassured her that all was under control. "Ardan was on his way with his troops. That's why he'd gone off-planet, to bring them from another project for an assault on the orphanage. He didn't expect us to get there before him."

Kat blinked a few times. *That must be why he hadn't revealed what he must have known. There'd been too many secrets.* "What about Matron and the Earthers?"

"Matron, Guirden and Bakker are trussed up like Gorind. They won't be able to give Hana any trouble."

They continued the drive back to the orphanage at a steady pace. As they neared, Kat thought she could hear weapon fire. "What's going on?"

Coren sped up. "No idea, but it doesn't sound good. Oh no! Hana!"

Struggling to a sitting position, Kat peered out of the window. Several armoured vehicles were in the compound where Bakker's vehicle had previously been. Groups of children—human, frenine, dineeth and other species—sheltered on the training grounds and by a small group of needle trees, each accompanied by a trooper dressed in grey. She heard sporadic firing coming from further away at the end of the compound near the kitchens.

Hana jogged along the corridor, avoiding the debris of the fighting while listening out for any sounds of children she had missed. She eventually found herself outside the matron's room, the wooden door still smoking from holes burnt through it. She listened carefully, hearing a clatter of machinery from inside the office against the distant cries and shouting from outside. Her communicator crackled, startling her.

"Hana. You there?"

"Relina?"

"Hana. Leave any more searching to the professionals. You should get out. I hadn't realised how many defenders there were."

Hana shook her head even though she knew Relina couldn't see her. "One of the kids must have released Guirden. I can't believe how brainwashed some of them are."

"All the more reason to get out of there. Get to The Agency vehicles. You'll be safe there.

"No, Relina. There's someone in the Matron's office. I'm going to check it out."

"Hana!"

She closed off the communicator's volume and pushed through into the destroyed room. A skinny girl with a dirty face glanced around before stabbing furiously at a button on the console.

"Get away!" she screamed in a high-pitched voice. "I've gotta get in. She won't let me."

"Who?" Hana asked as she walked closer.

"Her!" she jabbed a finger at the large screen in front of her.

"Guirden!" Hana breathed out seeing the familiar figure in the hidden laboratory. "What's she doing?"

As if in answer to her question the scientist looked up and glared as she recognised Hana. "You again. You dare to come and mock me, after all I've achieved. All my ground-breaking research is in jeopardy because of you and your friends. But it will go on and my name will be remembered. In spite of you!"

"Let me in. I can help you," the girl screeched, distracting the doctor's ranting.

"What? Too late. The timer's set. I will not let my work be taken. Join me, in immortality." The woman spread her arms wide and closed her eyes.

"Oh, shit," exclaimed Hana. "We've got to get out of here."

"No!" The girl leant over the console, gripping the edges with her fingers.

"Damn!" Hana yelled as she turned and ran for the door. She sprinted down the corridor before a vast push of air hit her in the back. The sound of the explosion rolled over her.

Whoomph!
An explosion rocked the flitter.

The administration building erupted in flames, clouds of black smoke billowing above. Screams came from every direction, boots pounding the earth, weapons firing.

"Ferking hell!" Coren swerved the flitter through the gates and pulled up next to another vehicle.

He leapt out of the flitter, but Kat didn't have the strength to follow.

Coren grabbed a grey-clad soldier's shoulder. "Where's Hana?"

"What?" The man pulled away from Coren's hand. "The young

woman? Don't know. In there, I think." He pointed towards the burning building.

Coren glanced back to Kat in the flitter. "I've gotta go! Find Hana! She's everything to me. I couldn't live if anything happened to her, especially as I left her alone."

"Go! I'm fine here."

"Coren! Where's Kat?" He swung around to see Ardan jogging towards them.

"She's here. In the flitter. I've gotta find Hana." He ran off.

"Are you alright, Kat?" Ardan bent down to her. "You look like you've been in your own fight." He grimaced. "Wouldn't have been with Lord Baden-Hauf, would it?"

Kat leant back into the upholstery, so tired that it took an effort to open her mouth. "Yes," she said.

"Where is he?"

"Coren told me he's grecka food by now. On the plains. He wanted to hunt me. But'—her eyes glistened—"I killed him."

"Ah," said Ardan straightening, "I see."

Kat turned her head, looking towards the burning building. "You better get there. Coren thinks Hana might be inside!"

"I've got all my troops searching so I'll stay with you. From what I understand there's been an explosion in the underground research complex."

"How?"

"Dr Guirden got away. One of my troops saw her go in but only got there in time to catch three tech assistants coming out. They're lucky they weren't killed in the explosion. Guirden must have blown herself up to avoid capture."

He rubbed his hand over his tired face. "We still can't locate Hana although the explosion seems to have been confined to one area of the building. I can't believe she was close to the blast, so we'll find her." He patted Kat's hand. "Unfortunately, we've lost some children, too. They were conditioned by the operations here and thought we were attacking them. We saved most with Hana's help."

Kat's ears still rang. Dots floated in front of her eyes. All the pain and suffering, to fulfil humans' lust for killing sapient species. She still couldn't understand why they did it. The loss of Tar and everything else, including the fight with Lord Baden-Hauf, overwhelmed her.

"Just find my friends, Ardan. Find them."

She lay back in the padded seat. She couldn't do any more. Even if she wanted to, her body refused to budge.

"Kat!" Hana's cry shrilled across the dusty yard.

Kat lifted her head.

Hana ran towards her, Coren close behind, then dropped down next to her. "Are you alright? What happened?"

Kat nodded. "Later. I'm so glad you're safe."

Coren kept both hands on Hana's shoulders. "What now?"

"I don't know," Kat murmured. "I've nowhere to go."

Coren grunted. "Neither have we. Time for Ardan to deliver on his promises.

Chapter 29

Kat pottered into the kitchen of the three-bedroom apartment in The Agency building that Ardan had made available for them. Usually it was used by visiting VIPs so it was luxurious but lacked the feel of a home. She raided the fridge for leftovers from last night's meal, too lethargic to bother making a fresh breakfast. Although her body was slowly recovering, her spirits held her down.

She poured boiling water into the teapot, the scent of peppermint tea reminding her of Mystic Nivlac. She needed to thank him for his support in gaining her revenge for Tar's murder, as hollow as that felt—nothing could return her lifemate and the love they'd shared.

Hana bounced into the kitchen, humming. "You're up, Kat. I didn't expect to see you before we went."

"Now my legs are stronger, I thought I'd go for a run."

"Great, that'll make you feel better. You should eat more, though." Hana busied herself toasting buns and juicing vegetables.

Kat did her best to smile at her friend. "What are you up to today? More shopping?" Since The Agency had paid them all for their work, Hana and Coren spent most of their time browsing the main shopping mall.

"No, we've got our appointment with Ardan this morning, remember?" Hana didn't seem surprised or upset that Kat had forgotten.

Kat poured herself a hot drink. "Do you know what he wants?"

"No, he just said something about our futures." Hana gathered up two plates and glasses and retreated to the dining area.

After only drinking half her tea, Kat slipped out of the apartment, not wanting to douse her friends' spirits. She hired a flitter and headed towards the mountains. Once away from Sensuna, she parked, stripped, and changed into hunting form.

As she stretched out her muscles, her breathing matched her rhythmic strides, her paws eating up the ground. As the incline increased, her breaths became deeper until she gasped for air. Twice she had to stop to rest. Pushing herself harder, she climbed the rocky slope, panting from exertion, and continued up the trail to the mystic's cave.

As expected, Nivlac wasn't surprised at her arrival. A pot of tea stood brewing on the rock shelf table just as it had the first time she'd visited.

"Kat, what a pleasure. You're looking well."

Kat caught her breath as she sat down, unsure how to start. "I'm getting better, thank you. Even though I expected to be dead when I used the diamond on the choker you gave me."

Mystic Nivlac tipped his head to one side, his furry ears poking out from underneath his floppy hat. "I warned you to only use it in a dire emergency."

Kat agreed. "I thought it was a suicide stone."

"No, no, no! I would never do that to you. Is that why you used it? That was never my intention. I'm glad you overcame Lord Baden-Hauf." Mystic Nivlac poured her a cup and handed it to her.

"The official line is that he's disappeared without trace, no one knows where." Kat wasn't really surprised that Nivlac knew more than she'd thought.

He sipped his drink, then sat back. "He was a nasty piece of work, but I'm sorry it had to end the way it did. For you, that is. I won't be shedding any hair over him."

Kat laughed, strangely easy in the dineeth's company. Maybe he'd put something in the tea again, to relax her. She sniffed at it.

"It's only peppermint. I know I had to drug you that once, but I had to be sure I could imbed the instructions in your mind. Will you forgive me, given what you know now?"

Looking back, Kat was glad she hadn't known about the dineeth and other DNA. The pressure to destroy it would have been too much. "Of course. I didn't come here to argue about the past."

"Good. So, to what do I owe the pleasure of your visit?"

Kat relayed what she'd learnt about the criminals' trials. "The list of accusations against Gorind grows every day. He's sure to end up on X-Astar9 for life."

Mystic Nivlac leant forward. "And the others? The HuX people?"

"They're being repatriated to Earth. They'll face justice there."

"And Sheenis Dines?"

"Who?"

Mystic Nivlac straightened up. "Matron. Gorind's mother."

"Is that her name? She'll be facing many years in custody. What a wicked woman. How can anyone do that to children? Some of them still can't talk about what was done to them, even now they're safe."

The dineeth shook his head. "She wasn't always like that. She was treated badly."

Kat's hand shook as she put down her cup. "You know her? How?"

He sighed and ran a hairy hand across his chin. "Gorind's father was half dineeth."

Nothing could have shocked Kat more. "Gorind is a quarter dineeth? So why did he do all those awful things to genoids?"

"Who knows? Hatred for his father, maybe. Hatred for himself, more likely. As head of the pack, I helped Sheenis establish the orphanage to give them a home, but I kept at arms' length."

Anger flared in Kat's stomach. "How could you let that happen? Gorind abused the children! Matron sold them to HuX! How could you not know what was going on?"

Guilt flooded Mystic Nivlac's face. "I should have had more involvement; I know that now. I started to get suspicious before you visited me. I did some digging, but before I could act through the law, you came along. The opportunity seemed too good to miss."

Kat leapt up, wanting to flee back down the mountain. "If HuX had been stopped earlier, Tar might still be alive!"

"You're right. I'm sorry, I would change the past if I could. As it is, I do what I can with the dineeth and frenine councils. We genoids need to stick together. There's a complex inter-species network on Crofta and across the galaxy."

Kat's mind raced, her fury simmering within her. "Is The Agency part of that?"

"One part, yes. It wasn't my place to tell you about Ardan and his activities. They prefer to operate behind the scenes."

Getting a grip of her emotions, Kat sat back down. She couldn't blame Mystic Nivlac for the actions of Gorind or HuX. "Thank you for what you, and the other dineeths, have done for me. I couldn't have coped with Tar's death without taking revenge. No matter frenine culture, I'm a predator at heart. And I'm glad I was able to destroy the DNA on Earth, though I think The Agency still has a lot of work ahead."

Mystic Nivlac agreed. "You still have an important role to play too. I told you before you are a catalyst for change. You're more than that, you're the hope of genoids everywhere."

"There's more for me to do? Haven't I done enough?" Chasing over the galaxy after humans who thought themselves superior was no way for a frenine to live. "What am I supposed to do now?"

After finishing the last of his tea, Mystic Nivlac rose. "That's up to you. Only you can determine what your next actions must be. Feel free to come and talk again when you believe you know the answer."

When it became obvious the mystic could share no more, Kat thanked him once again and left. As she ran down the hill, her thoughts bounced and whirled like the stones she deliberately knocked down along the way.

Hana and Coren accepted the seats Ardan offered in his office but turned down any refreshments.

Ardan cleared his throat. "Thank you for your patience while I sorted out a few problems. I didn't want to rush into anything without all the loose ends tied up."

Hana threw a quizzical look at Coren, who shrugged in return.

"I'm sorry, I shouldn't be so obtuse. I know you've been paid for your participation in bringing down HuX and its leaders, but I don't want to leave you with an uncertain future. I imagine you'll want a home, and a regular income."

"Sure," Coren said, looking bright. "Did you have something in mind?"

Ardan leant back and rocked his chair, his hands clasped over his stomach. "My people have been very impressed with you both, and from what I've seen, they have every reason to be. You are inventive, talented, and loyal. With more training, I believe you could be exceptional."

Hana smiled. "I've had lots of practice at hacking, since I was young. What I did to help was easy."

Holding up a hand, Ardan interrupted her. "I don't mean only what you can do at a keyboard. You've navigated across solar systems, taken adversity in your stride, and dealt with powerful men and women. Your life skills have been honed by living as you did after you left the orphanage."

Coren fidgeted. "I've always wanted to be an engineer. Can you help me with that?"

Ardan gave them the most genuine smile they'd ever seen from him. "I can do more than that. I want to offer you both full-time jobs."

"Really? That would be amazing! We could get ourselves a real home." Hana's mind was already imagining the type of house she'd love to live in.

"Would it be here on Crofta? We'd set our hopes on getting off this planet, away from our pasts."

Taking out two folders, Ardan placed one in front of each of them. "Hana, Relina would very much like to have you as her investigative technician. Coren, Velhker has agreed to take you on, primarily as a pilot and driver, but will support you through engineering studies. How does that sound?"

Silence descended. Hana looked at Coren, worry on her face. "But that means we'd be on separate planets."

Ardan held up both hands. "Not at all. Relina is the new Director of Operations on Earth."

"So, we'd both be going to Earth?" Coren's eyes widened.

"Yes. There's staff accommodation available if you want it, or you can have an allowance to set yourself up in your own home. You'll both get personal flitters, and annual salaries equal to the amount you received for the HuX project. It's all in here." Ardan patted the folders on his desk.

Both of them flipped open the dossiers and scanned through the information. With a grin and a single nod at each other, they said in unison, "We accept."

When Kat returned to the apartment, Hana looked fit to burst. "We've really exciting news, Kat."

Kat flopped onto the sofa. "What's happened?"

"Ardan has offered us jobs, with The Agency! I'm going to work with Relina! She's taking over from Trushaw on Earth!"

The three of them had discussed what they might do now, her friends no longer needing to live in hiding, and having credits from their part in bringing down HuX, but Kat had never imagined they'd want to continue a life of secrecy and adventure.

Coren grinned. "And I'm going to work with Velhker. To fly! I'll become a real engineer, and they'll train me in all the latest technology."

Despite being delighted for her friends, her first thought was that now she'd lose them. "I'm really pleased for you, but I'll miss you."

Hana grasped both Kat's hands. "You needn't. Ardan says there's a job for you too if you want it. He says to visit him whenever you feel well enough."

Kat shook her head. "I can't leave Crofta. Despite being an exile, this is my home. I've had enough of space travel. I'll work something out."

Her friends' smiles dissipated. She hadn't meant to spoil their joy. "But I'm not short of credits, so maybe I can visit once you're settled in."

"And with me being a pilot for The Agency, we might be able to return to Crofta sometimes, even though there was a time we never wanted to see Sensuna again. Now we have a reason to visit, to see you, and Ardan."

That was all very good, but where did that leave her? Kat's depression sank deeper. The years ahead loomed bleak and empty. "That's great," she said, faking enthusiasm.

Later that day, while Hana and Coren still buzzed with plans for their future, Kat hired another flitter. This time she headed in the opposite direction, out to the orphanage. She had always thought of Tar's murder as the start of all the trouble, but really it had commenced there, with the abuse of children. Back when she had been on the disastrous school visit, when Gorind had assaulted her, she could never have foreseen the way her life would turn out. *But how could she have known there was an organisation as degraded and perverted as Hunters Extreme?* Tar had lost his life for her to learn of its existence.

She wandered among the rubble, trying to imagine what life must have been like for Hana and Coren, and all the other children of various species who had passed through those gates. Now the fence was a tangled mess, the buildings wrapped up in danger-warning tape, weeds growing among the paths and outdoor areas. Even this soon after the explosion it appeared that wild animals had already moved in, scavenging for scraps and leaving their mess through the rooms. The Agency had stripped everything they could from the underground laboratory and Matron's room. *Maybe part of Hana's role would be to look through the files and track down the children represented?* The whole place sent shivers up Kat's spine.

The more she poked her head into rooms and explored, careful not to dislodge anything to cause herself harm, the stronger she formed an idea. By the time the red moon rose over the horizon, her step had quickened and thoughts whizzed like night insects through her brain. Kat almost ran back to the hire flitter and dashed back to Sensuna, certain Ardan would still be in his office; he couldn't go off-planet due to the court proceedings.

When she reached the office block, she sprang up the stairs instead of waiting for the grav lift, which was busy with people leaving work. As she'd hoped, Ardan was still there, his door ajar. She poked her head in.

"Kat! What a pleasant surprise. Come in." Ardan rose and ushered her to a seat.

Suddenly unsure of herself, Kat wiped at her whiskers. "Thank you. There was something I wanted to talk with you about."

"Of course. You're always welcome." When she didn't say any more, Ardan continued, "I presume Hana and Coren have told you there is a job for you at The Agency if you want it. Is that what you're interested in?"

Kat steadied herself with a deep breath. "No, not quite. Well, maybe. But not one you've probably thought of."

Ardan raised an eyebrow. "Very mysterious. Why don't you just tell me what's on your mind?"

The creak of Kat's chair sounded loud in the otherwise hushed room. Kat still hesitated to share her idea. Instead, she raised another topic that had been haunting her. "Did you know I've saved my ovaries and Tar's DNA? I have them in a lifeseal pac. I don't really know why. Do you think there's any hope—?"

After going to a cupboard in the corner of his room, Ardan extracted two glasses and held them up to Kat without saying anything. She nodded. He poured two drinks and sat back down. "It'll take a while for my team to fully understand Dr Guirden's work. Without her and her notes from the orphanage, we only have what wasn't destroyed on Earth. But you can be assured if there are ethical ways to use her knowledge and techniques for good, you will be offered a chance to participate in any trials."

"Thank you. That means a lot to me." Kat sipped at her drink, the strong spirit burning her throat. She braced herself to talk about the real reason she had visited Ardan. "I visited the orphanage today. It's so desolate, even worse than when the children were there. It seems a great waste to let the buildings rot. And although the kids are in foster homes, they're separated and it's only temporary. They must want something more permanent."

Ardan raked his fingers through his hair. "I'm sure they do. You know we're trying to find people to adopt them, but these things take time."

"Yes, and there will always be more children than homes, I expect." She took a deep breath. "What I'm proposing is that, with The Agency's resources, the orphanage could be rebuilt. Make it a place of education and provide a long-term home for those who want to stay. Give orphans a chance at a good life, among their own species, to learn their own cultures and not only that of humans." Kat's excitement came through in her voice, and she sat up straighter with every sentence.

Ardan drummed the desk. "I can see where you're going. But who would want to take on a project like that? It'd take vast dedication."

Kat shrunk back down. "I know I don't have the right skills yet, but I'm prepared to learn. I don't have a family anymore and there's no hint of them welcoming me back, not even with all the good we've done. Not yet, anyway. Maybe in time, if they see I can be constructive rather than destructive, the Council will allow me back into frenine society." The words rushed out of Kat in a stream.

"Oh, Kat. I didn't realise you were offering to take on the task. That's wonderful! I think you'd be brilliant. With The Agency's resources behind you, we can remake the orphanage how it should have been in the first place." Ardan jotted down notes in his personal device.

Sliding to the front of her chair, Kat swelled with excitement at Ardan's enthusiastic support. "I thought we could name it The Tar Memorial Children's Home."

Ardan beamed. "Excellent. Leave it with me. I'll get things started and draft a formal contract for you. Meanwhile, start gathering ideas for how you want things to operate."

Kat threw herself into her new role, discussing plans with architects while the rubble of the old orphanage was removed. She did her best to get to know all the children who'd been resident at the time of the bombing and let them share in how the new facility would evolve, taking their species' needs into account.

The building of a new family and a home for them helped fill the emptiness that the loss of Tar had left in her heart. Her hopes and dreams now had different horizons, including a multi-cultural school with well-stocked databanks, workshops where youngsters could learn trades, facilities for creativity such things as art and drama, plus places for relaxation and social events.

When she needed a break from her new fulfilling and busy life, she changed into hunting form and raced with the wind among the remnant catner bushes dotting the red and gold landscape. Sometimes she saw Tar out of the corner of her eye, or imagined she ran with him across the grassy plains, the smell of zeena, herbs and fresh grass wafting on the breeze.

The End